THEY CAME
FOR ADVENTURE . . .
TO CLAIM THEIR DREAMS . . .
AND FEED THEIR PASSIONS

ROYCE

The reckless young newspaper editor would risk his life to save this majestic land from a timber king's ax . . . and risk his heart to win the woman he loved.

LUCY

Lovely and impetuous, she was always the wild card in the deck, befriending outcasts and desperados, and falling for the worst man of all.

DELANEY

The ruthless Colorado businessman never paid for what he could steal . . . never walked away from what he wanted . . . and never asked for a woman—just took her.

THE MAVERICK TOUCH

CLYDE M. BRUNDY

AVON BOOKS ◆ NEW YORK

THE MAVERICK TOUCH is an original publication of Avon Books.
This work has never before appeared in book form. This work is a novel.
Any similarity to actual persons or events is purely coincidental.

AVON BOOKS
A division of
The Hearst Corporation
105 Madison Avenue
New York, New York 10016

Copyright © 1988 by Clyde M. Brundy
Published by arrangement with the author
Library of Congress Catalog Card Number: 88-91496
ISBN: 0-380-89600-1

First Avon Books Printing: August 1988

AVON TRADEMARK REG. U.S. PAT. OFF. AND IN OTHER COUNTRIES, MARCA
REGISTRADA, HECHO EN U.S.A.

Printed in the U.S.A.

K-R 10 9 8 7 6 5 4 3 2 1

Chapter 1

The westbound stage to Fort Crawford was already two hours behind schedule when it neared the tiny settlement of Barnum on the Lake Fork of Colorado's Gunnison River. Two of the passengers who were riding up-top beside the driver sat slumped in weariness and silence. It was late April, 1881, and the afternoon was unseasonably warm; the four-horse rig had fought sloppy muddiness most of the way from Cebolla Creek. Several times all of the passengers except one had been asked to help push the coach through nearly impassable spots.

Their journey had brought them from Pueblo, at the eastern base of the Rocky Mountains, by way of the San Luis Valley and the ten-thousand-foot heights of Cochetopa Pass. Off to the southwest stood the sawtoothed San Juan Mountains, dappled by sunlight and shadows.

Presently the young man sitting atop the coach began studying spots of mud on his plaid shirt, then brushed a couple of drier ones off his sleeve. His name was Royce Milligan. Every so often he glanced curiously at the cloaked and bonneted passenger seated beside him. An hour before, she had asked to ride for a time outside the coach. The reason she had given the driver was a desire to study the surrounding mountains; Royce Milligan surmised that she had really wanted to get away from one of her seatmates, the black-clad preacher, Lucian Goodfroe, who had been admonishing the passengers

1

within to mend their ways and help prepare the vast
frontier for the second coming of the Messiah, which the
parson held to be imminent. Also, she had possibly
spotted the lice leaping between the soiled collar and
beard of the ancient prospector sitting across from her.

At last Milligan reached a decision of sorts and let his
gaze fall steadily on the quietly poised young woman
beside him. Because the driver's handling of four leather
reins compelled him to occupy a good portion of the
wooden seat, Milligan felt his female companion press
against him at each curve of the rutted road. He noted
that she was deep-bosomed, and that a strand of her
copper-hued hair refused the restriction of her bonnet.

When she finally spoke, her gaze remained fixed on the
distant San Juan peaks, which now began to fade into
darkening clouds.

"There's a sense of loneliness and mystery about those
mountains," she said, almost to herself.

Her voice was deep and singularly attractive. The sound
of it made Royce Milligan snap to attention and look
closely into her face. Milligan was silent for a few
moments as he tried to recall her name. The driver, Ike
Fenlon, had used it once or twice already on the trip. At
last it came to him. "I know what you mean, Miss Lattamore. But those mountains are also today's land of
opportunity, rich in gold and silver and other minerals."
He paused, and then asked, "Do you have relatives in
San Miguel City?"

She shook her head. "I have a brother stationed at a
place called Military Cantonment. He is a lieutenant and
has been there since May of last year."

Ike Fenlon turned with a grin that lifted his handlebar
mustache and exposed the gap where he was missing a
front tooth. "That's right, Miss. The Cantonment was
established last spring about four miles north of the
Uncompahgre Indian Agency. Chief Ouray, and his wife,
Chipeta, both of the Ute tribe, headquartered at the
agency." Fenlon spat tobacco juice to the roadside below,

and then went on, "I figure you'll be a teacher or a governess at the post?"

"No, I won't, Mr. Fenlon. I am going there to file on some government land and start a farm, perhaps an orchard."

Milligan let out a surprised whistle. "Aren't you heading into pretty wild country for that?"

"Perhaps so," she answered in a spirited way. "But not so long ago my grandfather and grandmother ventured into the raw wilderness of Iowa for a chance to own good land."

Again Milligan was struck by the low and musical cadence of her voice. It was the kind of voice that belonged in a church choir, or better still singing solo.

"And just what brings you into western Colorado, Mr. . . . Mr . . . ?"

"Milligan. Royce Milligan," he said, politely touching the brim of his hat. "I am on my way to a place you likely never heard of. It is a new mining camp along a river downstream from San Miguel City. The camp is called Mesita; I'm going to start a newspaper there, provided the equipment I loaded onto a freighter's wagon back in Pueblo ever catches up with me."

As he spoke, Milligan realized that the driver had slackened the horses' speed as the coach approached a small building. They had come onto the only street of Barnum, where the passengers could stretch and eat and there would be a change of horses.

Driver Fenlon halted the team and then studied the western horizon. He frowned and finally said, "That preacher fellow inside just might get his chance to *clear the way.* Not for the Messiah, but to rid the road of snow hip-deep to a Missouri mule. We had best eat a bite and skedaddle."

"Snow?" the young woman said. "It seems too warm for that, doesn't it, Mr. Fenlon?"

"Miss Lattamore," he replied, biting into another plug of tobacco, "you got a lot to learn about them mountains.

It can be warm as toast down here, but up at the pass . . . well, I seen it covered in ten . . . twenty foot of snow."

Royce Milligan chose the driest spot he could find around the coach and dropped to the ground. Then he turned to help Miss Lattamore. Just then, the sun broke through gathering clouds and fell directly onto his face; it revealed eyes that were brown and lively, and neatly trimmed wheat-colored hair. He was nearing his twenty-sixth year, but the bridge of his nose still sported a band of boyish freckles.

The passengers spent the next fifteen minutes washing down tasteless sandwiches with black coffee, as a fresh team was hitched to the stage and another sack of mail heaved on board. With that, they moved again onto the road, which now began climbing toward the timbered upland known as Blue Mesa. At the driver's insistence, a change had been made in the seating, with the bewhiskered prospector Goetz by name, moving outside to occupy the seat next to Ike Fenlon, and Milligan and Lucy Lattamore again inside the coach.

The afternoon wore on, and their route took them along the southern face of a high ridge. The road had narrowed to a mere trail that often had a steep bank on one side and a drop into a rocky, timbered canyon on the other. They came to a somewhat wider spot and turned northward. It was then that the first wintery blast hit them. Atop the coach Ike could feel delicate crystals of snow light on his face. Before long it thickened to become a white, obscuring wall.

Royce Milligan grew concerned and yelled to the driver. When Fenlon drew the horses to a stop, Milligan jumped from the coach and peered upward. "This snow could be knee-deep in an hour, Ike. Hadn't we better try to find some sort of shelter before dark?"

Fenlon cast a searching gaze across his team and at the snowy road ahead. "I'd hoped we could make it through to a cabin a couple of miles ahead. But you're probably right. It's a steep and slow climb, with a couple of switchbacks before we'd get to the cabin . . . and this rig is loaded heavy."

There was an anxious silence during which Lucy Lattamore joined Milligan outside the coach. Presently she said, "Back down the road a little way I noticed a flat with a lot of timber. Maybe we can get back there. At least we would have wood for a fire; and we could throw up a pole shelter against this wind and snow."

Fenlon nodded. "It would be too dangerous to try to turn the coach around on this road, so I'll unhitch the team and we can lead the horses back there."

By now Parson Goodfroe had clambered out from the stage. "I'm certain, Fenlon," he observed, "no one is apt to loot the stage if we leave it here overnight. It will be snowbound within half an hour." He held out a delicate white hand to catch a few windswept flakes.

A stronger gust of snow-laden wind, whipping across the narrow roadway, made Lucy hurriedly turn up the collar of her coat. She walked toward the lead team of horses, speaking gently to them. To Milligan she said, "I will release the tugs while you unhitch the neck-yoke and drop the rig's tongue."

As Royce followed her suggestion, a curious smile played across his face. "You seem quite handy with horses, Miss Lattamore. Where did you learn?"

Ike Fenlon began looping the long reins over upthrust hames so that the horses might be led by their bridles. "She was raised on a farm or around a livery stable. I'd bet on it," he commented admiringly. He watched her grasp the bridle of one of the sorrel geldings comprising the lead team. "So, you're taking that one—" He nodded to Milligan. "You take the other sorrel and follow her. She sure seems to know what she's doing."

Saving her breath against the quickening force of the storm, Lucy plodded through snow already ankle-deep as she guided the horse back down the road. Presently, through the veiling snow, she glimpsed the stand of pine and fir trees she had noticed earlier. It lay scarcely a hundred feet from the road. She turned to Milligan and held out a gloved hand. "Here, let me have your horse too. Then . . . would you mind walking back up to the stage? Tell Fenlon to give you an axe and a bucksaw, if he has them. I noticed what I thought was a tool chest on the back of that stage. We've got to fix some sort of shelter and cut firewood before it gets dark."

Within ten minutes all of the passengers had abandoned the coach, taking with them only those items necessary for an emergency. The coach sat snow-plastered, blocking the road. In all likelihood no one would travel this route for days to come.

That night they huddled in the protection of a crudely built lean-to as a fire whipped erratically about near the structure's open front. They kept uneasy watch over the horses, worrying over the lack of forage for the animals. Their most valued possession that night was a heavy buffalo robe under which they sought refuge from the continuing storm.

Morning came as a vast grayness, with snow still falling. The wind had subsided somewhat but still moved the snow in white gusts. Lucy awakened from a broken sleep, stood up, smoothed her tangled hair, and then moved closer to the fire. Royce was already stooped beside the flames, attempting to brew coffee in an open pail. "You'll need more heat than that," Lucy commented.

"I know," he answered ruefully. "Ike Fenlon and that old-timer, Goetz, are already trying to rustle up more firewood. It won't be easy in this mess of snow."

Lucy gazed about and sensed the utter isolation of their camp. "How soon would you expect we can get out of here?" she asked.

"Not today. That's for sure. Maybe tomorrow or the next day."

Her face tightened. "But the horses . . . they have nothing to eat. And we have so few supplies."

"Before this is over, Miss Lattamore," he answered grimly, "one of the horses may be our food supply."

She received his assessment of their plight in silence, and finally said, "There is a slope over there to the left a little way. I am going to climb it and look around for a spot where the snow is light enough for the poor beasts to feed."

Royce nodded. "Sounds like a sensible idea. But don't go too far. Stay within calling distance. It would be easy to get lost.

Minutes later she struggled through the whiteness to where there was an area with just a few scattered trees. The snow was not so deep here, reaching just above her ankles. She began kicking some of it aside and smiled when tufts of grass came into view. Within ten minutes she had worked her way upward to what she surmised was the crest of the slope. It was then that she sighted the cairn. At first it seemed only a pile of rocks to which snow clung in an irregular pattern. But as she stared at it, somehow it came to her that this rock-heap was manmade and very old. She couldn't imagine who had placed it there and what purpose it might have served. She picked her way over to it, then reached out a tentative hand and touched some snow atop the cairn; she used the arm of her coat to brush it away, revealing a capstone. Her eyes searched along its length. At it's midway point was a V-shaped notch, carved in such a manner that when she stood on her toes, placing her hands on the foot-long capstone, the chisled notch became a sighting device. She peered through, at first noticing only that the snowfall had lessened, so that it no longer hampered her view. Southward, perhaps half a mile away, was a mountain slope with alternating timber and open areas now under deep snow. Higher still, she could discern the outline of a snow-capped peak. For quite a while she stared at the slope and what appeared to be a small ravine on its side.

At that moment she heard the concerned voice of Royce Milligan calling her name. The sound carried with unusual clarity through the chill morning air.

"Yes, Royce," she shouted back. "I'll be down soon. Save some coffee for me, if it is ready."

Again she bent to squint through the stone's notch. This time she sighted lower on the slope and into the ravine, at something she had not noticed before. Just a few yards to the right of the ravine was a splotch of blackness. It was hexagonal in shape, standing out in bold relief against the whiteness of the slope. Below it was a flat surface, perhaps formed by rock and refuse that had come from that spot of darkness. Lucy's face tensed in excitement; she was staring at a mine portal.

She would have continued to study this unexpected sight, but suddenly a gust of wind and snow blurred and then hid the nearby mountain. And Milligan was again calling for her. She looked quickly about the cairn, trying to fix its exact location in her mind. Then, almost reluctantly, she returned to the lean-to and her companions.

By the time she reached the camp, both the snow and wind had picked up again; the roar of the storm through the trees sounded like a dirge. With an excited gesture, she motioned the four men to her side and told them of the dark portal she had seen on the slope.

"It might be the entrance to an abandoned mine, a gold or silver diggings," Ike Fenlon said. "There was some prospecting activity up this way a few years back. A ruckus with the Ute Indians made the miners call it quits."

"Why don't we see if that tunnel might offer us greater protection?" she said. "There might even be some old timbers in there we can use to start a better fire." She paused and looked at the men's tensed faces around her. She was about to reveal her discovery of the monument with the chisled sighting V, when Ike Fenlon interrupted.

"What about my horses and the stage?" he demanded. "There's a United States Mail pouch in there."

His question was momentarily ignored, for Royce had turned to Lucy. "Are you sure there was a portal?" At her answering nod, he asked, "Could you find it again, Lucy? Lead us to it?"

She looked about, searching the storm. As she did so, she was oddly conscious of the way Royce was now using her given name instead of a more formal *Miss Lattamore*. "Right now I could lead you directly to it. But if this storm gets much worse I might get confused."

Milligan pointed to the lean-to. "If we use those poles to reinforce the horse pen, will the animals make out all right?"

"With snow for water," Fenlon began speculatively, "horses can go two . . . three days without fodder. Besides, there's some grass under the snow. I'll hike up to the coach and fetch the mail sack." He stared at Milligan. "Want to come along? There's a box with some odds and ends of eatables, maybe not all frozen."

They reached the protection of the mine tunnel an hour and a half later—and none too soon. All of them were near exhaustion from the laborious climb up the rough slope, through deepening snow. They would have missed the portal had Lucy not fixed its location so firmly in mind. It was now evident that the storm was a lingering and vicious one; they'd have had small chance of survival had they remained at the lean-to.

Chapter 2

As they struggled into the gloom and quiet of the tunnel, it was quickly apparent that it gave access to a mine that had not been worked for a great many years. The outer light filtered in only a short way, but it revealed that this tunnel was both narrower and lower-ceilinged than any mine entrance any of them had ever seen. There were no rusting iron rails or ore cars, yet worn spots in the rock floor gave evidence to the fact that at some time in the past a mine had operated in the depths of the mountain.

There was scarcely any light at all by the time they came to a small room about a hundred feet in from the portal, that had been carved out adjacent to the tunnel. After nosing around a bit, Goetz, the prospector, broke the silence that had descended upon them. "The air here is good and the ceiling dry and solid." He paused and pointed to the dark tunnel leading deeper into the mountain. "Back there, could be cave-ins or deep shafts. Dark as well."

"But can we start a fire here?" Ike Fenlon asked, and then shook his head as if in answer to his own question. "There is no fuel. And the trapped smoke would suffocate us."

Several long moments of silence followed, broken only by the sound of their breathing as their eyes slowly adjusted to the dark. Finally Lucy spoke. "Over here is another room, a smaller one. And there seems to be a cool draft and—and a stack of old poles."

Goetz and Royce Milligan moved quickly to her side and gazed about.

The cold air—" Royce began. "It has to mean that this room is somehow ventilated."

Goetz strode to one side of the room, dropped to his knees, and swept his hand across the stone floor. Then he peered at the ceiling. Taking another step as he rose, he thrust his arm upward. It seemed to disappear into the rock ceiling. "A perfect flue," Goetz muttered as he withdrew his arm. He turned back toward Lucy and Milligan, pointing to the surface he'd just inspected. "They must have built fires here before, because there's a vent here, you see? Maybe natural, maybe they dug it out. I don't know."

Lucy was lifting one of the poles as she asked, "Then we can start a fire here?"

"Yah, sure," the old prospector confirmed.

Soon a small fire was licking restlessly at the wood; true to Goetz's prediction, the smoke lifted and disappeared in the shadows of the ceiling. They fed the flames sparingly, not knowing how long the supply of poles might last or if more might be available in the deeper recesses of this strange old mine. Twice during what they knew to be the daylight hours outside, Fenlon and Royce made their way to the tunnel's portal. They could see only a short distance, for a heavy snow was still falling.

They kept close to the fire, prepared a meal from the diminishing contents of the grub box, and arranged their packs and few blankets so that all five might be warmed somewhat by the flames. Again, the buffalo robe was put to good use. There was no wind within the tunnel; the only sound came from the crackling fire and their own movements.

Naturally, Goetz seemed most at home in the long-abandoned mine. "The ceiling is of solid rock; there is no sign of chunking-off or caving," he commented at one point. "Still, we must watch out for drop-offs." He took a lighted brand from the fire and held it aloft. Then he cautiously moved further into the gloom of the tunnel. The others anxiously awaited his return until Ike Fenlon at last spoke up. "Don't be too concerned about Goetz; he has worked in mines for half his life."

"I wish we had a lantern or some of those special lights that miners fasten on their heads so that we could get around and explore," Lucy said.

"This is a strange place. I don't think I'd like to see any more of it than I have to," Preacher Goodfroe fretted. "It isn't like a regular gold or silver mine. It's more like a tomb. A sepulchre."

His remark brought a sober silence among them, for they were aware that hours, or perhaps a couple of days, must pass before they could continue on their journey.

To lessen the tension Royce looked at Lucy and asked, "Miss Lattamore, how about favoring us with a song?" When she seemed surprised by the request, he added, "Anyone with a speaking voice as vibrant and pleasant as yours must have sung many times."

Lucy's smile was visible across the wavering flames of their fire. "I did do some singing back home. Let me see . . ." She hummed a few notes, and then began the lilting melody of "Lorelei." When she finished it, at their urging she sang "Flow Gently, Sweet Afton," asking them to join in.

Afterwards Royce looked at Lucy admiringly. "Just as I thought. You've an extraordinary singing voice. Surely you've sung professionally."

She smiled modestly and replied in a casual way, "Perhaps once or twice."

Parson Goodfroe clapped his hands together. "I think it would be appropriate for us to offer a hymn unto the Lord. Miss Lucy, would you lead us in 'Lead Kindly Light'?" There was a low ripple of laughter at the aptness of the preacher's selection, but they all spiritedly joined in to sing. Later, it was Lucy who suggested Goodfroe offer a prayer of gratitude for their protection from the raging storm outside.

Midway through the prayer, Goetz returned, standing quietly apart until they had finished. Then he told them that he had located a shaft perhaps a hundred steps farther on. From the sound of a stone thrown into it, he surmised it to be very deep, much too dangerous to approach without sufficient light. He had also found a branch tunnel swinging off to the left, but there seemed to be some caving-in of its ceiling, so Goetz had not ventured into it.

"One thing I am sure of," the old prospector said firmly. "This mine is old. Very old. It has not been worked for fifty or more years." He dug a fist-sized piece of rock from his coat, and stared silently at it in the campfire's glow. "This is an amalgamate ore. Only an assay could establish what minerals it's made of. Some lead and copper, perhaps. A touch of silver. Maybe a trace of gold."

Lucy reached out. "May I look at it, Mr. Goetz?" When he placed it in her hand she murmured in surprise at its weight. "Is all ore so heavy?" she asked.

"It varies, Miss. The composition determines weight. Gold is the heaviest, always seeking the bottom—of a stream or the earth." He noticed the attraction the ore specimen had for her, and offered, "Keep that hunk of rock, if you want; I have plenty like it at home—mostly worthless."

Because of their fatigue, they all soon sought sleep, although it was scarcely mid-afternoon.

Hours later, Lucy suddenly awakened to the sound of footsteps. The fire was now only a pile of cherry-hued embers, but it gave enough light for her to make out the face and form of Royce Milligan passing close beside her. "Royce . . . wait," she whispered, hoping not to disturb the others.

He stooped over her. "Sorry to wake you, but I've just been up by the portal. The wind is down and the stars are showing through. Maybe we can be out of here and on our way tomorrow."

"I worry so about the horses," she replied.

"Well, don't. They can make out fine for a couple of days."

She was conscious of his warm breath against her forehead and that he was now kneeling close beside her. "I feel wide-awake now," she said quietly. "And there isn't an inch of space left under that old buffalo hide."

"Who has most of it?" He laughed softly.

"Right now Ike Fenlon seems to be winning. But the parson is yanking from one side and Goetz from the other."

"I'll lay my bet on the parson," Royce whispered. "He may invoke the aid of the Almighty." Lucy giggled and he went on. "You want to go up to the portal? Breathe the clean air and look at the stars?"

"That would be wonderful."

"Then just let me get a blanket or bedroll to wrap up in, and we'll be on our way," he said, helping her to her feet.

They covered the distance to the mine entrance easily, Royce leading the way. When they reached the portal they leaned against the stone wall, gazing silently at the white snow and star-strewn sky.

At last Royce broke the stillness and asked, "Lucy, where are you from that you know so much about horses and wagon-hitches and the like?" He had retrieved his own blanket and now sat close to her with it about their shoulders.

"I grew up on a prairie ranch northeast of Denver about eighty miles," she answered thoughtfully. "The nearest neighbor lived six miles away; we traded at a store known as Kate's Wagon, and it was an all-day wagon ride to reach it."

"But your voice? Surely you have had lessons . . . training."

"Precious little," she said wistfully. "My folks did

send me to Denver to a seminary when I was beyond grade school; a teacher there insisted I sing in the choir and a girls' sextet. I even gave a few concerts—'' She paused. ''But then my mother died and I had to go back home.'' Lucy's smile was a bit rueful as she added, ''Of course, I sang a lot to the cattle at home when Dad had me herding them. I even had a black dog that howled an accompaniment for me.''

Royce laughed, but didn't urge her to go on, sensing that his companion preferred not to dwell on the past. She confirmed it by quickly asking, ''How about you, Royce? I have already concluded that you are neither from the west nor a miner. Yet you spoke so knowledgeably of the mineral wealth of the San Juan Mountains.'' She paused and stared at him a bit impishly before adding, ''Besides, I detect something of the south—perhaps Virginia—in your voice.''

Milligan's gaze held to her face. For the first time he was fully aware of the shading of her eyes, gray and steady, but with a bit of violet when laughter or excitement played within them. Those subtly shaded eyes seemed to accentuate the copper hue of her hair and the fairness of her complexion, darkened a bit by the sun and wind. Instinctively, he edged closer, making sure she could share the comfort and protection of the blanket.

''Would you believe Alabama instead?'' he asked.

''All of you southerners sound alike,'' she said teasingly.

''Perhaps—except Texans.'' He chuckled. ''They are a breed apart and a sound unto themselves.'' Then, in a more serious tone, he summed up his years. ''My father inherited some land—hardly enough to be called a plantation, but it produced top-quality cotton. I was born there, and I still remember the fields and our white-porched house, shaded by cyprus trees. My father was killed in the fighting at Chickamauga Creek in September of '63.''

''I have heard of the carnage of that battle.'' Lucy shuddered, and then asked, ''And after that?''

"We lost the land to scheming carpetbaggers. After a year or so, my mother managed to house and feed us by selling farm supplies for a Birmingham wholesaler. I've a brother and a sister younger than I. We managed to stay together, and things got better when I found work with a little newspaper; I was just fourteen at the time."

"And you learned the printing trade?" Lucy queried.

"Yes . . . and publishing too. That's why I'm here. An old friend of my father's—his name is Tim O'Fallon—wrote to me asking for help in starting a newspaper. He struck it rich on a silver mine he won in a poker game. He has his own little town somewhere along the San Miguel River. Tim calls it Mesita, so he's determined to name the paper *The Mesita Times*. 'Mesita' is all right, but God forbid naming another newspaper the *Times*."

Lucy laughed aloud. "Royce, I know just what it should be called."

"What?" His reply was startled.

She was using a finger to sketch the newspaper's masthead in thin air. "How about this? *The Mesita Messiah*?" Lucy pointed to the slumbering Parson Goodfroe and explained. "The Reverend Goodfroe is preaching the second coming of the Messiah. Let your paper prove him more of a prophet than he knows."

Royce Milligan's eyes sparkled. "Why not? Lucy, you're a genius. *The Mesita Messiah*. The newest sheet along the San Miguel River—or even in Colorado. I'll talk to Tim O'Fallon about it just as soon as I arrive."

They talked for a little while in a quieter way, pondering the extent of the storm and the likelihood of a long delay, then returned to the cavern where the others still slept. It was Royce who first gave way to fatigue and sought the warmth of his blanket again. Lucy lay silently awake, the happenings of the day racing through her mind. The stone cairn she had stumbled onto . . . what could be its purpose but to pinpoint this long-abandoned mine in which they had found sanctuary and safety? Royce Milligan had spoken of a silver mine pouring out a fortune for his friend Tim O'Fallon. Could it have been a mine similar to this, one with the same eerie quality?

As the first wave of sleep swept over Lucy, she let her hand move to touch Royce Milligan's blanketed form and assure herself of his somehow protective presence. She had almost confided to him her knowledge of the strange rock cairn, but had not done so. Would she tomorrow? Would she ever? She was fast asleep when the last glow of the fire dulled, leaving the tunnel in utter darkness.

Unknown to Lucy, the storm blew itself out before dawn. The next morning a warming sun greeted the refugees when they gathered at the mine's portal and stared out. Lucy's thoughts turned to their meager food supplies, depleted now by a breakfast they had prepared over the rekindled campfire. She asked, "How soon do you suppose we can get on our way again, Mr. Fenlon?"

Their lanky driver combed a finger through his mustache and studied the depth of the snow both at the portal and in the distant timber where they had first thrown together a camp. Then he answered speculatively, "Likely the wind whirled a lot of snow off the road, but there will be drifts. Deep ones. Chances are, though, if we hitch up about noon and try it, we can at least get as far as the cabin. There's always some supplies stashed away there, and firewood too."

While they waited for midday to come, luck was with them. A freighting caravan of four wagons appeared, moving westward and breaking trail. Fenlon hastily called his passengers together. "We'll have pretty clear sailing after that outfit gets ahead of us."

"But Ike, our rig," Preacher Goodfroe remarked with concern. "It is snowbound smack in the middle of the road."

"Sure enough." Fenlon grinned. "But we can hurry down to get our horses, and be up there protecting our belongings when those fellers with the heavy wagons arrive. Then they'll have to help us dig snow to get us out of their way.''

Later, by following in the tracks of the freight wagons, Ike Fenlon brought his stagecoach safely to the shelter that marked the summit of the route across Blue Mesa. There he and his passengers remained overnight, knowing that the freighters would break the trail ahead.

Finally at noon the next day, the stage jolted its way through the muddy holes of the Uncompahgre Valley Road and came to the guard gate of the military outpost known only as The Cantonment. There was mail for cantonment personnel aboard the stage, so after undergoing a routine scrutiny at the entrance, Fenlon drove on toward the headquarters. Two of his passengers sat in awestruck silence beside him.

It seemed to both Lucy Lattamore and Royce Milligan that they had come magically from the winter-bound cold and isolation of Blue Mesa into the warm lassitude and luxury of spring. Ahead, as far as they could see, was a wide river valley hemmed in by mountains rising toward a cloudless blue sky. There was a tinge of green across the meadows; both the cottonwoods and alders strewn near the river held aloft budding branches. There were also stands of darker pine, spruce, and fir forests on the mountain slopes.

But the valley's most remarkable feature lay many miles to the south, where the high, snow-mantled peaks of the San Juan Mountains formed a rugged barrier on the horizon. After studying this vast highland, Lucy finally spoke with bated breath. "Royce, those mountains . . . they seem to go on forever. Remember? We saw them days ago from Cochetopa Pass.''

His eyes sought hers, and he answered, "I'm not likely ever to forget even an hour of this trip, or the way you saved all of our lives.'' She smiled and shrugged, and he added, "In a way I wish that I was starting *The Mesita Messiah* right here.''

"I imagine the military commander here at the Cantonment would have something to say about that." She laughed. Then as Ike Fenlon reined the team close to the headquarters building, she went on, more wistfully, "I'm sure you'll have plenty to keep you busy in Mesita. I wouldn't be surprised if ages pass before you get out this way again."

"I'll be back, Lucy." The words were simple, but his tone of voice was firm.

Moments later there was the flurry of arrival and unloading. From out of a small crowd that had gathered, a young, lean officer excitedly made his way, to enfold Lucy Lattamore in his arms almost before her feet were solidly on the patch of gravel serving as a pathway to the post headquarters. "Oh, Sis . . . Sis . . . at last! I was beginning to think you'd never get here." He held her at arm's length and searched her face. "You've gotten pretty, Lucy. Damn it, downright pretty. And your voice? Is it still the same? I've been bragging—"

Royce Milligan, standing nearby, broke in. "You've a right to boast; your sister's voice is beautiful."

As Lieutenant Phillip Lattamore stared, Royce thrust out a hand, and explained, "Lieutenant, I am Royce Milligan. I wanted to meet you before the stage pulls out and—unfortunately—I must be on it. Take good care of your sister. She is someone special—and particularly to every one of us on this stage. You see, she saved our lives."

Before the lieutenant could say a word, though, Ike Fenlon was shouting for everyone to get aboard. Lucy stood by to bid farewell to everyone: Parson Goodfroe, the white-whiskered prospector Goetz, and Ike Fenlon, before he climbed up to take over the reins.

"Mr. Fenlon, I hope my next trip over the mountains is with you," she said. The driver beamed.

Royce Milligan was the last to climb aboard. He looked for long moments into Lucy's eyes. "Know what?" he asked softly.

"What, Royce?"

"Tim O'Fallon has got to build an opera house—just for you." Before she could protest, he grasped her gloved hand in his and held it tightly; then, reluctantly, he turned away.

Lucy's gaze followed the departing coach until it was only a tiny spot in the vastness of the valley. Then she turned to her brother, who had started sorting her baggage from boxes left by the stage. "Phillip, your valley is so big . . . and overwhelming." Her hand lifted to sweep across the horizon.

"I know, Lucy. It makes you feel insignificant until you get used to the distances."

Her voice became practical as she asked, "Where on earth will I stay? Is there a guest house?"

"You happen to be my sister—the one that took a hell of a long time getting here," he teased. "We have an entire half of a two-storied officer's quarter—kitchen, bedrooms, parlor. And yes, our very own privy."

Then Phillip motioned two nearby enlisted men to his side. Pointing to Lucy's luggage, he said, "See to getting these things to BOQ number 5B and leave them just inside the door. It is unlocked. Then if you're free for a time this afternoon come by my quarters again. We may have to move some furniture around."

The men touched their temples in salute, and then one asked, "Lieutenant Lattamore, is this the lady who is going to sing for us?"

Lucy's mouth dropped open in surprise, but her brother took the question calmly. "You bet it is—my sister, Miss Lucy Lattamore. And if you're careful in handling her things, she may be persuaded to sing an encore at the concert."

Walking alongside Phillip, as soon as they were out of the men's hearing, she halted, caught his arm to swing him about, and demanded, "All right, Lieutenant Lattamore, what goes on here? Am I to understand that you have me scheduled for a concert?"

The sharpness of her words took him aback. "Lucy,

maybe I shouldn't have, but everyone here is starved for entertainment. And I remembered how you always used to love to sing.''

He looked so abashed that she hugged him. "Phillip, of course I will sing. But I hope that first I will have time to get settled and look about; this trip has been a tiring one.''

"Don't worry," he reassured her. "I left the date and time to your discretion.''

Arm in arm, they trod the short distance across the Cantonment parade ground to the row of officers' quarters.

That night they ate their evening meal at the mess hall, where Lucy was introduced to other officers and the two of their wives who were there. The conversation over dinner was mostly of military affairs, but Lucy joined in as much as she could. During the quieter moments, her mind turned to Ike Fenlon's stagecoach and his passengers. Where would they be now? And what of the bright-haired young newspaperman? Could he be thinking of her . . . ?

When she and Phillip returned to their quarters, he touched a match to paper and kindling beneath a log in a stone fireplace. Lucy found a rocking chair and settled into it. Phillip sat near the hearth, scanning her face. "Are you too tired to talk a bit?" he asked.

She sensed his hunger for news of their home on the grasslands of eastern Colorado. He had last been there almost two years ago, called home by the sudden death of their mother.

"It must have been hard for you, Lucy, pulling up stakes and leaving home—"

"No, Phillip," she began, and suddenly the words came tumbling out of her. "I was so happy when your letter came. Dad's new wife is a good woman, but somehow I think she wants him to herself." She sighed and gently shook her head. "But Dad is happy again and that's all that matters." Suddenly she brightened.

"Besides, your invitation to come out gave me the opportunity I've been wanting to make a way for myself in the world."

Phillip laughed, at the same time admiring the determination that gleamed in her eyes. "Does Dad still declare that you are a maverick?"

"Not so I can hear. Not since I surprised him by finishing school in Denver with good grades. But I am sure he still thinks of me as being—well, different."

"Well . . . weren't you, Lucy? Wanting to break and train horses when other girls were learning to crochet. And the way you finagled that deal to pick up mail and parcels at the Post Office at Kate's Wagon and deliver them to about a dozen ranches. And the way you managed to trip Bert Andrus so he would fall in fresh cow manure."

"He deserved it," Lucy flared, remembering the sly fervor with which young Andrus had tried to kiss her.

"Now, Sis, want to hear something of my plans for your big orchard?"

"Of course. Isn't that why I came to this great, bewildering valley?"

"Lucy, you probably noticed the Uncompahgre River as you were coming here. It is at flood stage just now, and is spreading across the valley meadows."

"And that is where you think fruit can be raised?"

"No, Sis. There is a peculiar geographic situation here. Most of the lowlands are on the east side of the river, and that area is clay-like and alkaline. Good for pasture but little else. But the west side of the Uncomphgre River Valley . . . what a difference." Phillip's voice became eager, and he clasped his hands tightly about his knees. "I have ridden horseback on that west side during my off-duty time. I could scarcely believe my eyes. Up above the river a mile or so there are some great flatlands . . . they are called *mesas* out here. On the mesas the soil is of a reddish color, and it is rich and deep. When it has sufficient water, it is excellent for growing fruits of all kinds. Apples, peaches, plums, pears, cherries, apricots. Just any kind of fruit. You name it, Lucy. Oh yes—and grapes too." Phillip rose and threw an arm across the mantel. "And the time is right. You can get hold of such land by filing homestead claims."

"But what about water for the trees, up on the level land so high above the river?" Lucy asked cautiously.

"There is talk of building a ditch to take water from the river to irrigate thousands of acres."

"But won't that take years to construct?"

"Exactly. So here's what you do. Just as soon as you can, ride into the little shack-town of Pomona. It's about four miles or so downriver. Then look up an old codger by the name of 'Pappy' Loutsenhizer. I understand he is the founder of Pomona."

Lucy's face was puzzled. "If you say so, Phil. But it all sounds crazy to me."

"Let me explain, Lucy. This Cantonment is here to make sure that the Ute Indians keep the peace. In fact, quarters were built for the Ute chief, Ouray, and his wife, Chipeta. A couple of months ago I got one of the older Indians to talking. He told me that off southwestward, along the mountains called the Uncompahgre Plateau, there are streams that flow year-round because they are fed by springs."

Lucy's head was whirling. "Yes . . . yes . . . but what does that have to do with the man you call 'Pappy' something-or-other?"

"Just this. Loutsenhizer is the one man who knows every inch, every stick and stone of this country. In fact, he's something of a legend in this part of Colorado. He has been here for God only knows how long. He was the sole survivor of the Albert Packer tragedy. Anyway, somehow you've got to get him to tell you, or better yet, to take us to some mesa land where we will have such a dependable flow of water."

"Why can't your talkative Indian do it?"

"Because he up and died two days after our little confab."

At that, Lucy's eyes widened in amazement.

"Once we find the right tract of land, you'll still have your work cut out for you," Phillip went on. "Fruit trees don't start yielding overnight, you know."

"I know," Lucy murmured.

"But I'll help out as much as I can—whenever I can get away from the Cantonment," he said, crossing over to his sister and taking her hands in his. Lucy's eyes were bright with anticipation now.

"I don't know how to thank you, Phil," she said.

"Maybe with a jar of preserves made from your first harvest." He laughed.

Chapter 3

At the small settlement of Dallas, Colorado, the stage-coach with Ike Fenlon at the reins took on two more passengers. Both were morosely silent men in their thirties who Royce Milligan pegged as either gamblers or confidence men. They chose to ride inside the coach, but clearly wanted no contact with Goetz, the unwashed and grizzly miner, who sprawled out over one entire carriage-width seat. The arrangement enabled Parson Goodfroe and Royce Milligan to enjoy the cleaner air and thrilling vistas from atop the coach.

It was just after they left Dallas and were driving for the turnoff that would take them across the Dallas Divide, that Royce broke the silence and asked, "Ike, isn't it unusual for one driver to take a stage so long a distance? I thought drivers were changed every few hours at inter-mediate points, but you've been atop this rig every step of the way from Pueblo."

"You're right, Milligan, but my bosses let me single-hand the outfit this time, after I told them I am in one hell of a hurry to reach San Miguel City." Ike had been chewing a quid of tobacco, and now spurted a mouthful of juice to the roadside.

"What's your hurry?" Royce asked.

"It's just that some of my friends are having a party at old San Miguel Town. They say I've got to be there."

As the hours passed and evening came on, there was

some talk among them of the frontier country into which they were heading, then periods of silence during which the noise of the wheels and the horses' hooves rang out loud along the lonesome trail. Soon Royce found his thoughts turning to their previous days of travel. Even now the sound of Lucy Lattamore's voice echoed in his mind. Her presence alongside him had made the trip seem short and enjoyable. He leaned back and closed his eyes, hoping to feel and hear her near him again, if only in his imagination.

They spent an uncomfortable night in a makeshift shelter near the crest of Dallas Divide. The following morning Fenlon reined his four horses down steep and zigzagging bits of road to bring the stage alongside the swollen and swift-running San Miguel River. They came onto the main street of San Miguel City shortly before noon. For all of them except Royce Milligan the arduous trip was at an end.

San Miguel City, the settlement that would later be moved two miles up the San Miguel River, was destined to become the fabulously rich mining town of Telluride, Colorado. On that spring day in 1881, though, Royce Milligan was appalled by its rawness and squalor. Ike Fenlon sensed the young man's dismay and made an effort to ease it, as he said, "It ain't much, Royce, but it sure can get lively. If you want better grub, lodgin' and entertainment, there is another town within walking distance. People call it Columbia. That's where my friends live, the ones who are so all-fired anxious for me to show up tomorrow night. Maybe I'll see you in Columbia." He laughed, then added, "Columbia ain't the gem of the ocean—but it's sure the hot spot of the San Juans."

In breathtaking contrast to San Miguel City's few log shacks was the natural setting—the mountains, the forests, and the snow-mantled peaks rising on all sides. Up the river valley a couple of miles, he could see vast canyon walls, from one of which a white, lace-like waterfall plunged hundreds of feet as part of the headwaters of the

San Miguel River. There were also greening meadows, encroached upon by coniferous forests.

Royce said a regretful farewell to Ike Fenlon and was standing hesitantly before a one-storied edifice bearing a HOTEL—BED AND BATH sign, when both Parson Goodfroe and Goetz approached him. Goetz was the first to thrust out a work-roughened hand. "Mr. Milligan, we've had quite a journey, haven't we? I hope that someday we meet again."

Royce laid his free hand on Goetz's shoulder. "I hope so, too. I will be in a place called Mesita. Look me up." He watched Goetz amble up the path that served as a sidewalk, and then he turned to Parson Goodfroe. "The same goes for you, Parson."

"It's possible that I might be in your part of the country." Goodfroe replied. "As you know, my circuit-riding takes me far afield sometimes. I travel many miles on horseback, in freighters' wagons, even on skis to spread the word of the Lord."

"Well," Royce went on, "should you ever find yourself in Mesita, you can reach me through my paper's owner, Tim O'Fallon—"

Because Royce was staring at a rider who had stopped beside him, he was unaware of the startled manner in which Parson Goodfroe had noted his mention of Tim O'Fallon's name. The rider had seemed to appear out of nowhere, mounted on a rangy sorrel gelding and leading two other horses. There was a gray mare, also saddled, and a heavier mare burdened with a packsaddle.

The newcomer, a suntanned man scarcely out of his teens, removed a hand-rolled cigarette from his mouth and asked in a cautious way, "Sir, would you happen to be Mr. Royce Milligan?"

Royce nodded. "That I am. Why do you ask?"

"I have been sent here to meet you. Mr. Tim O'Fallon told me to be sure and meet the stage every day until you showed up." He eyed the two travel-bags lying at Royce's feet. "Have you anything heavier?"

"Not with me. I shipped a couple of boxes. Maybe they will catch up before my socks rot off."

Goodfroe had stood silently by, gazing inquiringly at the young rider. Then, as if something had eased within him, the preacher said with finality, "Royce, if you have to ride all the way to Mesita today, I must not delay you. Besides, I have a sermon to prepare this evening." He held out a white immaculate hand. "God ride with you, my friend." Then without another word he walked away.

The route Royce and his guide followed toward their downriver destination of Mesita proved a rueful surprise to Royce. For almost twenty miles they doubled back over the exact river route by which the stagecoach had approached San Miguel City. The young man whom Tim O'Fallon had dispatched to meet the stagecoach was named Max Beasley. He explained that they had best stop for the night at a hamlet called Placerville and proceed to Mesita in the morning.

"Placerville!" a tired and somewhat bewildered Royce Milligan repeated with disgust. "That is exactly where we came onto this river earlier today. I could have gotten off there and saved hours of travel."

"Then you wouldn't have gotten to see beautiful San Miguel City," Beasley answered, smiling wryly.

There were a couple of tents set up in Placerville to do a sort of hotel business. The two men ate from tin plates as they squatted in the evening shadows of a towering spruce tree. Surprisingly, the food was good, and plentiful, causing Royce to wonder aloud what sort of person provided such accommodations. Then he added, "Getting food and supplies into such a place must be costly."

"I don't think that worries Mr. O'Fallon very much," his companion responded.

Royce's head lifted and he stared at Beasley. "You mean Mr. Tim O'Fallon—down at Mesita—owns this wayside eatery?"

"Sure. And just about everything else in these parts."

Royce had known O'Fallon years before the man had come west seeking his fortune; he'd also heard how O'Fallon had come by his money. "Some fellow told me that Tim O'Fallon got rich overnight. Is there any truth in that rumor?"

"You better believe there is," young Max Beasley assured him. "Mr. O'Fallon was a prospector when he came to the San Miguel River Valley. He didn't know much about minerals or how to locate them, but he sure knew how to make friends—and play poker. That's how he won the Jackass Lode. In a poker game. Five-card stud."

Royce whistled through his teeth.

"The Jackass claim was nothing but a probing pothole, sunk maybe forty feet into the mountain when Mr. O'Fallon won it." Beasley continued. "He won a couple of hundred dollars in the same game, and he spent it having a couple of muckers help him extend the shaft. After another twenty-some feet they hit a seam of silver. And you know what? It widened into about the richest vein of silver-bearing ore ever discovered in Colorado. Since making the first shipment to a smelter up in Leadville, my boss has sure made things hum. He started this town, Mesita, opened the hotel and saloon . . . and even a bank."

The extent to which "Lucky Tim" O'Fallon's sudden wealth was changing the aspect of the valley became more fully apparent as the two horsemen neared their destination. Another two hours' ride brought them to a tributary stream called McKenzie Creek near where the San Miguel River veered somewhat northward. Along it was a fainter trail, for the main road veered straight west and then began the twisting ascent that would bring it to the top of Norwood Hill.

Max Beasley led the way onto the fainter trail which twisted along close to the riverbank. The stream was still high and roily with spring runoff. There were mingled thickets and tall trees lining the banks, and places where large pine and spruce trees had been removed to make way for the road. On this day of stillness and sunshine, the swollen stream had spilled onto the road and they were forced to ride through water that at times came close to their horses' knees.

Within half a mile they came to a small open park. To their right a treeless but brush-covered hill sloped down from timbered country above. Suddenly Royce Milligan gasped. At the base of this hill, and bordering the trail they would ride, was a row of rounded kilns for the production of fired brick. About them, a dozen or so men were at work, shoveling clay from wagons, operating brick-forming machines, and making sure that a constant level of heat was maintained by burning logs within the kilns. The size and activity of the operation caused Royce to exclaim, "What will they do with a hundred thousand or more bricks?"

"Use them for building Mr. O'Fallon's town. It is only two miles down the river from here."

"Yes, but does he think he's building another Chicago?"

"Wait until we get there and you'll see. Lucky O'Fallon wants to build a better town than any other in western Colorado." Beasley paused to study this newcomer beside him. "Mr. Milligan, maybe I shouldn't ask, but what brings you to Mesita? All I know is that I was sent to meet you."

Royce laughed at his guide's hesitation. "I am going to work on a newspaper, help to get it started in Mesita."

"That is great," Beasley enthused. "I just hoped you weren't another gambler or gunslinger we would have to chase out of town."

"Maybe my news will get me run out," Royce parried.

As they passed the kilns, Beasley was greeted by several workmen whom it was obvious he knew. Several of them bombarded him with questions about news from the outside world. Others grinned and asked about the number and availability of whores in Columbia and San Miguel City. Also, was he lugging mail, snuff, plug tobacco or whiskey? He answered some questions and deftly fended off the more indelicate ones.

As they rode on, Royce asked his guide, "What brings so many men to—"

"This ass-end of creation?" Beasley cut in. "Money. Wages. Good wages. Mr. O'Fallon found a fortune in the Jackass workings. He told townfolks that right here it was found, and right here it would be spent. Those brick-making places we just passed furnish walls and foundations and a lot of other things for as pretty a town as you ever laid eyes on."

"But how many people can make a living? Will the town have work and business and trade to live up to Lucky O'Fallon's expectations?" Royce was still feeling lingering doubts as to the feasibility of a newspaper here in the wilderness.

In his reply Max Beasley revealed a keenness of mind. "Mr. Milligan, nobody knows how long the silver lode will support Mr. O'Fallon's ambitions. Maybe in five years . . . or ten . . . all this will peter out. But this is rich country. Good for timbering, ranching, maybe some farming. There is talk that someday we may have a railroad."

They rode silently for a while, for they were beginning to feel tired. The sun had dropped behind a western ridge when they broke from some timber, into the lovely glade that was becoming the town of Mesita. Already there were a few intersecting streets bordered by both log and clapboard buildings. Close beside such structures were some sixteen sizeable brick buildings, the windows of which now caught and reflected the afterglow of evening. There was a surrounding stand of both leafed and needled trees, sloping down to the San Miguel River as it seemed to circle around the townsite. On the gently sloping hill beyond the business blocks, there were already a few homes and a small park with a flagpole and bandstand. A

flag moved listlessly in the breeze. Tranquility and good
planning seemed to emanate from the place. "It is the sort
of town I have always dreamed about," Royce murmured
with reverence in his voice.

As they rode into the settlement's center, Royce looked
searchingly about, and then said, "Maybe you can point
out a hotel or rooming house where we can drop my stuff.
And how about these horses? Where do we leave them?"

Beasley's voice took on firmness as he reined his mount
close to Royce's mare. "Don't worry about lodgings, Mr.
Milligan; I was told to bring you to Mr. O'Fallon's house
as soon as we arrived. After that, I'll handle the horses.
That is part of my regular job."

Royce nodded agreement and then rode quietly alongside his guide. Within minutes they had left the small
business section and were ascending the hill where he had
previously noted the larger and more widely spaced
homes. Royce couldn't help but wonder at the newness
and orderliness of this town, so unlike the slovenly array
of shacks at San Miguel City, and he thought, *What a
difference a million or so dollars and a man of vision like
Tim O'Fallon can make.*

They came presently to the yard of an unpretentious but
spacious brick home set in a grove of scattered blue
spruce trees. There was a patch of lawn and several
flower beds, but the landscaping was largely that native
to the mountain slope. At that moment something close
to a premonition swept over Royce Milligan. It was as
though he had reached the place of his destiny, where
either success or failure would be thrust upon him in the
days ahead.

The eerie feeling fled as Max Beasley dismounted,
opened an iron gate, and motioned for Royce to ride onto
a well-graveled stretch of driveway leading to the veranda
of the house. And now Beasley fell back, for up ahead a
man had stepped spryly down the stone steps and was
approaching. Royce dismounted and waited, then smiled
to hear the Irish-accented voice of his father's old friend,

Tim O'Fallon. "Royce, welcome to Colorado. Lord, but I'm happy to see you." He clasped the newcomer's hand in the firmness of his own. "Boy, you're a lot taller—and a mite older—than I remember you. But that cornsilk hair and those brown eyes . . . just like your daddy's. They haven't changed."

"Mr. O'Fallon, you look fit as a fiddle too. You can't imagine how I have looked forward to seeing you." Royce's gaze swept over the older man, whom he had not seen for eight years; but O'Fallon, now in his mid-fifties, seemed still dynamic and vibrant. He was of medium height and weight; his eyes were blue and clear and confident, set in a face weathered by the wind and the sun. Only a touch of gray in the black, thick, unruly hair gave away his age.

Their mutual study of the changes eight years had wrought was interrupted as Max Beasley strode near and picked up the reins of Royce's mare. "I unloaded the packhorse and set your bags inside the door, Mr. Milligan."

Royce's jaw dropped in surprise. "But wait a minute. You mean to tell me I'm staying at the boss-man's house?"

"Damn it, Royce. Don't get difficult first thing off," O'Fallon chided him, his eyes twinkling. "We've got a lot of planning to do. Say, did you ever get your printing paraphernalia bought and started out this way?"

"It's trailing along," Royce assured him, as he watched Beasley ride away with both mares in tow. He then turned back to O'Fallon. That young fellow you sent to fetch me is competent. Knows how to think for himself."

"That's why I have him around." O'Fallon nodded. Then he added, "Let's go inside so you can freshen up before dinner. And another thing, Royce. Don't you think it is time to quit calling me Mr. O'Fallon? That was okay when you were a youngster, but let's make it Tim now. Tim and Royce."

Inside, there was a spacious living room furnished in mostly wood and leather. The walls were livened with handsome paintings of the Royal Gorge, the Maroon Bells Peaks, and the awesome sweep of the San Juan Mountains. There were also vases of fresh wildflowers. It seemed to Royce that this room, and those adjoining it, were an expression of Tim O'Fallon's love of and confidence in the west.

Royce was shown to his room by a quiet, pleasant-faced Mexican woman he judged to be in her thirties. He sensed she spoke little English, and so voiced his thanks in the few Spanish words he had picked up in Pueblo, where he had awaited the stage and arranged for the routing of his press. His bags lay on the bed and he noted with satisfaction and relief that there was an adjoining bathroom with a clean tub and towels. A bath was something he had sorely missed on the long stagecoach journey, so he stripped, bathed leisurely, and after shaving and donning a robe he stretched out on the softest bed he had felt since leaving Alabama, almost a month before.

After a few moments, a small, framed picture on one wall caught his eye, a daguerreotype portraying a girl of about twenty with shining eyes and a mischievous smile. Royce peered toward it in a fascinated way, and as he did, somehow the face became that of another girl, the one he had so reluctantly parted from at the Cantonment, the intrepid Lucy Lattamore. He smiled as he envisioned her staunchly making her way through the snow, whispering soothing words to the horse she led. And he wondered when he'd see the remarkable Miss Lattamore again.

Darkness had crept into his room by the time he realized that he must rouse himself and dress for dinner. He came suddenly to his feet, struck a match and touched it to a kerosene lamp. In the glow of its spotless chimney he saw his own face, and smiled. There was now a resolve and determination about him. *Somehow I will get*

back to the Military Cantonment and persuade Lucy
Lattamore to come to Mesita—perhaps for a concert!

He was still planning his strategy with Lucy when
fifteen minutes later, the soft ringing of a bell summoned
him to the evening meal. Tim O'Fallon was waiting for
him at the bottom of the stairs, and together they entered
the dining room. Royce looked about admiringly, for the
room's walls and ceiling were of fir slabs, expertly fitted
and stained to a natural luster. He eyed the table, which
was but a long bench of heavy, smoothed plank. The
seats were padded benches alongside, and instead of white
table linen there were colorful mats and napkins with a
Mexican motif. Light was cast by a candled table-fixture
atop a statue of a bucking bronco. On one wall was hung
the largest Spanish sombrero that Royce had ever seen.

There were already three other people in the room when
Royce entered. One, a woman obviously past middle age
but with a face searchingly alert, smiled in a manner that
eased Royce's reserve. "You must be the young publisher
Mr. O'Fallon has been waiting for so impatiently."

"I was even more impatient to get here, ma'am."

"This is Margaret Hendricks, Royce. She's been a
friend of mine and my housekeeper for more years than
either of us care to remember."

Before Royce could say more, Tim had guided him to
a tall and ruggedly handsome man, saying, "Royce, I
want you to meet Robert Delaney."

Royce accepted the man's offered hand, and was aware
of the strength of his grip. He judged Delaney to be
perhaps thirty-seven years old, with the robust physique
of an even younger man. Delaney's hair was reddish, his
eyes hazel.

"Tim tells me you are here to start a newspaper,"
Delaney observed.

"If my press ever makes it this far," Royce said. Then
he turned and saw Max Beasley, now out of his riding
gear and wearing dark brown trousers and a shirt of plaid
cotton, open at the throat.

"You don't look so trailworn," Beasley said.

"Thanks to a bath, some sleep, and the care with which you brought my suitcases through."

At O'Fallon's gesture, they all took seats on the benches.

"Margaret, would you say a blessing?" their host asked.

Her words were well-chosen, sincere, and of short duration. Their ending seemed a signal for food to be brought from the kitchen. Royce noticed that the woman serving them was the same one who had shown him to his room upon his arrival. She smiled in recognition and then busied herself serving. Presently she spoke in Spanish to an older woman who stood a bit uncertainly in the kitchen door. She was obviously the cook, and quickly retreated into her kitchen, nodding the while in understanding.

At Royce's stare of incomprehension, Tim O'Fallon chuckled. "*No comprendes*, Royce?"

Royce only grimaced.

"You will pick up Spanish . . . the curse words first, of course," O'Fallon assured him, and then burst into a flow of Spanish that sounded smooth and musical. Before falling silent, he turned to the woman sitting opposite him. "Margaret, do you care to translate?"

Laughter was in her eyes as she explained, "The boss-man says a Spanish lesson can come later, otherwise our beef and potatoes will be cold as a conquistador's sword."

The conversation then turned to Royce's trip, for all of those about him seemed starved for news of the outside world. He told them of the blizzard that had stalled Ike Fenlon's stage on Blue Mesa, and how the passengers had taken refuge in an abandoned mine. Throughout the telling, he dwelt on the courage and initative of the copper-haired girl who had likely saved their lives. "She was heading for the Military Cantonment in the Uncompahgre Valley; she has a brother there who is an officer.

When we arrived they gave her the royal treatment because they hoped to get her to sing for the troops. She's an accomplished songstress, you see.''

"How exciting," Margaret Hendricks commented.

Robert Delaney had listened in silence. Now he glanced curiously toward Royce. "Too bad such a fabulous creature wasn't headed this way."

"Perhaps later," Tim O'Fallon observed. "After our opera house is built."

Delaney's head jerked upward. "An opera house? God Almighty, Tim. What next? First a newspaper, and now an opera house we can't begin to fill."

O'Fallon's face was suddenly stern. "Bob, let me do the planning, the building . . . and the spending. You're doing very well, aren't you, with the contract you have to furnish logs to the sawmill?"

The reprimand was meant to silence Delaney; nonetheless he went on. "Mr. Milligan, I'll be interested in seeing what you find around here to put in your newspaper. Something about a horse going lame, or two soused miners brawling downtown? Maybe a couple of columns about how the honky-tonk women just about run things up at Columbia." He laughed sarcastically, then rose to his feet. "You'll have to excuse me; some things need attention down at the pole yard.' He turned to Royce Milligan. "I am glad to have met you, sir. Why not come by my office in a day or so. I have to be out of Mesita for two or three days, so why not make it early tomorrow, before I leave. I think we should have a talk."

The tension lessened with his departure, and Mrs. Hendricks said, "Don't pay any attention to Bob Delaney. He's just used to this valley being the way it always has been. But things change, don't they, Royce?"

"Indeed they do," the young man concurred.

Suddenly Tim O'Fallon spoke up from the far end of the table. "If that printing equipment isn't here soon, I've a mind to send Max to find out where it's stalled and speed it along."

His words brought a subtle smile to Mrs. Hendricks' face. "Tim, I need Max to help me plant a garden and do housecleaning."

O'Fallon stared at her. In all the years he had known this vivacious woman, she had never shown the least bit of interest in gardening. Their gaze met and Mesita's founder seemed to read her mind. He turned to Royce. "On second thought, I guess *you* ought to be the one to chase down your own confounded stuff. But give it at least a couple days to show up." With that, he grinned, touched a napkin to his lips, and asked, "Who's for an after-dinner drink?"

Chapter 4

Spring, it seemed, came a bit reluctantly to the valley of the Uncompahgre River. On the evening of the second day after Lucy Lattamore's arrival, dark clouds closed in and dropped six inches of wet snow over the valley. When the storm cleared, the brilliance of strengthening sunshine on the whiteness was almost blinding. Much of the work of the small military post was carried on inside to avoid the glare; those who went outside either wore dark glasses or attempted to shade their eyes with pieces of smoked glass.

It was through such an improvised filter that Lucy studied the skyward-jutting San Juan Mountains through the parlor window. The immense snowfields and forested stretches were an awesome sight. Phillip had gone somewhere within the Cantonment, and Lucy felt restless from being kept indoors. She laid the colored piece of glass on the table, sipped a cup of tea, and then studied the upper reaches of the valley again. Where, along the vast ridge, had Ike Fenlon's coach turned to climb into the dizzying heights of the wilderness?

Minutes later her thoughts were with Royce Milligan, wondering about his reaction to Mesita. Perhaps his equipment was there, she mused, and he was already writing news and setting type. Suddenly the sound of rapping on the front door broke her chain of thought.

Moving quickly, she opened it and peered out. A tall man in an army uniform was standing on the porch.

"Major Shores," she said with pleasure. "Do come in." She knew him to be the Cantonment commander, for Phillip had introduced them at the officers' dining table.

Hat in hand, he bowed a bit stiffly and then entered. Lucy waved him to a chair. "I'm sorry, Major Shores, but Phillip isn't here."

"That's no problem," he assured her. "It is you I need to talk with." His hand moved as though suggesting she sit down across from him.

She drew up a ladder-backed chair and eased down into it. "I am listening," she said quietly.

"Miss Lattamore, you are creating a problem," he began. "Ever since you arrived here I have been deluged—yes, practically overrun by men demanding that you sing for the garrison."

"But not one of them has ever heard me," she exclaimed.

"Likely not, but when the stage stopped here all Ike Fenlon could talk about was your fantastic voice. And that preacher, Goodfroe, bragged about it as well." He paused and smiled ruefully. "My men are bored stiff with this little Cantonment. They want entertainment—dancing, music, laughter, something of home, like a lovely-voiced . . . yes, and lovely-faced . . . woman."

"Of course I will—" Lucy began, then fell silent as the commander continued.

"And something else . . . something puzzling to me has come about."

"What, Major Shores?" she asked carefully.

"This morning I received a telegram. It came from the town of Columbia. A group of women who call themselves the Columbia Quality want you to sing there, too. Confound it, somehow they expect I can arrange it."

Lucy gasped. "Columbia Quality? What on earth could that be?" As he shook his head and voiced no reply, she recovered a bit. "Major Shores, if your men would like a concert, or a sing-along perhaps, I would be delighted to appear. Schedule it for a convenient time. Just let me know a day or so in advance.''

He smiled in a pleased way and rose to leave. "Miss Lattamore, I am glad you came to our little Cantonment. Duty here can be utterly boring at times." He had opened the door to leave when he asked, "Is there anything we can do for you?"

Lucy laughed softly. "Just try to unravel the mystery of the Columbia Quality. Perhaps it is a sewing circle.''

His eyes widened, but he did not comment as he took his leave.

Under a cloudless sky, the snow almost disappeared within two days. The roads became passable, and so on a Friday afternoon Lucy mounted a gentle black horse that Phillip checked out of the post stable. Within an hour she entered the shack-strewn settlement of Pomona. She scrutinized the place, recalling that the name *Pomona* was that of the Roman goddess of fruit. Yet there wasn't a fruit tree in sight. There was a wide and muddy street, bordered by perhaps a dozen log and slab cabins; on some of them dry reeds from the riverbank had been used to patch the roofs. She saw two men and three dogs lounging in the sun near a structure bearing a scrawled sign: LAND OFFICE.

She rode nearer, careful to keep a safe distance from the strangers as they stared at her. "Pardon me, sirs. I am looking for a Mr. Loutsenhizer," she said.

A boy of perhaps sixteen answered her, pointing as he spoke toward a sizeable cabin some distance from the others. "That's Pappy's place over yonder. Want me to fetch him?"

"No, thank you; I'll ride over and see if he is there."

"Should be. This time of morning he reads those funny-looking German newspapers he gets."

Lucy wheeled her horse cautiously away, and urged it down the road toward the cabin the boy had pointed out.

While still clutching the reins of her horse, she knocked firmly on Loutsenhizer's door. "Yah," came a voice, and moments later the door swung open. A tall and strongly built man peered at her from deep-set, intelligent eyes. She was aware of the thickness of his snow-white hair and beard, and of something else. . . . Instantly a sureness was upon her. This man had been through travail and suffering; it had imprinted itself indelibly on his face and lingered in his gaze. Maybe it had to do with the Packer tragedy Phillip had mentioned, she surmised. But now he was asking, "Young lady, what can I do for you?"

"Mr. Loutsenhizer, my name is Lucy Lattamore. I am staying at the Military Cantonment where my brother is an officer. We want to get hold of some land for an orchard. We were told to seek your advice."

His face showed animation as he replied, "Then why not hitch your horse to my fence and come in?"

Lucy's gaze moved across open space and became uneasy. All three of the loafers were still in place, and she sensed she and this elderly man were closely watched. Loutsenhizer seemed to quickly understand. "Perhaps it would be better," he said, "if I brought chairs outside for us." Then, as if to himself, he added, "God willing, someday our community will have enough women that the sight of one will not arouse evil speculation."

"Even Denver doesn't have enough females for that," was her rejoinder.

He seemed a bit startled, but observed, "I see you are blessed with humor. That is good. Now, about the fruit-lands? What do you need to know?"

"Mainly our problem is that of sufficient water. We know that the mesas west of here have deep and rich soil, well-suited to orchards."

He nodded knowingly. "Miss, I don't know of a single fruit, except oranges and lemons, that will *not* thrive on the mesas. You are right about the soil. Also the altitude and the climate are ideal. Someday there will be vast

groves of apple, peach, cherry, and other fruit-bearing
trees for miles up and down this Uncompahgre Valley.''

"If the water is adequate," she answered doubtfully.
"I doubt that the river, even if it can be diverted, will
suffice in this arid country.''

"You have given much thought to this, Miss Lattamore.''

"Enough that I'm positive I must have orchard land
where there is an independent source of water, say from
a creek or springs.''

"Spring Creek Mesa, about three miles west, is such
a place.''

"But the land has already been claimed—mostly by
you.''

"That is so." He smiled. "But there are other mesas
with sustaining water.''

"Where?" Lucy asked excitedly.

The old man was studying her intently. "Just a
moment, Miss. Your voice! Do you happen to be the
person everyone hereabouts is talking of . . . the one
scheduled to sing at the Cantonment?''

"It happens I am. Why?''

"You need to find orchard land. I need—for at least
one more time—to hear music sung by a gifted and
trained singer." He was close to laughter as he continued.
"Can we bargain? I tell you where to claim open land
with assured water, and you slip me tickets to each and
every concert.''

"Oh, but you offer so much for so little," she said in
wonder.

"Land can be had for filing on it and so can water.
But getting into the overcrowded hall when you sing
. . . Miss Lattamore, I am content. Do we have a
bargain?''

"Oh, yes, yes indeed," she rejoiced.

"Then listen carefully." From his pocket he drew a
stubby pencil and an old wrinkled envelope. "Maybe you
had best jot this down. Eight miles southwest of my

Spring Creek holdings is another mesa, flat-topped but with a gentle slope down from the band of cedars along the Uncompahgre Plateau. I don't know as it is named, but I think of it as Cedar's Edge Mesa. Back in the timber above it is a sizeable creek that headwaters up on the plateau in stands of magnificent timber. There is the water you are seeking, only you will have to dig about two miles of ditch to divert it onto your orchard lands.''

Caring nothing of what the three gawking onlookers might think or say, she impulsively leaned closer, to throw an arm about this strange man's shoulder and place her cheek against his. "Thank you . . . thank you so much, Mr. Loutsenhizer. And don't you dare miss my concert.''

"Do you know," he answered slowly, "I haven't talked this much with a pretty young woman in ten years.''

Already Lucy adored this man, and so a moment later words were pouring from her as she told him of her trip westward aboard Ike Fenlon's stage. Of the blizzard, and of the cairn by which she had sighted the life-saving mine shaft. She spoke too of the age and eeriness of the ancient shaft, with its telltale traces of ore. After mentioning their departure in the wake of freight wagons, she asked, "What do you suppose could have been the purpose and the origin of such a place? And what of the sighting device?''

He had removed his hat and now combed gnarled fingers through his mane of white hair. For perhaps a minute, he sat in thoughtful silence. Then he asked, "Would you mind if I call you Lucy?''

"I would like that.''

"Lucy, I believe that perhaps you stumbled onto a relic of the days when Spanish conquistadores pushed into this portion of Colorado a couple of centuries ago. If they discovered a sizeable silver lode—perhaps with some gold—they no doubt captured Indians and used them for slaves to open and operate a mine. I have come across other traces of those cruel and greedy Spanish noblemen."

"Where do you suppose they came from?"

"Perhaps from Mexico, or even South America. You have heard of Cortés and Pizarro? They had many henchmen."

Lucy rose reluctantly to leave, then said, "You are the first person to whom I have ever mentioned the cairn. Even those I took to the mine portal have no knowledge of it. Yet I had an urge to tell you, Mr. Loutsenhizer. You have told me of land that could mean everything to me."

He rose to stretch out a thin and timeworn hand, then replied. "Come and see me again, Lucy. And I will be watching Cedar's Edge Mesa."

"And you be sure and show up for my concert. There will be a front-row chair with your name on it."

Lucy had been heedless of the time as she talked with Pappy Loutsenhizer. As she mounted her horse, she realized the pangs of hunger were upon her. She looked about, hoping to catch sight of some sort of public eating-place, and it was then that her gaze fastened on a familiar object: the stagecoach by which she had arrived in this valley. It was drawn up beside a large tent through which a stovepipe was sending smoke into the breeze. Maybe, she thought, Ike Fenlon is driving it again. I can ask him about all of the others.

She reined her horse toward the tent, noticing with satisfaction that the coach horses had access to a trough of water and that hay was scattered about. She dismounted before the open flap of the tent and peered inside. This single canvas shelter served as both a kitchen and dining room. Far back, there was a great flat-topped iron range from which utensils of various kinds hung, and pots and pans gave off steam and aromas. It was flanked by tiers of wooden boxes on one side and dish-cleaning gear on the other.

At a planked table six people, four men and two

women, were seated on benches. Five of them she had never seen before, and she judged them to be stage passengers. The sixth one had already spotted her and now rose excitedly to his feet. "Hi . . . over there," Ike Fenlon called. "Damn but it is good to see you. Sit down so we can talk."

"And I'll eat while we chat, Ike," she smiled. "I am famished." She sat down and looked about as though seeking a menu.

"You won't find a grub list here," Fenlon warned. "It's take what they have. But usually it is pretty good."

A hefty woman wearing a spotted apron set a plate, cup, and bone-handled knife and fork before her, and advised, "Make them pass the victuals down your way. It's ham and beans today. With light-bread, molasses, and apple strudel. Eighty-five cents, please."

Before Lucy could reach into her pocket, Ike Fenlon thrust a dollar at their server. "Allow me, Lucy."

"Thank you, Ike. Oh, I am glad I came across you here. How was your trip to San Miguel City?"

He swallowed and turned to answer. As his mouth opened Lucy almost shrieked with surprise. "Ike, your tooth! The one that was missing. You have a new one and it is *gold*."

Her excited comment caused the others at the table to laugh aloud and stare at Fenlon.

"You bet I have. Take a good gander at it," Fenlon said, and pulled his lip up to allow the gleaming front tooth to be observed.

"Where did you get it? Was there a dentist at San Miguel City?"

"No, but there was one at Columbia. It was part of the surprise they wanted me there for." He lifted a foot so she could see it. "Look, I got new boots too."

"You mean your friends gave you all that—and a haircut and mustache trim too?"

"They did things up brown for me," he affirmed. Then

he nodded. "Those ladies of Columbia Quality sure know how to give a party."

His words caused Lucy to jerk in surprise and stare into his face. "Ike Fenlon," she half-stammered, "are you telling me there really is a group at some town called Columbia Quality?"

"Sure. How else could—" he began, surprised at her interest and reaction.

"Is it a sewing circle? Or maybe a sort of literary club?"

"Well, not exactly," he answered guardedly. "It's just some women I pick up packages and do errands for in bigger towns along the stage route." Fenlon gulped his coffee and started to rise.

Lucy laid a restraining hand on his arm. "Ike, it is important to me; I need to know what sort of community activities the ladies of Columbia Quality engage in. Are they employed?"

Fenlon's face reddened as he replied, "Well . . . yes, they are . . . sort of self-employed."

Those about the table had been listening in silence. Now a dark-faced man, apparently a mine laborer, spoke up in disgust. "For Christ's sake, Fenlon. Why don't you just out and tell her that those dames of Columbia Quality are the finest bunch of prostitutes this side of Omaha!"

His blunt words brought both laughter and startled gasps from those listening. Ike Fenlon took a little time to recover, and then said, "All right, Lucy. Now you know. My friends are ladies of the night."

"And of the daytime too, provided you've got the cash," someone leered.

Fenlon ignored the gibe. "Lucy, why are you so interested in Columbia Quality?"

"Because they have sent word to Major Shores at the Military Cantonment asking that I come over and sing for them." She paused to study Fenlon's face, and then asked, "Ike, did you put them up to this?"

Suddenly he banged his fist onto the table. "What if I

did? They have so little, and are branded as women to be kept away from almost everything worthwhile.'' He paused. When he went on he sounded defeated. ''But you won't do it—sing for them—now that you know?''

Her answer startled everyone at the table. ''The hell I won't! I will ask Major Shores as soon as I get back to the Cantonment, to send word that I will give an hour-long concert for the ladies of Columbia Quality at their convenience.''

Little more was said as they finished the meal, but when Ike Fenlon was about to leave to rehitch his team, Lucy asked him to stay for a few moments. Once the passengers were out of hearing, she asked, ''Ike, how do you really feel about my doing this?''

His eyes were shining. ''Lucy Lattamore, I am doggoned honored to have you as a friend.''

''Ike, have you seen Mr. Milligan lately?''

''Not since we parted at San Miguel City. Someone was waiting to take him on to Mesita. But don't worry, that hombre knows how to take care of himself.''

She came reluctantly to her feet. ''I mustn't delay you longer. But, Ike, when you see him, just . . . just tell him—''

As she struggled for words, he smiled and spoke to ease her self-consciousness. ''I will tell him that Miss Lucy Lattamore sends her regards.''

Chapter 5

Despite the request of Robert Delaney that Royce Milligan come and "talk things over" with him, Royce showed no inclination to do so. He had resented the manner in which Delaney worded the request and spoke of the paper's prospects in Mesita. There were other factors that forestalled such a meeting, too. Builders, employed by Tim O'Fallon, were in need of an interior layout for the printing plant and office. There was much Royce must do in a hurry, for if he failed to get matters well in hand, there would inevitably be further delay should he need to go in search of his printing equipment, which he believed—impatiently—should already have arrived.

It was mid-afternoon of the third day after his arrival before he felt that his affairs had any semblance of order. Feeling the urge to be in the open air for a time, he left the unfinished newspaper building and set out along the busiest of the town's few streets. With each step he became more and more conscious of the beauty of the town's location, nestling between the river and the encroaching mountain slopes.

The spring flooding had receded a bit, allowing him to tread near the rapidly moving water of the San Miguel. Perhaps he would seek out a trout pool. He had no fishing equipment, but he could note the spot and return with the needed hooks and line on another day. He soon realized

that fishing spots were in less accessible areas, mostly at
the bends of the stream. He saw also that there was a
well-worn and rutted wagon road leading downstream; he
followed it with growing curiosity, and after an hour, had
reached a point he judged to be three miles below Mesita.

There was an abrupt veering of the river as it swept to
the right, around a point of rocks several hundred feet
high. Royce plodded ahead, and then paused in astonishment. There was another river-side stretch of broad
meadow, somewhat smaller and more barren than that of
Tim O'Fallon's townsite. And here, it seemed at first
there was only noise and disorder. Sawdust filled the air
and logs were piled everywhere. All of a sudden Royce
realized that he had come to a lumber storage and
processing yard.

The entire operation was surrounded by a strong pole
fence, with barbed wire, clearly meant to turn any
trespasser back. At a locked gate in front, there was a
sign with bold black lettering: DELANEY LUMBER
COMPANY. K E E P O U T. THIS MEANS YOU!

With heightened curiosity, Royce stared about. There
were men working in the yard, unloading already trimmed
logs from the running gears of wagons and stacking them
close to a large building where he judged the preliminary
sawing was done. The source of power had to be some
sort of steam engine, Royce speculated, for black smoke
came belching out of the firebox of a steam-producing
boiler, sullying the otherwise pure mountain air.

Further observation made Royce practically certain that
no passerby, afoot, on horseback, or with a vehicle, could
proceed further down the river canyon without passing
through the private property of the plant. On both sides
of the river the high and discouraging fences reached from
the water's edge to as far back onto the slopes as he could
see.

What Royce couldn't understand was where these logs
were being hauled from. He could discern both pine and
spruce; he felt positive that such massive logs must come

from an area of ample moisture, probably high in the mountains. He had never seen any signs of such logs coming through Mesita or down the road by which he had come to this isolated sawmill. They have to come, he surmised, from further down the river, perhaps from some high forested slopes adjacent to the river.

But why all the privacy and need to keep everyone out? *Logging isn't unlawful, nor is sawmilling,* Royce mused. Yet Delaney sure discouraged visitors.

Just then Royce became aware of a man approaching him. The fellow was heavyset, in fact obese to the point of walking slowly and with difficulty. Finally he stopped just beyond the locked gate and the KEEP OUT sign. Royce could see that the stranger was middle-aged, and was clad in a jacket and trousers of tan corduroy cloth. A wide-brimmed straw hat was jammed low on his forehead, and streaks of sweat glistened on his florid face and heavy jowls. Upon the pocket of his black shirt was the badge of a deputy sheriff; there was a worn gun holster at his belt, from which the black handle of a revolver protruded.

His eyes swept Royce in swift, but exacting appraisal; then he said, in a voice somewhat high-pitched for so large a man, "What are you looking for?"

"Nothing in particular," Royce answered. "I am a stranger hereabouts, and was doing a bit of sight-seeing along the river."

"This is private property," the fat man advised. "Nobody comes in without written permission."

The warning tone accompanying the words rankled Royce Milligan. "I have no intention of trespassing, Sheriff," he said sharply. Then he added, "But maybe you wouldn't mind telling me something. Whereabouts do you get such huge logs?" He was pointing toward stacked tree trunks averaging two to three feet in diameter.

The badged man beyond the fence seemed to jerk in surprise, and his face tightened. "Listen, I don't know who you are or what you want, but I'll tell you two things. Those logs come from way hell-and-gone south of the river. And the other thing, mister. Folks around here don't like snoops. Don't come down this way again.''

Royce's temper flared, but he held himself in check as he turned to retrace his steps toward Mesita. Someday he would meet the overstuffed lawman again. In the meantime there was much to ponder. It was evident that Robert Delaney, with extensive lumber-milling facilities and some sort of contract with Tim O'Fallon, was firmly entrenched as an area business leader. But puzzling indeed was the seclusion of the lumber mill and the atmosphere of secrecy about it. And why had the fat man wearing a lawman's badge been so evasive about the source of logs?

Royce returned to the yet unfurnished quarters that would become his newspaper plant. Thus far, he was utilizing some empty packing boxes for a makeshift desk and chair. He sat tiredly down and let his mind search back across the events that had brought him to this strange settlement in the Colorado wilderness. He had been on the verge of accepting an editorial job with a Birmingham newspaper when Tim O'Fallon's offer of full publishing and editorial responsibilities had reached him. O'Fallon's pay offer had been excellent, but more exciting had been the thought of venturing to the western frontier.

He'd been ruminating like this for ten minutes or so, when the outer door opened and Tim O'Fallon stood silhouetted against the light of sunset.

"Come on in, boss-man, and grab an empty powder box to sit on," Royce welcomed him.

"Better not, Royce," O'Fallon replied, grinning, and then added, "We'd best be getting up to the house. Those Mexican ladies get pretty riled if I am late for dinner."

"Say, Tim, don't you think I have mooched bed and board long enough at your home?" He held up a restraining hand. "Don't get me wrong, I love the luxury."

"We will get around to finding suitable lodgings for you," O'Fallon answered. "But that can wait. I think that tomorrow morning you should leave for Uncompahgre country, or even back to Pueblo if need be to track down your press and gear." He paused and then went on, "And I have decided to send Max Beasley with you, Royce. Margaret's garden can wait. There will be no stage leaving for two more days, so you'll have to ride over; Max knows a few shortcuts."

"I would enjoy having him along," Royce replied. But he somehow felt that O'Fallon had some other, undivulged reason for having Beasley accompany him.

It wasn't until after their evening meal that Royce broached the subject of the off-limits sawmill he'd stumbled upon that afternoon. As they now sat in a den with leather chairs and big-game trophies, he told O'Fallon in detail of the guarded gate, the massive log-yard and the abrupt way the deputy sheriff had ordered him to leave.

O'Fallon sat quietly, and did not speak until Royce had ended his summary of the afternoon and had asked, "What do you make of all this, Tim?"

O'Fallon rose and thrust the poker thoughtfully at a flaming log in the fireplace. Then, choosing his words with care, he spoke. "It sounds as though you had a run-in with Paul Gribble. I suppose it was inevitable."

Royce looked up in surprise. "You know the man?"

O'Fallon reclaimed his seat, relighted a short-stemmed pipe and then cast a level, serious gaze at Milligan. "Royce, perhaps now is as good a time as any to explain how I conduct my business. This valley, and the entire western slope of the Colorado Rockies, is well-endowed, and sometimes fabulously rich in natural resources—minerals, forests, grasslands, fertile soil, heavy snowfall to provide an abundance of water. Yes, and a climate of temperate winters and yet a sufficient growing season." O'Fallon leaned forward with growing enthusiasm. "But of what use is all of that unless it's made to fill human needs? And to do that, mines have to be tunneled out, brickyards built, dams constructed across the streams, meadows plowed for crops or orchards, and, damn it all, mature trees have to be felled and sawed into lumber."

Royce listened in a sort of stunned surprise. He had seldom seen such seriousness, combined with animation, on a man's face.

Then O'Fallon laughed and looked a bit chagrined. "Sort of got carried away, didn't I? What I'm really trying to say is this. By a lucky chance, I am taking one hell of a lot of money out of a silver mine, right here in Mesita. Some fellows would run to Denver with that kind of money and build a mansion. I am different, I guess. I want to build a town right here. A place people can enjoy living in. And you know what, Royce?"

As Royce only stared, and remained quiet, Tim O'Fallon went on. "I'll tell you what. It takes lumber— maybe a million or so feet of it—to build a decent town. So when Robert Delaney offered to furnish all the lumber I would need, I took him up on the deal. Now, I know Bob Delaney isn't exactly what you'd call a pleasant man, but he serves his purpose. He knows the country better than almost anyone else around, and I figure he's honest enough. And I'm damn thankful for his logs."

"Makes sense, Tim. Something like the greatest good for the greatest number. But what about that Paul Gribble fellow down at Delaney's lumberyard and mill?"

"Just this, Royce. Delaney is a native of these parts. Maybe some of his deals in the past haven't exactly been on the up and up. He has enemies, and a sort of penchant for making more. He had Gribble sworn in as a deputy sheriff to protect his property." He paused then, and stared hard at Royce before going on. "But one thing, Royce. Always be on your guard if you should tangle with Paul Gribble."

"Why, Tim?"

"Because he is sinfully fast with a gun and damned ill-tempered to boot."

"I suppose he is a product of the valley, too?" Royce asked.

"No. He sort of floated into Mesita when we first opened up. There are always rumors about a man like that. Those about Paul Gribble aren't pleasant."

"I'll keep it in mind." Royce nodded.

O'Fallon poked again at the now-smoldering log, and his tone changed as he said, "I have gabbed enough. Royce, is there anything on your mind?"

"Just this, Tim. Does your stance on timber-cutting mean that I should avoid it in editorial policy?"

"Hell no, son. Do you suppose I would hamstring you that way first off? Your policies are yours to stand or fall by." He fell silent, and then asked, "What do you intend to call it?"

Royce's mind raced back to a dank and eerie mine tunnel, and to Lucy Lattamore tracing a masthead with her finger in the air. "Tim, I had thought of calling it *The Mesita Messiah.*"

The fire poker clanged sharply as O'Fallon dropped it on the stone hearth and bellowed, "The what?"

"*The Mesita Messiah,* with the subhead *A Mighty Voice in the Wilderness.*"

"*The Mesita Messiah.*"

And then Royce was telling how Lucy had come up with the name.

Presently O'Fallon laughed. "The *Messiah.* Isn't that another word for *savior?* And I like that *Mighty Voice in the Wilderness* thing. Go ahead, Royce. It's your paper." He waited a bit, then surprised Royce by asking, "How about this Lucy Lattamore person? Did she come on through to San Miguel country?"

"No, Tim, but I wish she had . . . and that you could have heard her sing. Her voice is positively thrilling. She used to sing professionally, though she's loath to admit it."

O'Fallon smiled in a knowing way. "I take it you hope to see her somewhere north."

"Yes, I do. Just now she is staying with her brother at the Military Cantonment in the Uncompahgre Valley."

"You wouldn't possibly want to ask her to favor us here in Mesita with a few songs?" O'Fallon asked with a sly grin, and knocked ashes from his pipe onto the hearth. After all, hadn't his trusted friend, Margaret Hendricks, suggested that Miss Lucy Lattamore be invited to Mesita?

"Tim, thanks. I'll ask her to come." Moments later he climbed the stairway and entered his room. A light was already burning, and in its rays he caught sight of the sliver-framed daguerreotype and the face with the haunting smile. Why hadn't he thought to ask Tim O'Fallon the identity of this appealing girl? He'd do so in the morning, he vowed.

Royce and Max Beasley left Mesita while the morning sun was yet a promise behind an eastward thrust of mountains. Max had saddled and prepared the same two horses they had ridden down from San Miguel City. There was no packhorse now to slow their progress; instead two more sturdy geldings were led by halter ropes as spare mounts. They were not saddled, but by means of belly-straps were made to carry clothing and small gear wrapped in a blanket and a rainproof slicker.

The speed with which Beasley arranged all this made Royce feel clumsy and a bit unnecessary, so he commented, "Max, you must have spent years learning about horses and riding gear."

"You are about right, Royce. I've always been around livestock; for all I know, I cut my teeth on a látigo strap."

As they mounted and moved away from O'Fallon's yard, Royce mulled over the probable use of a látigo strap. It abruptly came to his mind that Lucy Lattamore would know, which for some reason made him feel happy. "Max, how far do you estimate we have to ride before we reach the Military Cantonment?"

"It depends on which cutoffs we can take. This time of year, with snowbanks and such, we'd likely be wise to keep to the main route. Ike Fenlon told me a while back it is right at seventy miles.''

"How long will it take us?''

"Maybe until noon tomorrow . . . if this weather holds.'' Beasley was quiet for a time and then said, "Of course there is a chance we'll find mired-down wagons with your printing stuff aboard.''

But as it turned out, they met up with neither travelers nor printing press, and true to Beasley's prediction they came down the Uncompahgre Valley Road just after noon the next day. They had crossed the Dallas Divide, and behind them now were the white and soaring heights of the San Juan Mountains. In the valley were more areas of greenness and tokens of oncoming spring. Their way, as they rode steadily on, passed directly by the main gate of the Military Cantonment.

"I suppose this is where we part company for a time,'' Max Beasley said, and halted the horses.

"No, Max, I will ride on into Pomona with you. We'll need to find quarters. Since we're not here on military business, I don't think we can expect bed and board within the Cantonment.''

"Perhaps . . . Miss Lattamore . . . could arrange it.''

A surge of pride caused Royce's eyes to flash. "Not on your life. I'll ride on with you. Pomona isn't very far. It may be a shantytown, but I'm sure we can find beds there.''

Royce Milligan spurred his horse ahead. His manner was that of a man hastening to take action before his resolve should fail. *Tomorrow*, his mind tolled. *Tomorrow I will be shaved and rid of dust and horse sweat. Tomorrow I'll be fit to present myself to Lucy.*

They had ridden less than a mile toward Pomona when a figure appeared on the road far ahead. As they neared it, Royce saw that it was a man trudging along and leading a black-and-white burro. Then presently he gasped, "Why, I know that fellow. It's Parson Goodfroe!''

Beasley shaded his eyes with a hand, peering ahead, and affirmed, "None other. The Reverend himself. Black swallow-tail coat. Black beard. Bible. The self-appointed messenger of the Messiah."

Before Royce could say another word, they were interrupted by a deeply resonant shout as the Parson Goodfroe recognized them. "Ah, do my eyes deceive me? Two of my good friends journeying together toward Pomona." He thrust out both hands, one to Royce and the other to Beasley, and asked, "What brings about this good fortune for me?"

Beasley's response was practical. "We're looking for places to eat and sleep. Know of any, Parson?" He released the churchman's hand and stroked the ears of the donkey.

The parson smiled. "There is a new tent restaurant, with some sleeping quarters off to one side. And for twenty-five cents, a spell in a washtub of soapy water. But you'd best have a towel of your own; the other is common property." He turned his eyes toward Royce. "And Mr. Milligan, what of your adventures since we parted company at San Miguel City?"

"Just a short stay at Mesita, Reverend. Now I am backtracking to look for a long-delayed shipment of my newspaper equipment," Royce explained. "And what of you? Are you hereabouts to hold services?"

Goodfroe nodded. "Jehovah's hand has dealt well with me. For three nights I will be spreading His gospel here in the Valley. My good friend Pappy Loutsenhizer has found a vacant cabin for the services. I would be pleased to see the faces of both of you gentlemen in my congregation."

"I will be there" Royce said, "and I'll use mighty persuasion to get Max there also. But Parson, with a preaching coming up, how come you're hotfooting it out of Ponoma?"

"Because, Royce, there is one at the Cantonment

whom I must persuade to help me in this mighty effort for the Lord.''

"And who might that be?'' Royce asked affably.

"Your golden-voiced friend, Miss Lucy Lattamore. Her presence, to lead our voices in praise, and perhaps singing solo, will assure a tremendous gathering for my services.''

Before Royce could answer, Max Beasley snorted, "Hell's fire, Parson. How can you have a *tremendous gathering* when there aren't a hundred people living in Pomona?''

"Max . . . Max, son, why must you doubt?''

Royce listened with both amusement and irritation. This plodding preacher would see Lucy within an hour or so, while he himself must wait another day. In fear that his intense feelings might show, he touched spurs to his horse, and then said, over his shoulder, "Look for me at a service, Parson. Also, tell Miss Lattamore that I look forward to seeing her tomorrow.''

After Royce and Max had put about a hundred yards between themselves and the parson, Max turned and said, "Did you know that our esteemed parson is a compulsive gambler?''

Royce looked amazed, then shrugged. "Perhaps a poker hand helps him meet those he thinks require redemption.''

"Poker hand, my butt, Royce. Wherever there is a chance to win or lose a bundle, Goodfroe seems to be in the center of things. Horse races. Crap games. Roulette. Cock or dog fights. Blackjack. Shell games. You name it. The parson's hands are reaching for the stakes.''

"You mean he manages all of that on a preacher's stipend?''

"What stipend? Preachers don't draw salaries out here. They depend on the collection plate or the passing of the hat.''

"I suppose that can be a hand-to-mouth sort of existence,'' Royce observed.

"With Goodfroe it usually is *hat to table*. He preaches

the word, garners the coin and greenbacks, and hies
himself to the nearest game of chance. Double or nothing
is the creed of that servant of the Lord. Why, once the
gals up at Columbia—the Columbia Quality—chipped in
enough of their earnings to assure Goodfroe of being able
to build a chapel. Know what?''

"What?'' Royce asked.

"Goodfroe bet and lost every dollar of it. The Quality
gals still don't have their chapel. The hell of it is, Royce,
they still think of Parson Goodfroe as their escort to the
pearly gates of heaven.''

Royce Milligan scratched his neck and seemed to
ponder. "Maybe the ladies of Columbia Quality need a
means of special admittance to heaven . . .''

"Maybe.'' Beasley shrugged. "But there is something
you will learn as the weeks go by, Royce. Out here in
the wilderness, where there are still about half a dozen
men to every woman, life would be drab and boring—
yes, and downright unendurable—without prostitutes.''

They fell silent after that, until at last they rode into
the group of cabins, shacks, and tents that comprised
Pomona. They were fortunate enough to rent a sleeping
tent to themselves; for an extra dollar they were assured
of a tub of fresh water, bars of yellow soap, and clean
towels. After bathing, and a change of clothing, both men
rested for an hour on narrow, blanketed cots. Then hunger
caused them to stir and make their way to the adjacent
tent serving as an eating place. Darkness had come, and
their meal was served by the light of two kerosene
lanterns.

It was when they had finished helpings of tough
beefsteak, and were lingering over black coffee, that the
sound of approaching horses came to their ears. They
gave it little heed even when the pounding of hooves
broke off just outside the tent. It was when the canvas
flap, serving as a door, was pushed aside, that a startled
Royce Milligan rose to his feet. Two faces were at the

opening peering in. One was that of Lieutenant Phillip Lattamore.

But it was the second person who took Royce's breath away. "Lucy! Am I ever glad to see you. I was coming out to the Cantonment to look you up in the morning."

"I know." She smiled. "Parson Goodfroe told me of your coming. Why didn't you stop by on your way here?"

"Because I stank of trail dust and sweat. I was sure you wouldn't appreciate that," he said, grinning.

"Anyway, I couldn't wait to see you," she confessed, "so I asked Phillip to get some horses and ride into Pomona with me."

Royce turned to the lieutenant, and said, "Thanks for escorting Lucy." He turned to make way for the two arrivals at the table, and then, seeing the questioning in Max Beasley's face, he said, "Lucy, Phillip . . . this is Max Beasley. He's my guide." He turned back to Max, saying, "And these are the Lattamores. Have I mentioned them before?"

"Have you done anything else?" Beasley challenged, and then added, "Ma'am, sir, I am honored to make your acquaintance." He eyed the disarray of the table and asked, "Can we order anything for you?"

Lucy shook her head. "We were having dinner when the Parson arrived, so no, thank you." She turned to Royce, and let her hand rest on his arm. "How did you manage it, getting back so soon?"

"My boss, Tim O'Fallon, thought I should backtrack to look for my newspaper equipment; it is still missing." Royce could feel the touch of her hand all the way through his coat. They sat in silence for a moment until Max piped up.

"Did Parson Goodfroe persuade you to be choir leader and soloist for his three-night revival stand?"

"I limited it to one night . . . and just possibly two. Royce, it seems everyone wants me to sing. In a week I have to give a concert for the troops at the Cantonment, and then I am scheduled to appear as guest soloist for a group in a little place called Columbia. I was invited by a women's group—the Columbia Quality.''

"Oh, Jesus," Royce exploded. "Who talked you into that? Singing for Columbia Quality? Do you know who those women are?"

Lucy smiled amusedly at him. "You mean, am I aware that the ladies of Columbia Quality are members of the oldest profession in the world?"

"They are the prostitutes of Columbia's brothels," he said.

"To me," she answered spiritedly, "they are women reaching out for moments of forgetfulness and joy, for a chance to laugh and sing and escape from everyday drudgery and despair. Yes, Royce, I do understand. And I am going to Columbia to fulfill my promise to them anyway."

Royce looked steadily into her clear eyes, unsure for a moment how to respond to her announcement. Then Max broke in; his voice was low and full of feeling. "If only everyone could be as tolerant as you, Miss Lattamore, we'd be living in a better world."

"That may be true," Phillip said, "but no one could have kept my sister from doing what she had her mind set on, even if they moved heaven and earth to do it. I told her there'll be people who'll criticize her for this." Then he smiled affectionately at her. "But did she pay any attention to me?"

"It's true," Royce joined in. "I believe nothing could stand in her way once she decides to do something." They all laughed at that, Lucy included.

The four of them sat for a while chatting around the table. Royce talked the Lattamores into having a cup of strong coffee before heading back, and Lucy made him promise to attend one of her services.

"Now that Max has met you, I'm sure he'll want to come along, too."

"I will," Max replied, grinning from ear to ear. "The

Reverend Goodfroe's sermon wasn't much of an entice-
ment, but your singing sure is.''

"And once he hears you, Lucy, maybe he'll help me
convince you to come up to Mesita to give a concert. You
could do it a day or two after you finish at Columbia . . .''

"We'll see," Lucy said, pulling her riding gloves back
on in preparation for the journey home. "But in the
meantime, I want the two of you to put in an appearance
at the Cantonment just as soon as you've taken care of
your business." And with that, she and her brother
climbed onto their mounts and disappeared down the trail
leading out of Pomona.

Chapter 6

As it turned out, Max and Royce were at the Cantonment the very next day, when a small miracle occurred. They'd planned to visit with Lucy briefly before heading off toward Blue Mesa to hunt down the press, but while Lucy and Royce sat on a porch swing on the veranda outside the Lattamores' quarters, and while Max was getting a tour through the stables conducted by Phillip, a train of several wagons pulled into the camp, sending dust flying as they approached. The freighters' wagons held some soldiering supplies and, lo and behold, Royce's printing equipment.

He couldn't contain his relief and joy, and Lucy sat smiling as he obtained the head freighter's promise that the shipment would reach Mesita within a week. After he'd sent the wagon train on its way, he dashed up the veranda steps, and without a word, pulled Lucy out of her seat and into his arms. Behind her the porch swing rocked crazily.

"Royce Milligan," she breathed into his ear, "what are you doing? When things work out well for you, do you always embrace the first lady your eyes happen upon?"

Royce threw his head back and laughed; she joined him, but then, suddenly, his mood changed and his tone became serious. He led her back to the swing. "You must know, Lucy . . . You must see," he began, "how I feel about you."

For once, Lucy Lattamore held her tongue and let her companion speak his peace.

"I love you," he finished simply.

She drew a deep breath. She felt at once lightheaded and blissfully happy over the sincerity of his words. Her face lifted for a kiss. "Royce, how did this happen to us so quickly?"

"Perhaps it was meant to be—you and I together. Perhaps that's why we both ended up on Ike Fenlon's stage."

There was magic about the moment, as both Lucy and Royce realized that what had begun days before in the quiet of an old deserted mine had now blossomed into something of glory and wonder. Tenderly, Royce touched his lips to hers.

Minutes passed and then Lucy sat upright on the swing, clinging to his hand. "Royce, my brother and Mr. Beasley will be back any minute, and we have so much to talk about."

"I know, my love," he said, gently stroking a wisp of hair that played in the breeze.

"And once you return to your newspaper, and I to my plans for my orchard, so many miles will lie between us . . ."

"Never fear, Lucy," he whispered. "I promise to stay until the day you sing at Parsen Goodfroe's service, at least. We'll have plenty of time to talk. And I swear we'll find a way to be together."

The evening of the revival service at Pomona was pleasantly warm, and as a crowd gathered at the cabin loaned by Pappy Loutsenhizer, it soon became clear the building would not hold all of those attending the event; so chairs and benches were brought from all parts of the settlement and placed outside. An improvised pulpit was arranged, to which the San Juan Mountains, bathed in the hues of evening, lent an inspiring backdrop.

Royce and Beasley sought out seats beside Lieutenant Lattamore; Lucy lingered with them a while before being escorted to a chair near the pulpit. Royce looked about at the rows of people, wondering silently where so many might have come from.

There was a sizeable group of military personnel, both officers and enlisted men. Off to one side, standing reservedly apart, were about twenty people with darker faces, and clothing that singled them out as Indians. Max Beasley identified them as being of the Ute tribe, some of those who had been allowed to remain in the Uncompahgre Valley.

At last Parson Goodfroe walked to the pulpit, laid his Bible upon it, and said, "Brothers and sisters, welcome to the first of a three-day opportunity to renew our faith in the Lord." He signaled with his expressive hands for everyone to stand, and then said, "Let us pray." Royce found this invocation meaningful and not unduly long. He also noticed the compelling quality of Goodfroe's voice as it carried clearly across the room and through the door to those assembled outside.

Presently Lucy Lattamore came to the pulpit on the arm of a stout, elderly man for whom a seat had also been placed close by. Max Beasley leaned forward in surprise, and then touched Royce's knee. "Does Miss Lattamore ever rate high! That old guy, her escort, is none other than Pappy Loutsenhizer, the most respected man of this region." Royce nodded, but kept silent, for at that moment, the hauntingly beautiful voice, he remembered so well from that night of the Blue Mesa blizzard, began singing. For her opening selection, she had chosen "I Know that My Redeemer Liveth." As her words poured forth, both awe and pleasure filled those listening. She concluded with stronger and deeper contralto tones, in a way that seemed to confirm the Lord's nearness to each listener.

Even before they could show their approval with applause, Lucy spoke up. "Let's sing together. Everybody join me and sing." Her voice seemed the call of a trumpet as she began: "Mine eyes have seen the glory of the coming of the Lord. . . ." She led them in "The Battle Hymn of the Republic," and close to two hundred voices joined in to make the music ring out across the little settlement.

Royce looked about. He was entranced by her voice, and by the song, which reminded him of the tragic conflict in which his own father had died. Among those in the crowd, he saw others, like himself, who seemed to be too moved by the music to sing along.

Lucy's two selections were followed by Parson Goodfroe reading several verses from the Book of Ezekiel. As he began, Lucy rose from her chair and made her way to Royce's side. Those near him on the bench made room to allow her to sit down.

"You held me spellbound," he whispered, then reached for her hand. "What a wonderful voice. I want to be hearing it for the rest of my life."

Wisely, Parson Goodfroe kept his sermon to thirty minutes. It was thoroughly prepared and thoughtful, tinged with the speaker's conviction that the second coming of the Messiah was fast approaching.

The inevitable passing of the hat followed. Royce surmised the offering would be a generous one, more in tribute to Lucy's voice than to Goodfroe's apocalyptic preaching. Briefly he wondered whether the entire collection was now destined to become Goodfroe's stake in a poker game. *Even if he wastes it all,* Royce realized, *these people, entranced by his words and Lucy's lovely voice, will be flocking back to his revivals—just as the members of Columbia Quality will continue to place utter trust in this bearded prophet of the wilderness.*

All this was resurgent upon Royce Milligan's mind as he and Max Beasley rode reluctantly out of Pomona the

day after Lucy's triumph. Her face appeared before him
at every turn in the road. The two of them had made no
firm plans, but they both knew they'd see each other
again soon.

During moments when the two of them had been
together over the last few days, Lucy had told him of her
visit with Pappy Loutsenhizer and of the way he had
described Cedar's Edge Mesa, its potential as an orchard,
and its constant supply of water from high atop the vast
Uncompahgre Plateau. As yet, she and Phillip had not
had time to visit the mesa, and Royce detected her
lingering anxiety about the feasibility and the cost of
building two miles of ditch to divert stream water onto
the land.

Royce had not considered visiting Cedar's Edge Mesa
himself until the morning of their departure, when Max
had squatted down and drawn stick scratches in the dirt
to signify their route.

"You know, Royce, it is some seventy miles to Mesita
by way of Dallas Divide. But as the hawk flies, on a
straight line over the Plateau, it can't be more than
forty."

"But could we get through that way? The Plateau is
high and mountainous. There may be cliffs and snow-
slide—" But even as he spoke, Royce was thinking about
something else. So he asked, "Max, if we go home that
way, over the Plateau, is it likely we can find a place
called Cedar's Edge Mesa? It should be about twelve
miles that way." He waved vaguely toward the southwest.

"Mesas have a way of showing up," Max laughed.
"As for the Plateau, it'll be rough going, but I imagine
we can make it through."

So they mounted their horses, fastened the halter ropes
of their spare mounts, and made their way across the
Uncompahgre River to begin the climb onto Pappy
Loutsenhizer's Spring Creek Mesa. Royce was already
planning how he'd surprise Lucy by showing up at her

concert in Columbia a week hence with news about Cedar's Edge Mesa.

Before long, they crossed Spring Creek Mesa, noting Pappy Loutsenhizer's property markers. On the largest section of this gently sloping area, brush had already been cleared, irrigation ditches dug and experimental plantings made of various fruit trees. The trees seemed to have survived the winter in good shape and were now putting out new growth.

With Spring Creek Mesa behind them, Royce and Beasley started a steeper climb, which would eventually bring them atop the Uncompahgre Plateau. For a time they traveled through grassy areas and small brush, and then, as they ascended the slope, they came to trees that Beasley identified as juniper. With increased elevation, the timber attained greater diameter and height. Max Beasley stopped his horse near a large piñon pine. "The Indians eat these things," he said, handing Royce a piñon nut. "Here, taste one, and be sure to spit out the hull."

They realized presently that they were already too high on the slope for a fruit-growing enterprise, and had likely bypassed Cedar's Edge Mesa. But by studying the terrain lower down on the slope, they could clearly see a level area that seemed to fit the description Lucy had gotten from Loutsenhizer and passed on to them. To reach it would mean doubling back and losing at least a couple of hours, but Royce was determined to do so.

They rode back down to the mesa and found it considerably smaller than the one watered by Spring Creek, but the plant growth and soil appeared to be identical. Cedar's Edge Mesa was somewhat higher, but probably within the limits of elevation for producing hardy varieties of fruit.

As Loutsenhizer had indicated, a small, fast-moving stream came out of a small ravine, crossed the mesa, and dropped toward the lowlands. "This isn't the sort of creek that would sustain an orchard or farmlands year-round," Beasley pointed out. "This is water from the spring snow melt. Within a couple of weeks this patch of ground will be high and dry.''

"You're right, Max," Royce answered. "But Lucy said there was a dependable water supply. I remember her saying that a ditch would have to be built to fetch water. But from where?''

Beasley glanced at the midday sun. "Suppose we stop here and fix something to eat where there's water, wood, and grass. We wouldn't make it across the Plateau by nightfall, anyway. So let's spend the afternoon looking for that bigger stream, the one Loutsenhizer says can be diverted this way.''

They came across the larger stream by mid-afternoon. Royce recalled how Lucy had learned that its source was high on the Plateau in a dense stand of timber. At its nearest point, its course was roughly two miles from Cedar's Edge Mesa. There would be no great difficulty in trenching out a canal to carry much of its flow to the potential orchard site. But as Royce studied the terrain, a new thought occurred to him. Why couldn't a flume be used to carry the water? Such a wooden waterway would avoid a lot of rock-blasting. Also, he reasoned, since the soil along the two-mile route was so porous, much of a trench water-flow would be wasted before it ever arrived at the orchard site. But because the idea seemed both speculative and expensive, Royce did not mention the possibility of a flume to Beasley.

They camped that night on Cedar's Edge Mesa. Its isolation and quiet intrigued Royce, as did the clearness of the stars above and the sprinkle of lights, far below, marking Pomona and the Military Cantonment.

They awakened early, prepared their breakfast over a small fire, and then packed their few trail necessities. The sun was just breaking over a line of peaks to the east as they sought out the possible route of a canal and rode along it. Royce was sure that Lucy would want every bit of information regarding this water source that he could gather.

Within an hour they reached the larger stream. Here they spent half an hour determining a possible point of diversion and a likely place to begin construction. Royce drew a rough pencil sketch, using a huge rock formation above them as a point of identification.

With this task completed, Royce and Beasley turned their horses upstream to explore the course of the creek and its source. It proved to be a slow and difficult ride, made even slower by having to maneuver their extra horses through clumps of brush and along the rock-strewn banks of a narrow ravine that led to the crest of the Uncompahgre Plateau.

About them, the stands of brush and juniper gave way to pine and fir trees. This area held every appearance of being virgin wilderness.

It was shortly after noon when they came up a final long slope and arrived at the top of the Uncompahgre Plateau. The air was still cool at midday, and Max Beasley estimated they had reached an elevation of at least 8,500 feet.

Royce wondered whether a finer stand of coniferous trees might be found anywhere else in Colorado. The well-formed trees surrounding them reached upward to fifty or sixty feet, with trunks a couple of feet or more in diameter. There were smaller pine and fir and spruce trees, too, all with a healthy appearance that spoke of both fertile mountain soil and ample moisture from snows and rain.

There were also small parks, free of timber, but with native grass growing tall and just now moving restlessly in the breeze. It was in such a clearing that they reached the place they'd been seeking. Here three small watercourses, coming from varied directions, joined to form the stream they had been following since early morning. From here would come the water for the orchards of Lucy Lattamore.

This confluence had inevitably attracted a family of beaver, but there was no sign of their still being about.

Max Beasley reasoned that these animals had stayed for a time and then left this well-watered park. "Probably not enough timber close to the streams, and too high up for their old reliable the aspen trees." He paused and then nodded toward the south. "But we've got company, Royce," he said, pointing. A bull elk was standing close to the timber, watching them curiously.

They were content to silently study the grandeur of his rack of antlers. Later, their attention turned back to the stream, with its abandoned beaver dam. Its water was deep and clear enough for them to make out the shadowy forms of a dozen foot-long trout.

"Right here we have a fish fry," Max said in a decided way. "Royce, you rustle wood for a fire. I've got a lure that should prove fatal to a couple of these rainbow beauties."

Royce nodded his approval of the idea, but his mind was suddenly elsewhere. How greatly would Lucy enjoy such a spot. And how beautifully suited this remote place would be for their honeymoon.

Then another thought that was less pleasant struck Royce. What if someone else were to happen upon this spot and claim it? That would surely mean an end to Lucy's dream of orchards upon Cedar's Edge Mesa, for only irrigation could render the soil capable of nurturing fruit trees.

Perhaps I should advise the Lattamores to lay claim to this bit of forestland also, he thought; *their livelihood will be dependent on it. But yet,* Royce reasoned, *neither Lucy nor Phillip can spend time up here. Young Lattamore's army commission dictates what he will be doing for a couple of years at least. Lucy will have her hands full with the fruitlands . . . and with her concerts.* Abruptly Royce jerked his head up in amazement. "Damn!" he said aloud.

Beasley was busy preparing a line, but when he heard Royce's oath, he looked up, startled. "Now what, Royce? Squat on a thistle?"

"Maybe something worse. I've decided to homestead this park, maybe a couple hundred acres. How do I go about it, Max? Oh, I don't mean to live here necessarily, but I do want to make sure Lucy has access to this water."

Beasley was silent for a moment. Presently he said in a slow, thoughtful manner, "Perhaps there is a better way. File on a few acres of this little park as a mining claim."

"But mining for what?" Royce answered doubtfully. "What ores—if any—might possibly be found in a place like this?"

"Coal, my friend. Maybe down a few hundred feet there is a vein of coal. By the time you're through doing exploratory work, you'll for damn sure have legal title to a slice of land."

Royce eyed him in open admiration. "Max, I know now why Tim O'Fallon keeps you around."

The words brought an unexpected seriousness to Max Beasley's face, but he said nothing.

They spent another half-hour setting boundaries for Royce's claim that encompassed the confluence of the three tributary streams. For markers, they blazed small patches on four trees. Then, at Max's urging, they left the park and entered the dense timber to the south.

They had ridden less than two miles, through timber so tall and magnificent it filled them with awe, when abruptly the trees and greenness stopped. Both men halted their horses in utter astonishment. Now, instead of rich and virgin woods, they gazed upon a denuded waste-land—raw stumps, piles of dry and rotting branches, and an occasional scrawny pine or fir. Only one thing could have brought this about. Not fire. Not flooding. Not winds of tornado force.

Staring at the desolation, fury rose in Royce's heart. This was the work of *men,* men who had, in days or weeks, wrought complete destruction through unheeding and indiscriminate logging. "Max, I hope whoever did this burns in hell for a hundred years."

"Why not two hundred?" Max growled. "It takes that long to grow a mature tree up here."

They veered eastward, determined to ride through the desolation. "Who do you suppose owns this land?" Royce asked.

This Plateau is government land. Probably a logging crew came, raped the place, and then got the hell out."

Little more was said as they picked their way through the small park. Here the water of a pond lay scummed and stagnant.

Before them now was a steep hillside that blocked their view ahead. Here too was more devastation. The logging method had been ruthlessly efficient; even smaller trees had been cut down and cast aside.

All the while, a thought had been lurking in Royce's mind. Again he pictured the carefully guarded sawmill downriver from Mesita. Could it be that he had stumbled onto the source of Delaney's lumber? He turned to Max, saying, "If we come across a logging road, I want to follow it every damned step of the way, wherever it takes us."

When at last they crested the hill and stared down its southern exposure, their suspicions were confirmed. Before them lay a small logging camp, with three roughly-built shacks; from the stovepipe of one, a curl of smoke lifted up into the sky. Men were moving about, and there was a great deal of logging equipment; the sound of saws and axes could be heard, and presently the crash of a great monarch spruce.

The presence of Royce and his companion was quickly noted by a man who seemed to be strolling about the logging grounds. He stared toward the newcomers and then entered one of the shacks. When he reappeared, a rifle lay across his arm. Then he signaled for Royce and Beasley to ride on down the short stretch of slope between them.

Ignoring the gesture, Royce turned in his saddle and said, "That's the sort of summons I think over before responding to. That fellow's looking for trouble, Max."

"You're right, Royce. We should do our talking from here," Beasley answered. With deft movements he removed a short-barreled repeating rifle from the scabbard hung low on his saddle.

Royce noted that the man below was already moving cautiously up the slope. And abruptly he was aware of something else—the utter transformation of Beasley's face. Moments before, he had seemed boyish and friendly; now there was grimness, and a touch of cold and calculating anger about his eyes. He positioned his rifle to cover the man, who had now stopped and was shouting, "Where are you heading?"

Beasley answered. "We're riding through to Mesita."

"The hell you are! This is private property," their challenger flung at them. "How did you get here? Where did you come from?"

Max Beasley's dark eyes narrowed as he replied. "Not that it's any of your concern, but we came up from Pomona. Now, suppose you just stand aside and we will be on our way."

"You're trespassing on land that's off-limits."

"Whose land?" Royce demanded.

"This is the property of the Ponderosa Land and Cattle Company." The fellow's voice became impatient and ugly as he added, "Everything for five miles or so north and west of here is a cutting area. We don't cotton to snoops. Now get going. Back off easy-like, before I—"

In defiance, Beasley touched spurs to his horse and moved down the slope. At the same time, he said softly to Royce, "If you're carrying any kind of weapon, get it handy."

What ensued came so fast that Royce could scarcely follow the action. The man below, tall and bearded, started to lift his rifle. The motion gave Beasley just time enough to get off the first shot, which tore through the stranger's arm and broke his grasp on his weapon. He staggered backward, then fell to his knees, cursing furiously.

The sound of the shot swept the clearing and seemed to echo from the dense stand of timber beyond. All at once, men were yelling and running as the loggers cast aside their tools and sought firearms. Max sensed how little time remained in which to escape a hail of bullets. "Royce, let's get the hell out of here." He managed to flail the pack animals into a burst of speed to keep them close behind the nervous mounts.

They galloped down the slope, past the still-kneeling, bleeding fellow Beasley had wounded. They heard him shout, "You two will roast in hell for this." And Royce was startled to hear him add, "Wait till Gribble—" The words trailed off as they came into the camp, raced between two shacks, and made for the cover of timber. Just as they reached it, two bullets whined past them. One went harmlessly into a tree trunk; the other sang wickedly close to Royce.

In minutes, they'd put a good bit of woodland between themselves and the logging camp. Royce felt sure the loggers would send someone after them, so they kept riding hard.

Their progress was speeded when they came upon a level reach of timberland through which a narrow swath had been cleared to serve as a logging road. The marks of horses and of iron-tired wagons confirmed that it had been used lately, perhaps as recently as the previous day. At first the significance of this rutted, stumped way did not occur to Royce. Instead he was thinking about the deadly quickness with which Max Beasley had fired. And now he asked wonderingly, "Max, where did you learn to shoot like that?"

"Maybe you should ask Tim O'Fallon about that, Royce." There was cautious restraint in the words, but Beasley's face brightened as he added, "But now you know why he keeps me around."

They rode steadily on. The sun was scarcely an hour above the horizon when they realized that they were nearing the southern flank of the Uncompahgre Plateau. Already there was a slight sloping of the terrain and a thinner and less majestic stand of timber. Once they caught sight of a distant range of mountains, and Max explained that likely the peaks were in Utah.

Both men rode for a time silently immersed in private thoughts. Royce couldn't stop hearing the logger's words: *Everything for five miles or so north and west of here is a cutting area.* Such destruction would encircle and devour the lovely glade where they had stopped for lunch; soon there would be no source of water for Lucy's orchards on Cedar's Edge Mesa. The realization caused Royce to straighten in his saddle, and ask, "Max, is there any chance we can reach Mesita tonight?"

"Perhaps. Why?"

"I want to file claim to every possible acre around that spot where the streams come together. That so-called Ponderosa Land and Cattle Company won't waste any time in logging and laying waste to the area . . . unless they are stopped."

"They will be tough to stop."

Royce looked at him shrewdly. "Max, I think you have a damned good idea who is ramrodding this cutting. Besides, aren't these wagon tracks leading right down into the San Miguel Valley, say a few miles below Mesita? Yes, by God, Max, they lead straight to Delaney's big log-yard and mill."

Max made no comment, only studied the descending sun, and then veered due south.

Suddenly Royce asked, "Max, why does Tim O'Fallon think I should have a bodyguard? Because that is just what you are, one hell of an efficient bodyguard, and, incidentally, one great friend."

Max smiled and then let himself laugh. "Mr. O'Fallon knows you are independent and obstinate and that your paper's editorial policy will be the same way. That means trouble, most likely from some pretty well-heeled and prominent people.''

"Like Robert Delaney and his henchman, Paul Gribble?''

"To name a couple.'' Beasley nodded, and then fell silent again.

An hour later, in deep twilight, they rode tiredly down a small timbered canyon. Emerging from it, they heaved a sigh. The sprinkled lights of Mesita told them that their journey was at an end. Royce glanced back over his shoulder and laughed. "Nary a pursuer hove into sight,'' he quipped.

"You never know . . .'' Beasley answered quietly.

Chapter 7

During the days after his return from Pomona and the Military Cantonment, Royce found himself working long hours, supervising a small crew of carpenters who were trying to complete the interior of the newspaper office before the press arrived.

Despite this, he took time to write out in longhand what he hoped would pass for a mining claim on the plot of land he had come to think of as Three Rivulets Glade, the source of Lucy's irrigation water high on the Uncompahgre Plateau. He had it in hand one night when he came down to dinner at Tim O'Fallon's. O'Fallon studied it for a time and then passed it to Margaret Hendricks, saying, "It looks legal enough to me, Royce. But let's have Margaret run her eagle eye over it; she is the document-scanner around here."

The pleasant-faced woman donned a pair of spectacles hung by a chain from the lapel of her jacket. Then she read quietly, stopping twice to make small pencil-marks in the application's margin. Finally she looked up at Royce. "This is a competent piece of work, Royce, but I think that a couple of small changes would clarify and perhaps strengthen it."

"By all means then, let's include them. Can we do it after dinner? I am anxious to get this filed at once. And by the way, where does one file such a document?"

"The nearest United States Land Office is in Gunnison," O'Fallon answered.

"Then I will have to apply by mail." Royce looked disappointed. "I bet it'll take weeks. . . ."

"Not necessarily, Royce," O'Fallon said. "We have a town clerk, who also serves as justice of the peace and can attest legal papers. Because we are so far from Gunnison, the county authorities there approved the arrangement."

"Who is this life-saving person?" Royce asked, relieved.

"Who? You're looking at her. Mrs. Margaret Hendricks." O'Fallon chuckled.

"Pretty handy, isn't it?" she commented. As the three of them went in to dinner, Mrs. Hendricks laid her hand on Royce's sleeve and looked at him speculatively. "It would be interesting to know, Royce, why you want to get hold of land—more than you'd ever need for a mining claim—up there on the Uncompahgre Plateau. And why all this haste?"

Royce told them everything then: his and Beasley's ride to Cedar's Edge Mesa, their scouting of the area and discovery of the stream's source at the small glade. Then he added, "It's not that I'm planning to abandon the paper for this, Tim. It's just that the success or utter failure of Lucy Lattamore's plans for an orchard depends on that water. And I want to do what I can to protect it."

"Lucy Lattamore. . . . Is she the young lady with the beautiful voice?" Mischief was dancing in Mrs. Hendricks' eyes.

Royce nodded; he knew that his face was turning crimson, but he had more to say. "Max and I discovered something else, too: Some damned logging outfit is laying waste to hundreds of acres up there. Unless there is a way to stop them, they will plunder and ruin the stands of timber bordering the little meadow and the streams."

"Well," O'Fallon began slowly, "if they own the land, I guess it's their prerogative—"

"The thing is," Royce interrupted, "Max and I think it's government land, and if it is, whoever's responsible for the logging is nothing more than a common criminal."

O'Fallon was staring at him. "How in hell do you intend to run a newspaper, investigate all this, and work a mining claim all at the same time?"

"Maybe on Sundays, during the winter—" Royce began lamely.

"Sundays! Winter!" Tim O'Fallon roared. "Boy, have you got a lot to learn about the Uncompahgre Plateau! Come winter, the snow will be ass-deep to a grizzly bear up there."

"Are you saying you think I shouldn't file?" Royce wasn't about to give in on this, but nonetheless he wanted to hear Tim out.

"Sure you ought to file. But plan to hire some hard-up prospector or mucker to dig a few feet of shaft every summer, just enough to satisfy a claim examiner."

Mrs. Hendricks had listened with interest, and now she nodded and spoke. "That makes sense, Royce. And just maybe I know an old codger who'd do the job. His name is Goetz."

Royce's head jerked up. "Goetz," he repeated. "Does he happen to have a bushy beard, and generally need a bath?"

"Exactly." She laughed. "Do you know him?"

"Sure, Margaret. He was on the stage when we got marooned on Blue Mesa. He definitely seems to understand mining and ores and such."

"I only wish he were as familiar with soap and water," she joked.

The following morning Royce had two callers. The first was Ike Fenlon, who tethered his lead team to a hitching rail and left three passengers to wait impatiently as he sought out Milligan. "I take it you're in the newspapering business now," he said after barging into Royce's shop and shaking his hand.

"Ike, sit down." Royce pushed a chair toward him. "Where are you coming from—and heading to—this time?"

Fenlon bit off a chew of tobacco, looked for a cuspidor, then hastened to the door. When he returned, wiping his mustache, he said firmly. "You gotta get a spittoon for this here office."

"Just so you take good aim when I do, Ike."

Fenlon cocked his head, and answered, "Milligan, I have a mind not to tell you the good news I brought."

"I suppose the gals of Columbia Quality gave you another party," Royce jeered.

"The news ain't that good. It is just that a certain young lady will be aboard my stage when I come back from Pomona."

Royce wheeled about. "Ike . . . you mean Lucy?"

"Yep," Ike affirmed, twisting one side of his handlebar mustache. "Her singing engagement for the Columbia Quality is set for Friday evening. She'll be staying in San Miguel City. Columbia Quality's putting her up in the best rooms the town has to offer."

"My God," Royce said, almost to himself, "that's the day after tomorrow. And I'm expecting my press to arrive then—"

"Calm down, boy," Ike said.

"You don't understand, Ike. I'm going to be up to my ears in work, sorting out equipment, getting the presses rolling . . . And I told Tim O'Fallon I'd get my first paper out early next week if the shipment showed up."

"Looks like this is one concert you're gonna have to miss."

"I'll be dammed if I do," Royce exclaimed, pounding his fist onto the desk. "Listen, don't say anything to Lucy," he went on. "I don't want her to get her hopes up about me being there. But Ike, if I don't make it to the concert, promise me you'll bring her here as soon as you can after the concert. Kidnap her if you have to, but get her here."

Before the stagecoach driver could reply, though, one of the stage passengers stuck his head in the door, saying disgustedly, "Driver, are we going to dally forever? Either you get a move on, or I'll demand my money back!"

For a time after Ike's departure, Royce went about his work in a sort of trance. Only a few days had passed since his parting with Lucy, but now there was a chance he would see her again soon. He'd be able to tell her about Cedar's Edge Mesa and the possibility of a flume. And he couldn't wait to describe Three Rivulets Glade to her. With its clear blue waters, luxuriant grass and wildflowers, towering trees and mountain peaks, it was fast becoming his favorite spot in the world. Equally exciting was the prospect of escorting her about Tim O'Fallon's incredible little town, and introducing her to O'Fallon and Margaret Hendricks. *If they hear her sing,* he thought, *they're bound to want her for a concert. Knowing Tim, he might even start construction on an opera house!*

Royce's euphoric thoughts were abruptly brought to an end by the opening and closing of his outer door. He spun around to see a man striding toward him. It was Robert Delaney, tall, well-muscled, and smooth of movement. He was clad in riding breeches and boots, a white shirt and a leather jacket. He looked arrogantly about the still-disorganized shop, then spoke. "Good morning, Milligan. I thought we had a meeting planned for several days ago. But since you never showed up, I thought I'd put in an appearance over here."

Royce motioned for him to be seated. "I had to go out of town, Mr. Delaney," he explained smoothly.

"So I gathered."

Royce flushed. "Just what is it you believe we should discuss?"

Delaney said icily, "Just this, Mr. Milligan. I'm not a man who craves publicity. I sure wouldn't like to see anything concerning me or my affairs turn up in this paper of yours.''

The implication of Delaney's words stuck like a lump in Royce Milligan's throat. His eyes narrowed. ''All right, sir. You have had your say. But I want you to understand my point of view, too. You're a public figure here, and people have a right to know what you're up to.'' At that, Delaney started to speak, but Royce refused to back down. ''Mr. Delaney, I will publish a newspaper in Mesita, and I will be the one to determine its content, and guide its destiny.''

Delaney glared at him. ''Why, you simple bastard . . . If you don't keep your goddamned nose out of my business, I'll have you and this stuff out of Mesita so fast you won't even know what hit you.'' He strode toward the door, but halfway to it picked up a short board from a packing box and with it swept two cases of assorted papers to the floor. He would have left then, but Milligan's voice, harsh and loud, checked his steps. ''Pick it up, every sheet of it. Put it back in the boxes.''

''And if I don't?'' Delaney raged.

''Then your right hand will never pick up another damned thing. I'll put a bullet through it.''

Delaney's face whitened in shock as he noticed the derringer Royce held in his hand. ''And don't be tempted to draw your own gun, Mr. Delaney, because if your hand comes any place near your coat, I'm going to pull the trigger.''

Mesita's handsome lumberman stooped then and retrieved most of the papers. When he rose, his gaze raked over Royce. ''Keep something in mind, you smartass,'' he snarled. ''You're gonna pay for this. You ought to get out of Mesita while you're still able.'' Delaney turned and with an attempt at dignity, made his way for the door and the street.

When he was gone, Royce sat for a time on the corner of the desk. He felt no triumph in what had occurred. Delaney had come looking for trouble. But he had made no mention of Royce's downriver jaunt; nor had he said anything about the wounding of the man at the Ponderosa Land and Cattle logging camp. In all likelihood Robert Delaney hadn't heard about that yet, but once it was brought to his attention he'd be even more infuriated than he already was.

But I have to be my own man, and be my paper's decency, good sense and conscience, Royce told himself. *Tim O'Fallon would want it that way . . . and I will work and publish under no other conditions. If something ought to be published, I'll do it, and let the chips fall where they may.*

Royce stood up and swept his gaze over the rooms that would be the home of *The Mesita Messiah*. Then he knelt to retrieve the remaining papers.

Chapter 8

Word rapidly got around the Uncompahgre Valley that Parson Goodfroe had found a gifted soloist for his revival gatherings at Pomona. This caused a jump in attendance and an urgent plea from Goodfroe that Lucy Lattamore let her voice ring out at each of the three services. She agreed, and luckily, the weather held dry and pleasant to accommodate the gatherings.

The crowds listened with quiet respect to the sermons of their circuit-riding preacher. When he called for converts, a sprinkling of those most moved by his messages approached the improvised altar. But it was Lucy's voice, strong and lovely in the gathering darkness that really swelled the numbers seeking spiritual solace. When she led the worshippers in song, eager smiles replaced lines of worry and anxiety on many faces.

With the revival meetings over, and a sizeable polk of money from the collection hats and plates, Reverend Goodfroe, made it immediately known that a conference of his denominational coworkers was about to convene in the silver camp of Aspen. So he struck out with his burro for the Roaring Fork Valley.

The day after the reverend's departure, Lieutenant Phillip Lattamore was off-duty, so he and Lucy rode over to Spring Creek Mesa, through meadows dotted by sage clumps and wildflowers, and found their way to Cedar's Edge Mesa. They came upon the large stream that dropped from the Uncompahgre Plateau, but made no attempt to push on and seek out its source. They sat for an hour in the shade of a large juniper tree and made plans for Lucy's orchard. Then they rode leisurely homeward.

. Along the way, Lucy turned to her brother, and asked, "Phillip, what can we do to show our appreciation to Mr. Loutsenhizer? His advice proved so sound . . ."

"Let me give it some thought, Lucy."

"You know, Phillip, I haven't been able to get Pappy Loutsenhizer off my mind. He seems different somehow. Branded. Almost as though he's been through some sort of hell that sets him apart from other people."

Phillip gaped at her. "You mean you don't know? You haven't heard?"

"Heard what?"

"The incredible story of Alfred Packer—and the part that Loutsenhizer played in the tragedy."

"Go ahead. I'm listening," Lucy answered curiously.

"I don't know all the details, but the story's told over and over in this part of Colorado. Back in November of 1873, twenty-one prospectors came up this river valley on their way from Salt Lake City to a settlement called Saguache over in the San Luis Valley. They intended to search for gold. They were just about half-starved when they got close to where the Cantonment now stands. Chief Ouray, of the Ute tribe, advised them against trying to cross the San Juan Mountains so late in the season. He told them they should stay here in the valley and wait out the winter.

"Some of the prospectors took Chief Ouray's advice and lingered until spring. But Loutsenhizer and four others rested a couple of weeks and then trudged on toward Saguache, a hundred winter-swept miles away. They got lost in the mountains, and for three weeks had no food except a half-starved coyote Loutsenhizer shot; in the coyote's mouth was a shank of sheep. They lived on that for another five days.

"They were skeleton-like and close to death when they happened to find the cow camp of the Los Pinos Indian Agency. They rested a few days there, regained strength and pushed ahead again. But then they hit a stretch of incredible storms and subzero temperatures. They couldn't find game. Loutsenhizer, their leader, fashioned snowshoes and stubbornly went from one mountaintop to another, breaking a way for his followers. Finally the party won through to Saguache.

"Five days after Loutsenhizer's party left the Uncompahgre Valley, six more of the prospectors also took off for distant Saguache." Phillip paused, drew a deep breath, and asked, "Are you sure, Lucy, you want to hear the rest of this? It's gruesome as hell."

She shrugged. "If I don't hear it, I will always wonder what happened next. Go on."

"This party also got lost in the mountains. They didn't have a resourceful leader like Loutsenhizer, and failed to find the cow camp. In desperation, they stopped on the Lake Fork of the Gunnison River. For all except Alfred Packer, it was a final camp. Packer murdered his five companions and survived on their flesh for two months. With the coming of better weather, he made his way to Saguache."

"Did they hang him there?" Lucy's question was a whisper from a white face and tightened lips.

"Nope. It was summer again before people found out what Packer had done. He spent fourteen years in the penitentiary. Then they pardoned him. But about Loutsenhizer, Lucy, I have an idea Packer's cannibalism was on his mind a long, long time. He's a decent, sensitive man who was driven close to insanity himself. Likely some of the murdered men were close friends of his."

Lucy gazed with mixed emotions at her brother. "Phillip, now I understand. Much of the horror of his ordeal is etched on his face . . . and those sad eyes of his."

They rode the remaining miles to the Cantonment in

almost complete silence. The following day they sought
out a Cantonment officer with two years of legal training.
He aided them in preparing legal forms by which they
might make homestead claims for six hundred-forty acres
of land on Cedar's Edge Mesa.

Two days later, the four-horse stagecoach of Ike Fenlon
brought Lucy Lattamore across Dallas Divide. It was
Thursday—the day prior to her scheduled appearance
before the Columbia Quality group. Fenlon had asked her
to ride beside him atop the coach. The two of them talked
the whole way, under a sky holding only fleecy white
clouds against its azure blue, surrounded by the peaks of
the high San Juans. "You know, Ike," Lucy said, "I said
something on that first day I rode with you down Cochetopa Pass, and it holds true now more than then."

"What's that, Miss Lucy."

"I said these San Juans seem lonely and mysterious."

"I hope they stay that way. There's sure a passel of
newcomers pouring in since gold was—" Fenton's words
broke off. With the butt of his whip he was pointing into
a stand of aspen close to the road. "Right over there,
Miss. See . . . a doe and two little fawn." He slowed
the team, and they watched until the deer bounded away.

"Ike, that proves something," she said. "Not all
newcomers to the San Juan Mountains are undesirable."

"Not when they are as pretty as those fawn." He gave
her a quizzical grin. "Or as pretty as a young lady that
Royce Milligan says I'd better show up with."

"Will we see him today?" A glow was creeping across
her cheeks.

"My, my, aren't you the impatient one," Fenlon
chided teasingly. "You want I should delay the United
States mail, a dozen express packages, and those three
gents riding down below, just to skedaddle over to
Mesita?"

"But don't we come to Mesita first?"

"The schedule doesn't work that way, Lucy. Today we

ramble up to San Miguel City and Columbia. Then on Saturday we head for Mesita."

Lucy said nothing; she was too filled with hope to speak. Perhaps Royce Milligan would somehow already know of her coming and be on hand at San Miguel City . . . or show up for the concert. On the other hand, perhaps he'd be too busy . . . The thought distressed her. She consoled herself by studying the narrow, twisting valley along which the stagecoach was now descending toward the San Miguel River. There was a stream off to her left, swift-moving and stirred to a white froth by rocks impeding its way.

It was where this creek merged with the greater flow of the San Miguel River that Ike Fenlon reined his team onto a straighter road leading up the wide and heavily timbered valley. He turned to Lucy. "Your trip's pretty well over. About twelve miles more—a little over two hours—and we'll be in San Miguel City."

"Then how much farther to Columbia?" she asked.

"Just a couple of miles . . . but you won't be going there today."

"Why, Ike? That's where I am to sing."

"So it is. But accommodations have been set up for you at the hotel in San Miguel City. It is clean. Comfortable. And you'll like the food."

His words affirmed something that she had already suspected. Although she would sing for the women of Columbia Quality, she would be given little opportunity to mingle with them. By staying in San Miguel City, she would practically be sequestered. The idea irked her.

Presently a turn in the road brought them to where the entire upper San Miguel Valley lay revealed in mellow afternoon sunlight. Within sight now were the buildings of San Miguel City, and those of Columbia. Almost instantly, the magnificence of the valley cast its spell upon her. Close by there was a vast natural amphitheater, from one height of which Bridal Veil Falls plunged hundreds of feet. There were cliffs and hills, vividly red in the waning sunlight.

At San Miguel City, Lucy found her hotel room to be both spacious and comfortable. There was an iron bedstead, enameled white, with supporting sturdy springs and mattress, and made up with thick blankets and white linens. There was also a matching commode, a dresser with a tilting mirror, and a wooden rocking-chair. The curtained window offered a view of the valley that encompassed the great rock walls of the amphitheater and a zigzagging tracery of roads climbing toward the gaping mouths of mine tunnels.

Lucy napped during the rest of the afternoon. When she wakened, the shadows slanting across the room told her that the sun was near to setting. She spent the next hour paging through songbooks and sheet music, making selections for an hour-long concert. She chose them with care, for an idea had come to her as to how she might best entertain the special group that would comprise her audience.

With the concert outlined, she rose and moved about the room. All afternoon she had hoped that by some chance Royce Milligan might come tapping at her door. It had not happened, and now she felt a tiny bit of disappointment at his absence. Gathering darkness caused her to light a kerosene lamp; then she changed to a warmer dress. It was already chilly, and she surmised that the night would be even colder at this elevation.

It was well into the dinner hour, so she walked down a stairway to the hotel's lobby and sought out the dining room. It was small, with only four tables, covered in red-and-white checkered cloths and illuminated by lamps on each table. Only one table was unoccupied; she hesitated to claim it, but a middle-aged, blue-aproned woman came from the kitchen door and waved for her to sit down. The woman turned as though to leave, then swung about and studied Lucy. "My goodness, Miss," she exclaimed, "that dress . . . sort of ivory-colored and with the flared collar. It is just right for your copper-toned hair and hazel eyes. Sort of reminds me of a bouquet of mountain wildflowers.''

"Thank you," Lucy murmured, and would have added some sort of pleasantry, but at that moment the outer door opened. It admitted a gust of chilly air and a tall man clad in a gray suit and matching cloak. He quickly closed the door, swept off his hat, and then gazed about.

A fluster of surprise ran through the woman standing at her kitchen door. "Why, Mr. Delaney, how nice to see you here in San Miguel City. How are things down in Mesita?"

"So-so, when I left this morning, Nora." His eyes rested on Lucy. His black hair shone in the lamplight. "And who do we have here?" he asked as he approached her table.

Lucy looked startled at first but then took his curiosity for friendliness. "I doubt that she, or anyone else here at the hotel would know my name," Lucy explained. "I arrived but a short time ago. I am Lucy Lattamore; just now I call the Military Cantonment home."

"Miss Lattamore! Of course . . . you will be giving a concert at Columbia tomorrow—part of my reason for traveling this way." He shrugged free of the cloak, threw it carelessly across an unoccupied chair, and then asked, "Would I be presumptuous in asking to share your table?" He smiled in a hopeful way, and added, "By the way, my name is Delaney—Robert Delaney. I am in business downriver at a town called Mesita."

"Do sit down, Mr. Delaney," she offered. "Dining by oneself can be a dull affair."

As he took his place across the lamplit table, Lucy studied the stranger. He seemed somehow of a far more sophisticated world than this small frontier hotel. Would he attempt a conquest? His awareness of her forthcoming concert made her uneasy. She would be singing for women of easy virtue. Would Robert Delaney readily classify her in the same category? Her mind turned for an

instant to Royce Milligan and her yearning to have him
near, to feel the wonder of his arms and his kiss.

Just then, the waitress reentered with glasses of water.
Apparently there was no written menu, for she said,
"This evening we have either chicken and dumplings or
ham and yams. Dessert is apple pie. You can have either
coffee, tea, or fresh-churned buttermilk."

"Would you mind if I suggest the ham and yams?"
Delaney grinned. "Voice of experience, you know."

Both of them ordered the ham special, and coffee along
with the pie. As they waited, Delaney observed, "Miss
Lattamore, I have an idea your audience at Columbia will
have a delightful experience. There is something singularly attractive even about your speaking tones."

"Thank you." She nodded. There was nothing
menacing or even presumptuous about Robert Delaney,
and soon she found herself glad for his dinnertime
companionship. His casual but somewhat reserved manner
caused her to ask, "Are you a native of the San Juan
area, Mr. Delaney?"

"Born and bred here, Miss Lattamore," he replied
affably.

"Haven't I heard . . . or read . . . something about a
man—I believe his name is Tim O'Fallon—planning to
start a newspaper in Mesita?"

For the first time, Delaney's face took on hardness, and
his eyes narrowed. "Hell yes. It is true, all right. Old
Tim will squander piles of money on it. He's trying to
turn Mesita into New York City—but, by God, what's he
going to put in his headlines?"

Lucy Lattamore scanned his rugged face. She had
intended to mention Royce to him, but given his attitude
toward the paper, she now thought better of it. Instead
she asked, "What sort of business do you have in
Mesita?"

"Lumber. Building materials," he said brusquely.
There was a lull in the conversation as Nora placed plates
of food before them. To ease the unexpected tension,

Lucy asked, "What sort of songs do you suppose I should sing for Columbia Quality tomorrow night?"

"Oh, I don't know," Delaney began slowly, then smiled, clearly pleased to be asked for his opinion. "Civil War songs are still popular. And anything written by Stephen Foster . . ."

They chatted on like this throughout the meal, Lucy carefully avoiding any further mention of developments in Mesita. Delaney told her a little about his childhood in the San Juan basin, and Lucy related amusing bits about hers in the grasslands of northeastern Colorado. An hour passed and then Robert Delaney drew an expensive-looking pocket-watch from his coat pocket. "Miss Lucy, thank you for sharing your table and for your enjoyable companionship. I have to meet a business associate shortly." He rose to his feet and extended a firm hand to the one she offered. Then he asked, "Tomorrow, say at four in the afternoon, may I escort you to Columbia? I can arrange for a rig and a team of horses."

It was in her head to refuse, to say that Ike Fenlon's stage would take her, but suddenly—and as a surprise to even herself—she nodded, and said, "Mr. Delaney, I would like that." After he had reclaimed his cloak and disappeared through the outer door, she sat musing. Mr. Delaney seemed courteous, interesting, and agreeable, save for his bitter outburst about the newspaper. Nonetheless, she couldn't say she liked him exactly, though she couldn't put her finger on what was holding her back.

The thought persisted when she left the dining room and mounted the stairs to her room. Soon fatigue and a mountain chill caused her to seek the comfort and warmth of bed. For a time her thoughts raced. What would her concert be like? Was there a possibility that Royce might show up for it? And why should a man as intelligent and charming as Robert Delaney object so strenuously to a newspaper in his hometown? Before she fell asleep, a firm conviction was upon her. If Royce didn't turn up tomorrow, after her singing engagement, she would board

Ike Fenlon's stage to Mesita. She'd waited long enough to see the young editor, and besides she had some questions that seemed to need answers.

The following morning passed quietly; Lucy spent much of it walking outdoors, where she could revel in the awesome beauty of the valley and surrounding mountains. Shortly after noon, a horseback rider appeared, tied his mount to the hotel's hitching rail, and sought her out. He was of slight build, balding, and wore thick-lensed spectacles. He stared at Lucy somewhat uneasily before saying, "Miss Lattamore, my name is Gerald Whitestone. I have been asked by a committee from the ladies of Columbia Quality to act as your piano accompanist this evening."

"I am glad you came," she said, smiling, and motioned to a plank bench on the hotel's porch. "Let's sit down there. We can run over these." She placed a sheaf of sheet music in his hand.

Whitestone glanced through them and seemed relieved. "Wonderful, Miss Lattamore. This is the sort of thing I play at the saloon every night. I . . . I was afraid you would insist on operatic or classical selections."

"You see, there's no need to worry about that," she consoled him.

"Just hope for a calm evening and no showers." His voice carried a hint of anxiety.

"But we will be inside, out of the weather . . . and where your piano—"

"Oh, no. It's to be at the amphitheater, Miss Lattamore, a sort of rock formation where they are setting up benches and a stage."

Lucy gasped. "All of that . . . just to allow me to sing to a dozen or so women?"

Whitestone rose to his feet and stared at her curiously. "Haven't you been told? Your coming is the talk of the San Miguel Valley. They're expecting hundreds of people to show up."

"My God—from where?" Lucy asked in amazement.

She swept a hand across both San Miguel City and the distant rooftops of Columbia. "There aren't that many people in this whole valley."

"Perhaps not. But tonight men and women—yes, and children too—are going to pour out of these San Juan mountains. People are starved for entertainment, Miss Lattamore. And you've had the best press-agent around in Ike Fenlon. He's been telling everyone that you sing like an angel—and you know how fast word can get around."

At that, Lucy's eyes swept the glistening whiteness of the high peaks. "Give me something of your steadfast strength," she murmured. Then she caught her visitor's hand in hers. "If I should sing a few extra numbers, Mr. Whitestone, would you stay to help me out?"

He peered into her face, a smile starting at the corners of his mouth. "Not one minute past three o'clock in the morning—unless we take time out for a barley bracer."

The sun was just touching the western horizon when Lucy stepped from the shining new phaeton, with a fringed top, in which Robert Delaney had brought her from San Miguel City to Columbia. The trip had seemed short, riding behind a pair of matched black horses, with Delaney using his buggy whip only to point out various prospect holes and piles of mine tailings. "Right here there's going to be some of the richest miles on earth," he said proudly. "Fortunes are going to be made."

When they reached the hamlet of Columbia, a welcoming committee of both men and women escorted her from the phaeton to a large circular tent, which stood on the edge of some clustered buildings. Just beyond the tent was an open area leading gently up from the river. Higher was a precipitous mountainside; from it, in some long-past time, rocks had tumbled, coming to rest in a semicircle. Here wooden benches, chairs, and even powder boxes had been arranged for seating. All faced a plank stage where a canvas-covered piano and a few stools had been placed. Lucy sensed that her voice would resonate from the surrounding rocks in a most effective way.

Within the tent were lanterns held aloft by poles. Immediately, Lucy was introduced to several community leaders, and then guided to a table where a buffet dinner awaited her. *They must think I sing best with a full stomach,* Lucy mused to herself. *And maybe they are right!*

Presently Robert Delaney rejoined her. He was wearing a dark blue suit that was neatly pressed, and shoes with a luster that caught even the dimness of lantern glow. He carefully filled a plate, then slid into a chair beside Lucy. "The crowd is gathering outside. There is a pit barbeque going on too."

"I would like to meet those outside at the barbeque," she responded.

At that, he laughed gently and replied, "I can't allow that. I feel I must protect you from the unwashed masses."

Lucy felt like saying that it was the unwashed masses she was most interested in, but she held her tongue and let Delaney play the part of her Sir Galahad.

For some reason, it pleased her—almost perversely— that he should do so. Delaney was an opportunist, but a charming one. She scanned the crowd for Royce's face, then turned back to chat with Delaney until several local dignitaries came over to lead her to the amphitheater platform. Her accompanist, Gerald Whitestone, bowed and then took his place at the piano. Lucy had chosen a woolen dress, rose-hued with long sleeves. Her dark coppery hair cascaded loosely to her shoulders; her eyes gleamed with excitement. After taking a deep breath, born of the size of the crowd before her, she smiled and waved. There was an answering wave of greeting. And the next moment Lucy Lattamore tilted her head to pour out the stirring notes of "The Star Spangled Banner."

She sang steadily for almost half an hour—songs of

love, Irish ballads, marches, hymns. The clarity and wide range of her voice seemed enhanced by the rocks, the trees, and the silent darkness of the night.

There was a short intermission, during which a portly stranger with Scottish accent made a surprise announcement. A committee had only yesterday voted that the villages of San Miguel City and Columbia would merge to become a town known as Telluride. The announcement drew a mixed reception.

It was during an ensuing moment of silence that Lucy first noticed a girl in the audience who had risen and was approaching the stage. Several hands were extended in an attempt to stop her, but she eluded them and drew nearer. The darkness of her hair and complexion told Lucy that she was Mexican. There were teardrops on her cheeks, but across her face was something close to ecstasy. She was clad in a thin and rumpled black dress; in her hands she held an alabaster carving of a dove with outstretched wings, bearing in its beak a short stem of wheat.

The girl, seemingly in her late teens, pushed through the crowd to stand before the plank stage. A tall man, wearing a lawman's star, moved to intercept her, but Lucy spoke quickly. "Let her come to me . . . please." She stooped down and laid a reassuring hand on the girl's shoulder. "What is it, honey?" she asked.

At Lucy's words, the girl's face filled with wonder and adoration. She held the dove out to Lucy. "Señorita, my name . . . it is Felicidad. I must give this to you. You have brought beauty into my life. For this I must thank you."

Lucy accepted the gift, keeping her eyes all the while on the waif-like Spanish girl before her. Then she kissed her on the brow, backed away, and launched into the haunting strains of an old Spanish love song she'd learned many years ago.

The beauty of Lucy's voice and the drama of the moment brought the audience to utter silence. When she was through, Lucy turned to Gerald Whitestone at the piano, and asked, "Will you see that Felicidad gets safely back to her seat?" She watched them move from her, and as she looked out over the audience, she noticed where the women of Columbia Quality were sitting.

She sang for most of the following hour, often urging those gathered to join in, and closed the concert with a stirring rendition of "Rock of Ages," then called her accompanist to her side to share in the final applause.

Later she mingled with the crowd, making sure to shake the hands of the women of Columbia Quality. When the time for her departure was at hand, Robert Delaney was there with his phaeton, ready to return her to San Miguel City.

Chapter 9

The next evening, Royce Milligan sat exhausted at his desk in the office of the newborn *Mesita Messiah*. In the pressroom behind him, a tall youth was moving about the press that had, at long last, arrived the day before, and would print the first small weekly edition. Royce had thrown open both a window and the door facing Mesita's main street. Now the sun was dropping behind wooded hills to the west, and shadows crept across the quiet town.

From time to time Royce searched the street with an expectant gaze. Ike Felon's stagecoach was due within half an hour and Royce had every reason to hope that Lucy would be on it, for Fenlon had promised to see her safely to Mesita and the newspaper office. Now Royce forcibly turned his thoughts to the few things remaining to be done before he could complete the first pressrun of *The Mesita Messiah:* arranging type cases, inking devices, and page-forming plates. It would be a run of scarcely three hundred copies, and Royce knew that flaws would inevitably show up in both composition and printing. Yet despite this, and even in his fatigued state, there was excitement in the venture; Royce had heard enough people living in and about Mesita say how eagerly they looked forward to having their own newspaper to know it was true.

During the past two days Tim O'Fallon had showed up repeatedly at the *Messiah* plant demonstrating an almost boyish enthusiasm about the activities, anxious to hold the very first paper, warm off the press, in his hands. To Royce's amusement, Mesita's founder and most prominent citizen had seized a broom and window-polishing gear and worked until the rooms were spotless.

Tim O'Fallon and Royce were united in their determination to meet a first-edition deadline, and that, combined with the recent arrival of the press, had caused a flurry of activity in the newspaper office. Royce had had to act as reporter, editor, and pressman—though he *had* managed to find himself a young assistant for the printing phase of the operation—and he still had a raft of stories to go over before they'd be ready to run. For this reason, he'd missed Lucy's concert, but he felt that he'd been with her in spirit.

The event had become the talk of the valley; he was planning to get a firsthand account from Lucy herself to go in the paper. He wondered whether she had been amazed at the great size of her audience, what she had chosen to sing, and whether she had actually met the ladies of the infamous Columbia Quality.

If he hadn't been able to be present last night himself, he took consolation in the fact that he'd broached the subject of a Mesita concert for Lucy with Tim O'Fallon; his employer had been receptive and, above all, anxious to meet Lucy once she arrived.

Royce hoped Lucy wouldn't think him too high-handed in having Ike Fenlon collect her after the concert and bring her on to Mesita. Part of him was sure that she'd enjoy a spur-of-the-moment change of plans, especially if it brought the two of them together again.

He now let his eyes search again along the street, but the stage had not yet come into sight. He stood restlessly at the window as deeper shadows engulfed the town. There was so much he had to tell Lucy, so many questions he must ask her. Already, he almost felt her presence about him. He closed his eyes, remembering their moments together at Parson Goodfroe's last revival meeting. Both of them had talked a little of their future plans, but they had been largely content to sit in the enchantment of the summer night and the knowledge they had come to mean so much to each other.

It was the pounding of hoofs and the rattle of stage-coach wheels that brought Royce abruptly back to the present. Already Ike Fenlon's rig was drawing to a stop just outside the door.

"Come along," Royce shouted to his youthful helper. "They are here. You can hold Fenlon's lead team while he and Lucy and I talk." Royce's gaze swept the top of the coach, but the two figures seated close to Ike Fenlon were both men in miner's garb. Impatiently, Royce positioned himself to open the rig's door and help Lucy Lattamore to the ground.

Fenlon's voice sounded testy as he dropped to the ground, his whip still in hand. "Hold on, Milligan. She ain't aboard." As though to emphasize his disgust, he snapped the whip against the hitching rail of *The Messiah*.

"You mean she isn't—" Royce said disbelievingly.

"Oh hell, yes. She will be showing up directly. But likely he will take her flying past here and up to Tim O'Fallon's house. I heard him say he wanted to be the first to introduce the two of them."

A look of utter bewilderment was stamped on Royce's face. "He? Who? Ike, you don't make sense."

"Neither does Miss Lucy, Royce . . . promising to ride down with me from San Miguel City—"

"You mean she agreed to come?" Royce interrupted.

"Oh, sure. She was excited as can be about seeing you again, but then she let that son of a bitch—" Ike paused, spitting a mouthful of tobacco juice for emphasis. "—Delaney, entice her into his phaeton."

"She took a ride with Robert Delaney?" Royce said, stunned.

"Yeah, but you can't blame her. She doesn't know what kind of bastard he is, and I didn't have the chance to tell her." With that, Fenlon climbed back onto his rig.

Suddenly another rig, a phaeton drawn by a team of fast black horses, came into sight. Fenlon waited for it to sweep by before urging his team into motion. By then, though, a dazed and furious Royce Milligan had turned his back to the street and reentered his office.

Once inside, Royce touched a match to an oversized kerosene lamp, and in a heedless way watched the flickering glow it cast over his desk and a couple of locked-in pages of type, ready for the press. Minutes passed and he became aware of Andy Parnell, his young helper, standing in wordless perplexity nearby. "Andy, we've had a long day; tomorrow is apt to be even longer. Why don't you head for home and get your supper and a night's rest?"

"All right, Mr. Milligan . . . if you're sure you won't need me." The youth hesitated, as though wishing to say more, but then turned silently and started toward the door.

Royce dropped with tired bewilderment into a chair, propped his elbows on the desk and wiped a hand across his forehead. Still seared into his brain was the sight of Robert Delaney's ostentatious phaeton careening by his newspaper office.

He glanced at a wall clock and noted that already it was almost seven o'clock. By now Tim O'Fallon would be expecting him to appear for the evening meal, escorting Lucy. Well, they'd see Lucy, all right, but not him. He'd plead newspaper business—anything to keep him away from a meeting with Delaney that could only lead to trouble. Hastily, he scribbled a note to Tim explaining his absence, asking him to explain it to Lucy, as well. He went to the door and called back Andy, who agreed to deliver the note. Then Royce dropped his arms onto the desk and lowered his head into them, but abruptly jerked back up and banged his closed fist down hard. *Why in hell didn't I take time to go to Columbia . . . to her concert? Instead, I was so wrapped up in my own little world that I let a bastard like Delaney . . .*

He stared at the printer's gear about him. The locking

metal frame meant to hold page one of his first issue was only half-full. He had hoped to report the success of Lucy Lattamore's concert in the remaining columns.

Given greatest prominence, just below the masthead, though, was an article on the devastation of the forests on the Uncompahgre Plateau. Royce hadn't been able to make an ironclad connection between it and the Delaney Lumber Company, but he'd printed what evidence he had. He'd been scrupulous about including only the facts; he was proud of that. Nonetheless, the article was damning to Robert Delaney, and the lumber magnate was bound to be furious.

Royce reread the piece, searching his soul to clarify his motives for printing it. He had personal reasons for loathing Delaney now; the man was obviously doing everything he could to win Lucy's affections away from him. But dammit, the allegations in the article were valid and the public had the right to know!

He then put the frame holding the incomplete page one aside, and set about proofing other stories. He was beginning to feel cold in the unheated office, so he sought out a heavy sheepskin coat from his storage room and draped it about his shoulders. Gradually, he felt his weariness begin to overcome him, and his eyelids drooped and his pencil fell from his hand. His head dropped to the desk and he slept.

He was awakened by morning sunlight pouring warmth into his *Messiah* building. He dashed water from a wooden pail onto his stubbled face to drive sleepiness away, wishing for his razor and a change of clothes.

He was rubbing cold water from his neck and arms when the outer door opened and Tim O'Fallon walked briskly in and stared at him. "Well! You're still among the living," the older man observed.

"Right now," Royce answered, smiling ruefully, "I'm not so sure."

O'Fallon peered at him in a measuring way. "Royce,

Margaret says you'd damn well better get up the hill for breakfast with us in half an hour.''

"Lucy—" Royce began.

"She'll be there. We got her to stay over with us." O'Fallon's voice took on a note of wonder. "God, Royce, that voice of hers! Even when she is speaking you sense its beauty and power."

As he spoke, O'Fallon was craning his neck as he attempted to read the locked-in type of page one. "That stuff is put in there backwards," he commented.

"Sure," Royce joked. "You have to stand on your head to read it until it shows up in the paper." His voice took on seriousness as he thrust a sheet of page-one copy into O'Fallon's hands. "Read it if you wish, Tim."

Moments of silence elapsed as the builder of Mesita—and owner of the newspaper—read thoughtfully. Then he handed the sheet back to Royce, and said, "We agreed, son, that I would keep my hands off your pages. That still stands. But Royce, I want you to know that I think this piece on Delaney is powerfully written. It's nothing short of a declaration of war." O'Fallon put the paper down and clapped Royce on the back. "Where is your write-up of the concert at Columbia?" he queried.

"Coming—as soon as I talk with Miss Lattamore."

"Well then, let's get on up there," O'Fallon urged.

Royce entered O'Fallon's house by a side door and quickly sought out the second-floor room where he bathed, shaved, and quickly changed clothes. As he moved toward the door to leave the room, his gaze came to rest once more on the small daguerreotype of the girl with the appealing smile and dark eyes. He'd forgotten to ask Tim about it. Would O'Fallon think he was prying if he did? Yet something of the picture's mystery was with him as he went slowly down the stairs to meet Lucy.

When he entered the dining room, O'Fallon waved him to a place next to Margaret Hendricks, then said, "No need for introductions, that's for sure. Just eat hearty, Royce, because today we have to make sure our *Mesita*

Messiah is born. It's a challenge, and we're all ready to lend a hand.''

Royce recognized his friend's words for what they were, ice-breaking banter to ease the tension. Then Margaret Hendricks laid an envelope beside Royce's plate, and said, ''Here's an item for your premiere edition, Royce. But don't open it here. Save that for office hours.''

During these moments of casual talk, Lucy Lattamore toyed with a napkin ring. Now she looked directly into Royce's face. ''Good morning, Royce. I am glad these gracious friends of yours insisted I stay over for your opening day. And my congratulations.''

His first impulse was to reach out, grasp her hand, and cling tightly to it, for there was a troubled and reserved undertone to her words. But then his mind reverted to the means by which she had come into Mesita, side by side with a man for whom he held only the deepest loathing. ''Good morning to you too, Lucy,'' he murmured. ''You will enjoy your stay, I am sure.''

The chill born of this meaningless exchange of words lingered throughout the meal, and only impersonal topics were mentioned. After a time Lucy excused herself and moved quickly from the room. But when Royce left the house, bound for the newspaper office, she was awaiting him on the walk leading to the gate. ''Royce,'' she called.

He stopped and looked into her pale, determined face. ''What is it?''

''Just answer me this: Why are you suddenly treating me like a pariah? Am I to believe that you no longer care for me? Is that why you didn't come to Columbia?''

Her words broke through the fragile barrier of his reserve. ''God, no, Lucy. Didn't Ike Fenlon explain? My press had just arrived . . . there was no way I could get away. And then, when you swept by the office last night in Delaney's phaeton . . . I had been waiting for you to arrive.''

She moved her hands in helpless gesture. "But I did come to Mesita at your bidding, didn't I?"

He said nothing, only stared deeply into her lustrous eyes.

"Royce, you resent my having come down from San Miguel City with Mr. Delaney. Isn't that it?

"Delaney is a son of a bitch in my book, a crook and a despoiler."

Lucy's face reddened. "I confess I know nothing about Robert Delaney beyond what he told me—that he's a native of the Valley and in the lumbering business. Nor, I must assure you, did he make any attempt to despoil me!"

Royce stood silent for a time, knowing that an explanation was due her. Presently he said, "Lucy, listen to me. I simply could not be up river for your concert, and also meet my announced publication date for *The Messiah*. And don't, for heaven's sake, think I was accusing Delaney of attempting to seduce you. He *is* a despoiler, Lucy, but of another sort. He lays waste the countryside for personal gain."

"You expect me to believe that?" she said somewhat scornfully. "Mr. Delaney furnishes materials for every one of Mr. O'Fallon's projects. He told me so."

Royce Milligan noted the stubborness of her defense of Robert Delaney. The anger had drained from him and he started to move on toward the street, feeling at wit's end. Then abruptly he turned and grasped her hands. "God, Lucy! Are we going to let this come between us?"

She let her gaze sweep over him, then placed a hand on each of his cheeks. "Royce, perhaps you and I have been thoughtless and jumped to conclusions. Go ahead to your office and your big first day. I will see you later. But right now let's both do some clear thinking." With that, she turned and moved swiftly toward the house.

At the *Messiah* office, Royce went about his work with a thoughtful expression. He pondered the reason why he was feeling little elation in the fact that today his newspaper would become a reality. With the help of his young assistant, he moved the finished pages of type close to the press and made sure an ample supply of newsprint paper was on hand. There was a delay about midmorning when Mesita's grocery-store proprietor rushed in with last-minute changes to his advertising copy.

It was while changing this type that Royce suddenly recalled the envelope Margaret Hendricks had put near his plate at the breakfast table. He completed the rearranged advertisement and then dug out the letter. It contained two pages of clear, legible handwriting: a concise and interesting summary of Lucy Lattamore's concert at Columbia. He knew it to be Mrs. Hendricks' own composition, and that she must have attended. Here, then, was the rest of his front page. He glanced at a clock. It would take an hour to hand-set the type for the concert story and get it into the proper locked frames.

A thought struck him. Andy Parnell, his young apprentice, had shown considerable skill in hand-setting type. "Andy, get over here," he called. "Grab a type-stick. Here's a page of copy. Let's get busy."

Within the hour the story, with Margaret Hendricks' byline, was set, beginning with nearly a quarter of page one, and carrying over to page two.

As noon approached, Royce knew that the pressrun must begin within an hour. It was while he was mulling over the idea of sending Andy out for sandwiches, that the door opened and three people approached him. Margaret Hendricks led the way, clad in a serviceable-looking calico dress and blue apron. She was carrying one handle of an apple basket over which a tea towel had been tucked. The other handle was in the grasp of a slightly embarrassed Max Beasley, whom Royce had not seen for several days. And immediately behind the basket-burdened twosome, Lucy Lattamore trudged in, her arms wrapped about a jug as though to maintain the warmth of the liquid refreshment it contained. She too had changed into clothing suitable for work, and about her copper-hued hair she'd pinned a white cloth.

Mrs. Hendricks was the first to speak. "Well, Royce, look us over. Lunch-toters, and your first-day labor brigade."

Her words, together with their motley appearance, caused Royce to break into laughter. "Whose idea is all this?" he asked.

"Not mine," Max Beasley hastened to assure him. "I would be up on the high divide napping under a pine tree, except—"

"Except that Mr. O'Fallon decided all of us should help you out," Margaret interrupted.

"And you?" Royce was staring at Lucy as he spoke.

"I am just a slave," she murmured impishly. And then added, "Besides, I expect this printing establishment to pass my personal inspection."

Royce would have returned her banter, but suddenly he was staring at Max Beasley and recalling how together they had stood, aghast at the wanton destruction of forestland atop the Uncompahgre Plateau.

He was so absolutely quiet for a time that Lucy found herself asking, "Royce, are you all right? Perhaps I should leave."

Her words broke his reverie. "Don't you dare leave. Not one of you—until we've a chance to empty that basket and jug."

He heard their sudden laughter, but his mind was working. *That is it! Somehow get her up there on the Plateau to where Max and I saw the hell Robert Delaney and his crew are creating. Let her see for herself how a whole forest is being raped . . . and the havoc that is moving toward the place from which water for her own orchard lands must come.* Royce glanced from one to another of them. *Now isn't the time to ask her to go up there into the woods. Not while others are about. But I must suggest it soon. Today.* Then he said, "Actually, folks, I can sure use all of you the rest of the day. We've got to midwife a newspaper onto the street. But not until we clear the gear off the worktable and dig into the grub." He paused, then added, "Damn, but I'm hungry!"

It was the determined work of *The Messiah*'s editor, apprentice printer, and what Beasley termed "slave-labor force," that made *The Messiah* a reality and the chief topic of conversation in homes throughout the town of Mesita that night.

Much later, as Lucy stood scanning the finished product, Margaret held another copy aloft. "Fame at last," she shouted. "See, right here on page one . . . the first byline ever to be awarded by *The Mesita Messiah.*"

"And for a job well done," Royce commented. "And my thanks to all of you for some fine help this afternoon."

"Your paper will thrive and grow," Margaret predicted. "You have already made some thought-provoking comments, Royce."

He knew that she was referring to his first-page article on Delaney and the challenge inherent within it. His gaze moved to Lucy, seated nearby; she'd flung aside her headcloth, allowing the coppery cloud of her hair to tumble freely across her shoulders. She had the stain of printer's ink about her, but at that moment it seemed to Royce that she looked lovelier for the disarray. Lucy was still engrossed in the first page of the paper, and he knew she was carefully reading the already controversial logging piece.

Moments later Royce was called to a rear area of the building, where an excited boy was demanding to see him. The lad appeared to be about ten years old. "Mr. Milligan, my name is Tony Lucero. I can sell maybe thirty or forty papers down at the saloons. Can you let me have them? I'll bring back money to you first thing in the morning." He was proudly displaying a bag he had fashioned from burlap to carry the papers.

Royce counted out fifty papers and helped stuff them in the boy's bag. "Good luck, Tony. How about our splitting your sales money fifty-fifty for tonight? Then perhaps we can work out a regular route for you.''

When Tony Lucero had started hastily on his way, Royce returned to the office. He looked about, realizing that both Margaret Hendricks and Max Beasley had left, taking the lunch containers with them. But Lucy sat quietly with her *Messiah* still in hand as she watched Royce's approach.

"Well, that's it for the first week, Lucy. And now for your opinion of its contents.''

"You should build a subscription list quickly, and attract plenty of advertising. Royce, your *Messiah* is lively and timely.'' She paused, and then stood up close to him. "Royce, your own article . . . on this front page . . . it is a sort of clarion call. But isn't it also a direct challenge to Robert Delaney and his means of livelihood?''

He motioned her to again be seated, then drew up a chair, which he sat on backwards, throwing his arms across its top. "Yes, Lucy, the piece is a challenge to Delaney and those associated with him. I have a gut feeling that either he or I will cease to do business in Mesita—and I myself propose to remain. But the issue goes far beyond his hellish timber-felling practices. It goes beyond Delaney himself. It calls for scrutiny of the means by which every natural resource of western Colorado is being utilized—or exploited.''

"But isn't there some personal feeling against Mr. Delaney in this?'' There was no anger in her words, only persistent probing.

He countered by asking: "Lucy, has Delaney suddenly become all that important to you? So much so that you constantly seek to defend him?''

Her eyes were perplexed as she answered. "Royce, I don't know. Honestly, I don't. Robert Delaney has been kind and courteous to me. Did you know he persuaded Tim O'Fallon to put me under contract for a series of concerts? There is talk that a music hall might be built within a year.''

"Lucy . . . Lucy." He laughed. "Delaney is an opportunist. How damn clever it was of him to make it seem that all this about your concerts here in Mesita was his doing. But Tim O'Fallon makes his own decisions and runs his own affairs. He had decided long ago to build a concert hall. Weeks ago he urged me to have you come here so he could hear you sing." He waited a few seconds, steeled his mind, and then asked, "And what about me, Lucy? Am I no longer a factor in your life?"

A devilish glint came into her eyes. "What a question, Royce, and what a way of asking. Listen, Mister Obstinate, why not find out by getting out of that chair and kissing me?"

He obliged, and as they clung together the matter of Delaney's play for her attention seemed unimportant. But something else reoccurred to him. It caused him to ask, "Lucy, can you spare three days? I want you to ride up with me onto the Uncompahgre Plateau. To the source of the water for your orchards."

She thought a moment, then asked, "Wouldn't we be able to ride on down to the orchard lands themselves? Follow the route of the water?"

"Every step of the way," he assured her, at the same time thinking, *She must see for herself . . . the wanton destruction . . . the waste of forests that can't be replaced for another two or three hundred years.*

Chapter 10

They rode out of Mesita at dawn two days later. Preparations for the trip had kept them busy since Lucy's arrival in Mesita. Royce had had to get ready for the next edition, as well, a task made easier by the appearance of Margaret Hendricks at his shop. "If you are going to be gone for a time, someone has to run this shebang," she'd informed him. Working long hours with this aging but spry woman, Royce became confident that she could indeed fill in for him, especially with the help of young Andy Parnell.

Meanwhile, Lucy Lattamore had found it necessary to search the handful of stores in Mesita to find apparel suitable for the journey by horseback. She'd picked out serviceable overalls and a couple of denim jackets. Tim O'Fallon had offered suggestions as to other gear and suitable bedrolls; he also had his household help prepare what he termed a *jackass grub-pack,* food that could readily be carried atop a packsaddle. Fortunately, no one had seemed overly concerned about the propriety of the two of them traveling alone together. Lucy had brought it up tentatively to Margaret, who'd laughed and assured her that out west, folks were more practical about such things.

Morning sunlight was still a narrow band along the higher ridges when they came to the base of the Uncompahgre Plateau and began the steep climb. As nearly as

113

possible, Royce followed the little-used trail by which he and Max Beasley had descended into Mesita after their troublesome encounter with the loggers. His plan was to detour around the operations of the timber crew and yet find his way to the three-streams glade. Before leaving Mesita, he had learned that his application for a mining claim there had been approved. Likely after this trip he would follow Margaret Hendricks' suggestion and hire someone like Martin Goetz to do assessment work in the area, thereby firming up his claim.

They rode in single file, picking their way through thick brush, with the packhorse bringing up the rear. Little was said, but Royce was aware that Lucy was both surprised and elated by the cool green growth of timber about them, and by the beauty of the distant peaks of the high San Juan Mountains.

When the trail widened for a time, he checked his mount to allow Lucy to ride beside him. Then he said, "In about five miles we will come into true forest, up where timber stands straight and lofty, thousands of acres of it. You'll see all kinds of animals, and birds too."

They stopped momentarily at a bend of the trail; as she lifted her face toward the rising sun, a pattern of restless aspen shadows danced across her features. On impulse, Royce leaned close and let his lips touch hers. She sighed in what seemed to him an enchanted way, and then said, "Mr. Milligan, you know the perfect time and place to reach a lady's heart, don't you?"

He would have gone on kissing her, but abruptly he rose slightly in his saddle, and turned. His eyes searched the trail over which they had just come, visible far below. "Damn it!" he said sharply.

"Royce! What's wrong?"

"Maybe nothing. I don't know. I thought for a minute that we were being followed."

"What makes you think so?"

He pointed. "See that break in the timber about a mile and a half back of us? A rider just passed it . . ."

Presently they urged their horses into movement. The magic of their moment of peaceful togetherness had somehow vanished. They rode quietly for a while and then Lucy asked, "Royce, what are we really up here for? You've more on your mind than a simple outing."

He began slowly. "Lucy, there are things up here on this plateau that are apt to play an important part in your life and in mine." He hesitated, striving to find the right words. "You see, I have a mining claim about a good day's ride from here. I filed claim to the land, a small park-like area, because of you. It likely controls the only water source you have for your orchard lands on Cedar's Edge Mesa."

She stared at him in an uncomprehending way. "But why, Royce? Why would you want to control water that's so important to me?"

"Because of the vulnerable spot you would be in should somebody else get hold of it."

"Who on earth would want to do such a thing?" she asked in disbelief.

His answer caused her to jerk her horse to a halt as he said, "The same men who tried to kill Max Beasley and me when we rode across this forestland a couple of days ago."

"You mean Robert Delaney's employees? They tried to murder you just for traveling through?"

"I admit I don't have proof, Lucy. But that is why I am here, to find out for sure. And to have you see with your own eyes how a forest . . . as well as men . . . can be murdered."

Comprehension was flooding her face.

Royce shook his head tiredly and went on, "Lucy, maybe it isn't so important after all, your knowing that Delaney really is a thief and a spoiler. But I do want you to see the source of your irrigation water, the beauty of the spot. I intend to gain full title to it—and then give the damned water rights to you and your brother. In their entirety. In perpetuity."

Lucy's face whitened in shock. For moments she remained silent, as Royce urged his horse ahead. She caught up with him after a while, to seize and hold his free hand. Then in a voice scarcely above a whisper, she said, "Royce, I want to see whatever it is you have to show me, even if it proves that I have been a blind, silly idiot."

During the day's ride that followed, Royce was silent about those harvesting timber on the Uncompahgre Plateau. He had stated his case; now Lucy Lattamore must see for herself the devastation that would, if not halted, inevitably destroy the glade and its water sources. But that must wait until tomorrow, after she herself had seen the forest-ringed park and reveled in its pristine beauty.

Well after midday they stopped atop a rocky spur near the trail, for close to its base a trickle of cold spring water began its downward way. Again Royce studied the trail behind them, sensing that they were not alone. He would have been more concerned, except that he felt certain that if they really were being followed, it had to be Max Beasley, Tim O'Fallon's troubleshooter. *And sly old Tim expects there may be trouble ahead for Lucy and me,* Royce speculated. *More trouble than we can handle. Max won't catch up with us, or camp where we do, but he'll be close by if trouble brews.*

As they ate lunch, Royce asked, "How come you have never told me anything of your concert for the Columbia Quality?"

"It was just a friendly little get-together." She smiled evasively.

"Not from what I read in that story Margaret wrote. They estimated you sang to almost three hundred people. The Quality group must have lots of friends." He paused, then added teasingly, "And customers."

She smiled, but then turned serious eyes toward him. "There were lots of fine and friendly folks there, and I was treated like royalty. But you know, Royce, one incident lingers in my mind. Sort of haunts me."

"What was it?"

"There was a young girl there, poorly dressed, clearly distraught. She couldn't have been a day over sixteen, and I believe she was Mexican." Lucy paused, then went on, telling of the strange and timid approach of Felicidad, her gift of the alabaster dove. Presently she asked, "Could she have been a prostitute? She was so young and piteous."

"I don't know, Lucy. I guess it's possible," he said sadly.

They reached the glade of three streams just as the sun dropped behind a timbered ridge to the west. They had met not a single person on the day-long ride, nor had they broken from green and growing timber into the desolate reaches of plundered woodlands. Once Royce had noticed a smoke plume off eastward, and the acrid scent of burning spruce needles, but he had steered away from it.

Now, dismounting from their horses, they stood ankle-deep in the lush grass and meadow flowers of the glade. There was a brisk coolness in the air and the sound of birdcalls from the timber. After a short time, the evening light laid a silver sheen across the three merging brooks and the creek born of their union. Lucy's face seemed to take on the quiet tranquility of the place. "Royce, this glade is almost unreal in its loveliness. Why can't we just stand here and let our eyes drink it all in—at least until darkness comes?"

He grinned, delighted with her words, but shook his head. "The horses have to be unsaddled and our gear unpacked. Then we need to rustle up wood and water. Besides, your tent has to be set up."

"All right, boss-man," she replied. "But you know what?" Suddenly her arms were about him and her face upturned in rapture. "Thank you, Royce, my kind and thoughtful Royce, for bringing me here."

They both began preparations for their meal and for the

night. By the time darkness came on, Royce had securely staked a small tent on a dry knoll. Before it danced the flames of a fire that would serve both for warmth and cooking. Royce had not pitched a tent for himself, for there seemed little chance of a nighttime shower. He did unroll a bedroll, thinking how nice it would be to have Lucy with him under the stars instead of inside the tent.

It was after they had eaten, and the fire had become a pile of glowing embers, that Lucy suddenly came to her feet. Her hands were folded; her gaze seemed to rise and seek out some distant star. And now the magic of her deep, expressive voice filled the glade. Royce quickly realized that her words were Latin, but nonetheless their meaning was obvious: they expressed certainty of God's love and protection.

Later, both of them seemed intent on avoiding sleep. They sat side by side by the fire, and after a while Royce drew a blanket about them. "Remember the last time I did this?" he asked her.

"Of course. In that spooky old mine."

"And lucky we were to be there, Lucy, thanks to your sighting that mine portal through the storm. You must be clairvoyant."

Lucy was very quiet for a time, then suddenly she pressed closer to him. "You won't believe this, Royce, but I was pointed to that mine. Remember when I climbed the ridge looking for grass to kick aside for the horses? Right then I found it."

"Found what, Lucy?"

"A pile of rocks, Royce. A cairn. Right up there atop the ridge."

"Rocks . . . piled up," he repeated. "Could be a grave, Lucy."

She shook her head. "I thought that too—at first. Then I noticed a sort of V carved in a smooth rock, and something made me stoop and peer through it. And Royce, it directed my eyes to the mine portal."

Royce shook his head in wonder, and said, "Why

would anyone want to set up a device that gives away the position of a mine?'' He paused thoughtfully and then added, ''Lucy, that mine was old, and hadn't been worked in Lord knows how long. I've always felt pretty sure it was an old Spanish workings. But why would they have built a marker pointing to it?''

''I don't know, Royce,'' she murmured.

''Lucy, have you told anyone else of this?'' he asked intently.

''Just Pappy Loutsenhizer. Why do you ask?''

''Because I think this mine may deserve further investigation. We had little chance to look around inside, you'll recall.''

She shuddered a little, and spoke again. ''Royce, it is all sort of weird—and frightening. I am not sure I would ever want to go inside that tunnel again.''

''Poor, Lucy,'' he teased. ''Scared of a deserted mine?''

She laughed and then he pulled her to him and kissed the warmth of her lips. He felt her respond to him and he clasped her to his chest. But then, breathless, she pulled away. ''I guess we'd both better get some sleep now.''

As much as he wanted her, he acquiesced. He didn't want to rush things with her, and possibly jeopardize their love. So he rose and drew a lantern from the saddlepack, saying, ''Here, I'll light this for you; it'll be handy if a packrat decides to bunk down inside the tent with you.''

''Oh, damn it,'' she exploded. ''Now I won't get a wink of sleep all night!''

He chuckled, and then took off into the darkness to check the horses. He stood for a little while on the edge of the clearing, pondering the brilliance of the stars, feeling more restless than he'd ever felt before.

He started to return to the dying campfire, but then stopped abruptly. Royce caught his breath, for as Lucy moved the lantern about inside the tent, the canvas wall seemed a lighted screen upon which was an entrancing

silhouette . . . that of Lucy naked to the waist as she
knelt combing her hair. He was conscious of her uplifted
face, the gentle swell of her breasts, and the litheness of
her body.

He was silent for a time, struggling with an
overwhelming desire to enter the tent and take her in his
arms. Then he steeled himself and moved toward his own
bedroll. Sleep eluded him, though. With his hands cupped
behind his head, he lay recalling what a lighted tent wall
had revealed. He turned to gaze toward it again, but now
there was only darkness and the quiet of the night.

The next morning he and Lucy arose early. By sunup
they had broken camp, packed their gear and moved
northward along the creek flowing from the glade. It took
four hours of steady riding to bring them to the spot
where he and Beasley had determined that water could be
diverted from the stream's course and led to Cedar's Edge
Mesa. Royce carefully pointed out the advantages that a
flume would offer. "I don't believe that material would
be too hard to come by," he explained. "There are two
or three sawmills in the vicinity of Pomona and the
Cantonment. And there's a decent road most of the way
to your orchard lands. From there, it will just be a matter
of clearing away some piñon trees and a few rocks to get
wagonloads of lumber and other supplies up to the diversion point."

After a while they turned reluctantly back toward the
high and level reaches of the Uncompahgre Plateau. Both
would have liked to continue northward, to Cedar's Edge
Mesa, Spring Creek Mesa, and the Cantonment. But
Royce had another plan.

They came again to their campsite at Three Rivulets
Glade by mid-afternoon. As they were riding clear of the
dense surrounding timber, suddenly they halted their
horses and stared about, surprised. There were saddle
horses and half a dozen pack burros grazing along one of
the three streams. Also, a tent had been pitched less than

three hundred feet from their own, and now smoke drifted lazily up from a stovepipe thrust through the tent's canvas roof and secured by guy-wires staked to the ground. Judging from the setup, it looked as if the tent's occupants planned to stay.

Royce and Lucy rode quietly forward, but anger was growing within Royce. These newcomers were trespassing upon his property; he would quickly send them on their way. And then Lucy yelled in an excited way, "Royce, I'll bet it's Mr. Goetz . . ."

"Well doggoned if it isn't." Royce grinned. "Margaret Hendricks must have sent him up here." As they rode close to the camp, Goetz himself pushed back a tent flap and appeared, grinning broadly. There was a round of hand-shaking, during which Goetz introduced his companion. "This is Luther, my younger son. I have two boys—both dunderheads." Goetz was shaking his head dolefully, but there was pride in his eyes.

"Mr. Goetz, what brings you and Luther up here?" Lucy asked.

He seemed taken by surprise. "Why, Miss, don't you know? Mrs. Hendricks, down at Mesita, sent for me. She told me we should heist our rumps up here and start digging a shaft for Mr. Milligan. One big enough for coal." He paused and peered about the timberlands, then added, "But what anyone needs coal for up here, I sure don't know. Wood burns too, you know, Royce."

Royce laughed, then explained the shaft's primary purpose, which was to enable him to claim the source of irrigation water for Lucy's fruitlands.

Goetz nodded understanding. "If we do just the digging needed for assessment work every summer, likely we'll be busy a hundred years before we run into the coal," he observed, and then asked, "Will that be long enough?"

"Ask me fifty years from now," Royce gibed back.

He and Lucy spent another night at the quiet glade that had come to be precious to them both. With others about, there was no lingering over a campfire; Lucy and Royce went their separate ways to bed after a few moments of smiling and looking deeply into one another's eyes.

Lucy was awakened early the next morning by the sound of hammers and a saw. Lifting the tent flap, she saw that already the two Goetz men were at work, staking and framing a small rectangular area that she surmised would mark the beginning of a shaft. She dressed hurriedly and joined Royce, who was pouring coffee from a pot at the Goetz's campfire. He greeted her eagerly. "They're getting started, Lucy. And every shovelful of dirt they bring up will strengthen my claim to the land—and yours to the water."

She moved close and let her arm encircle him. "Royce, thank you. Thank you for putting my need for irrigation water ahead of everything else, even your newspaper. Are we going back home . . . back to Mesita, that is . . . today?"

He was quiet for a few seconds, knowing that the time had come for utter honesty. "Yes, Lucy, we will be riding out of here after a bite of breakfast. But I want you to brace yourself, my dearest, for desolation . . . for utter plunder and chaos brought about by greedy men like Robert Delaney." He hadn't meant to mention the logger to Lucy again, but the words had been spoken before he could stay them. Now he said no more, but with a sweep of his hand indicated a breakfast that he'd prepared for her. Then he began packing their gear for the journey before them.

Lucy ate sparingly, her mind alive with thought. *It is easy to accuse a man of anything if he isn't present to defend himself,* she reasoned angrily. *Logging is going on all over America. Why does Royce have to single out one operation—and one man.*

She was still silent when he finished loading their packhorse and saddled her mount. She rode beside him into the timber after bidding farewell to Martin Goetz and his son. Royce guided their way in a direct line toward the area claimed by the Ponderosa Land and Cattle

Company. He made no effort to bridge the chasm that had opened between them, and kept moving through dense timber in a grim and determined way.

And within the hour they broke into the logged-over area. Before them lay the miles of desolate, treeless ruin he knew must be crossed to reach the lumber camp.

"Look around, Lucy," he said in a quiet and oddly toneless voice. "This is what the entire Uncompahgre Plateau—and our Three Rivulets Glade—will become unless somehow the plunder is stopped."

She did not answer him immediately, but sat scanning the vista of destruction. At first her face was bewildered, as though she could not comprehend that such wanton slaughter of a woodland could take place. Presently, though, both anger and revulsion filled her. She lifted a steady hand that moved to encompass the whole chaotic scene. "Royce, how can you think that Robert Delaney would condone this?"

His answer came in a tired way. "Lucy, ask yourself just this: Where else would all of the big logs be coming from for Delaney's sawmill down close to Mesita? For the lumber that is building the town of Mesita?"

"But Royce, Mr. O'Fallon wouldn't be a party to such destruction."

"Not if he were aware of it. But O'Fallon has never been up here . . . nor has he any idea of what is going on." As he finished speaking, Royce was reining his horse back toward the lush greenery of the uncut timber they had left. "At least we can ride around all this on our way back to town, by backtracking along the same route we followed to reach this plateau."

She did not turn to follow him. Instead, she said with determination, "No, Royce. I want to ride across this logged-over area, whether it is three miles or thirty. There must be a road off this mountain, and I want to follow it, to make sure . . . to learn the truth, once and for all."

"I can't let you do that, Lucy. That's how Max Beasley and I ran into trouble, and gunfire. The men at the camp would recognize me . . . those loggers of the Ponderosa Land and Cattle outfit.''

Lucy's face was grim. "Then likely I should ride on by myself and meet you somewhere beyond.''

"Nothing doing,'' he growled. "Where you go, so do I.''

She smiled. "I knew you would say that.''

No further words passed between them as they rode deeper into the desolate timberland. It was half an hour later when they spotted a still-forested area which Royce judged covered about two acres. Apparently it had been left uncut because it was split by a steep-sided ravine that made logging difficult.

It was by entering the ravine that they rode into a trap. Suddenly riders emerged from the little grove to surround them. Staring as they closed in, Royce felt fear. The face of the nearest horseman—the man Beasley had wounded on their last visit up here—was etched by both triumph and fury. His words echoed in Royce's mind: *You will roast in hell for this. Wait till Gribble hears.''*

There were other riders crowding in, but Royce paid them scant heed—except for one, a fat man wearing the star of a deputy sheriff, astride a black gelding. *Paul Gribble!* Royce's mind warned. *Here for a showdown.* For an instant, Royce considered reaching for his derringer. But there wasn't time.

Suddenly the man closest—the one whom Beasley had wounded—swung a riding quirt, driving the leather thongs to cut a bloody path across Royce's face. Royce felt a searing pain; he swayed in the saddle, and would have fallen save for Lucy's steadying arm. Her face had paled in shock, but there was nothing of fear in her voice as she demanded, "Just who are you? Half a dozen of you, yet scared to give one man an even chance.''

There was no answer, but when the quirt was lifted for a second time, Paul Gribble knocked it away. "Hold up, Buck,'' he ordered. He rode close to peer into Royce's

lacerated face. "I'm told you like to shoot a man's hand
with that little toy gun of yours. Want to try it now?"

When Royce remained silent, Gribble quickly reached
out and snatched the derringer from its holster beneath
Royce's jacket. He turned it over in his hand. "Piss on
such a toy." With a contemptuous gesture he tossed it
aside, close to a clump of dry grass. "Now, Mr.
Newspaper Man, just where you and this woman
headed?"

"We've been over toward Pomona. Now we are on our
way back to Mesita."

"Oh, just a nice little outing with the little woman, eh?
Bullshit, Milligan. You've been sizing up land you filed
claim to on this plateau. And you're digging out material
for another story about something that doesn't concern
you."

"You seem to have it all figured out," Royce
commented. Then he asked "What do you intend to do
with us?"

A cold savageness marked Gribble's reply. "Right now
I plan to turn you over to Buck and his whip while the
little lady and I—"

At that instant Royce's fist crashed into the fat man's
mouth. Gribble had his revolver out in the blink of an
eye.

"Hold it, Paul!" The words, spoken with steely
coldness by one of his own group, caused Gribble to
hesitate.

"What the hell, Plover," he growled. "No man hits
me in the face and lives."

The man called Plover sat erect in his saddle. He was
older, mustached and steady-eyed. "Gribble, don't be a
fool. Suppose you gun him down. What then? This man
runs Tim O'Fallon's newspaper. And the woman, she's
the singer who gave the concert in Columbia. Delaney
won't like it if you mess with her."

Lucy's eyes were wide with comprehension. Here was

damning proof of Robert Delaney's connection to the operation.

There was a moment of silence, during which the quiet old rider's eyes seemed to search a dense clump of mountain alder nearby. His face was grave and thoughtful as he heard Gribble curse loudly and then say, "Milligan, never get in my way again. If it hadn't been for the woman—"

"Hey, Gribble," the calm old rider said quietly. "Take a look over there. See? In them bushes. There's a rifle pointing at your guts."

"What?" Gribble exclaimed, swinging around. When he caught sight of the barrel, he sneered and said, "That's got to be that young punk Max Beasley."

But Royce could see naked fear in his eyes, so he decided to make his move. "We'll be riding on now. We have learned what we came to find out." He broke from the group, urging his horse a dozen steps toward the timber. Lucy followed. Then abruptly she halted, reined her horse back toward the group and quickly dismounted. When she regained her saddle, Royce's derringer was in her hand.

"Now, Royce, let's be on our way. Perhaps Max Beasley will see fit to join us."

There was no move to restrain them as they rode from the wasteland, nor did Max Beasley make his presence known.

When they were well into the concealing forest, Lucy drew nearer to Royce, scanned his face and gasped. The furious whip-stroke had bitten deeply across his nose and cheek.

"Do you suppose, Royce, there is a stream close by, where we can bathe and tend your face?" she asked anxiously.

"We will come to water before long," he assured her.

They rode through a deeply shaded area and for a time neither of them spoke. Then abruptly Lucy asked, "Oh, damn it, Royce, why don't you say it—tell me what a blind fool I was to keep believing Delaney had no part of the rape of this forest?''

He lifted his still-bloodied face. ''You had no way of knowing . . . You had only my word for it—and surmised, rightly, that my opinion came partly from personal bias.''

They rode on, talking easily now as they went.

''Royce, do you suppose Max Beasley was really hiding back there?''

''Probably,'' he answered. ''I've had an uncanny sort of feeling that Max has been nearby ever since we came onto the Plateau.''

''You know, somehow Max Beasley reminds me of a legend my mother spoke of years ago.''

''What was that?'' Royce asked, and let his hand search out hers. He was again noting the singular strength and richness of her voice.

''It was about a woodsman, a frontier scout, in the early days of West Virginia and Ohio. His name was Lou Wetzel, and the Indians feared him more than any other pioneer. They called Wetzel the 'Death Wind.' Whenever they raided, Wetzel trailed them and took bloody revenge. He could move through the forests without sound.''

'' 'Death Wind,' eh? That sounds like Beasley, all right,'' Royce agreed.

''But Max is quite young,'' she pondered. Then she caught the sound of running water. They veered toward a ledge and found a clear pool and small sandbar at its base. ''Let's stop here for a little while, Lucy.'' Royce said.

Quickly she assessed the spot's possibilities as a camp, then said firmly, ''Right here we stay until you are rested and patched up a bit. There is wood for a fire and a place to set up the tent. Also, we still have odds and ends in the grub box.'' She swung from her saddle to the ground, then caught the reins of Royce's horse. ''Now,'' she urged, ''you lie down while I tether these horses and unpack some things. I have a bottle of salve that will burn a bit, but will help heal your face.''

As she helped him from his horse, he protested, ''But we can't get to Mesita before dark if we linger here.''

''Need we?'' she demanded. ''Your newspaper will still be there tomorrow. And . . . and, Royce, right now there is no place I would rather be than here with you.''

He reached out and pulled her to him. ''God, how I love you, Lucy . . . the maverick,'' he said almost fiercely.

''I love you too, Royce,'' she answered softly, and lifted her lips to his. Then she drew away, saying, ''But this doesn't do much to get that nasty cut cleaned up.'' She retrieved a small pail from the pack filled it with water. Then her fingers moved about his face, at times soothingly and often in a probing way. When she had finished, they spread his bedroll on the sand and he sank tiredly down. Moments later he was asleep.

Evening had descended upon the Uncompahgre Plateau when Royce awakened. Now he propped himself up on one elbow. ''Lucy,'' he said excitedly, ''most of the pain is gone. That salve sure must be potent.''

''It and several hours of sleep,'' she agreed. ''Are you hungry?''

Before answering he stared about their camping spot. Already the tent was set up and the horses picketed in a grassy spot; a small fire lifted smoke lazily into the evening air. ''You've spent the whole afternoon working, honey!''

''Hardly,'' she laughed. ''I'm not that slow. I had time to do some thinking, Royce.''

''Such as?''

''Suppose I tell you while we eat. I have hot biscuits, a pot of beans, and cold tomatoes ready.''

Royce was spreading honey on a third biscuit when he asked, ''Now, what's on your mind, Lucy?''

''Royce, my dear, how does one go about claiming title to land up here on this Plateau?''

"I am still not sure, Lucy. I finagled title to our Three Rivulets park by means of a mining claim."

"Royce, I want to somehow get valid title to every possible acre I can. Mostly between here and Three Rivulets. I want to protect the Uncompahgre Plateau. Maybe it will take dozens of acres . . . or hundreds . . . or even thou—"

"Whoa." Royce laughed and raised a protesting hand. "There is a limit to the size of any claim, whether it is for mining, timbering, or plain homesteading."

"I know." Lucy nodded. "But likely this is government land, for which no definite usage has yet been set. If so, Royce, perhaps larger areas are for sale."

"That's possible," he agreed. "But I think such a deal would have to be worked out either in Denver or Washington, D.C. Besides, it would involve considerable sums of money."

"Royce," she said firmly, "Tim O'Fallon wants to put me under contract for a series of concerts. Some in Mesita. Some elsewhere. I believe he would agree to as much as five hundred dollars for the series. And I want to buy timberland up here with every cent of it."

He stared at her in amazed wonder. "That sort of money should buy a hefty number of acres—if the woodlands are for sale. But what would you do with it?"

"I'd put a damned quick stop to timber plundering," she vowed.

Their fire had burned down to almost gray ashes, and now a cold wind was rising. Royce looked about with concern. "If you'll help me get this bedroll tarp straightened out, Lucy, I will crawl in. And you had best tie down the flaps of your tent tonight; there could be snow before morning."

She rose to her feet, then looked down at him shyly. "I think it should be *our* tent tonight, Royce."

Royce got up and wrapped his arms around her, let his lips linger at her soft white throat before finding the sweetness of her lips. There was no need to say more.

They carried his bedroll into the small tent and placed it beside hers. Then in darkness he discarded his clothing and wordlessly helped her out of hers. Her camisole was incredibly soft beneath his fingers. When he'd finished undressing her, he went to light the lamp, for he wanted to be able to see her when they made love for the very first time. As he rose from his task, she stood before him in all her loveliness: her skin was like alabaster, her breasts high and firm. He pulled her almost roughly against him. "Lucy, Lucy . . ." he murmured. Gently he let his fingers slide between her thighs. She moaned and reached to stroke his wheat-colored hair.

They came eagerly into union that night high on the Uncompahgre Plateau—Lucy tentative, Royce guiding her tenderly. Afterward, their passion spent, they slept, wrapped in each other's arms and in the fullness of their love. At one point an owl disturbed Lucy's sleep and she snuggled closer to Royce. He stirred, woke to cover her body with kisses, and then made love to her again.

They awakened to find that dense fog had descended on the Plateau. Lucy studied it in exasperation. "Look at this soupy stuff, Royce," she complained. "And I was hoping we could survey some timberland this morning. Land that perhaps I can buy . . ."

"Likely this fog will burn off in a couple of hours," he assured her. "But honey, I have to get back to Mesita today. Besides, I am pretty sure there are maps in Margaret Hendricks' office. We might even use the legal description of my mining claim as a starting point. Then later we can send a surveyor up here."

She placed her arms about his neck and then leaned back to study his face. "Did those lash-cuts hurt much during the night?" she asked.

"Nothing hurt last night," he said, and kissed her forehead.

Her fingers caressed his cheek. "Just the same, Mr. Milligan, I am going to wash and tend to those cuts and bruises again before we leave.'' She was very quiet for a time, and then added, ''But I . . . I don't want to leave. Royce, why are people's lives so complicated? You must get back to your newspaper. And I need to arrange for the concerts with Mr. O'Fallon, and then get on Ike Fenlon's stage headed back to the Military Cantonment. But my heart urges that we stay here, or at the Three Rivulets park. All by ourselves. Together. For a day, a week, a . . .''

He lifted her into his arms and strode toward the tent. ''At least, Lucy mine, we have the hours until the fog lifts.'' His breath quickened at the urging glow of her eyes.

Chapter 11

On that same morning, as fog shrouded the Uncompahgre Plateau, the little town of Mesita lay drenched in sunshine. A mild but steady breeze out of the southwest stirred the broad leaves of cottonwood and oak trees and assured that the day would not be unpleasantly hot. Tim O'Fallon, out for an early stroll, stopped to study the progress of workmen using cement and boulders from the river for the newest of his downtown buildings. Minutes later his attention turned to a young man running up the street toward him, shouting his name. He quickly realized that the approaching youth was Andy Parnell, the apprentice printer at *The Mesita Messiah*.

Parnell, coatless and bareheaded, slid to a stop facing O'Fallon. He was breathing hard, clearly agitated. "Mr. O'Fallon, sir," he panted. "It's awful! Stuff broken and strewn everywhere. Windows broken. The press dumped over on its side."

O'Fallon laid his hand on the boy's shoulder. "Now just take it easy, Andy. Let's go take a look together."

One glance around the rooms that had so recently been an orderly publishing office confirmed Andy Parnell's report. Whoever had wrought the damage had doubtless been intent on putting *The Mesita Messiah* out of business. Grimness settled across Tim O'Fallon's face, and presently he said, "Andy, I am going to have people here within an hour to help clean up this mess. Leave it to me and to them. I have something more urgent for you."

"Whatever you say, Mr. O'Fallon." Parnell's voice was still shaky.

I want you to round up whatever copy Royce had ready for printing. You're going to take it to the nearest print shop—maybe in Columbia, or over at Montrose—and have it printed. *The Messiah* may be a day or so late, but by God, it's going to be published."

Young Parnell looked about, and a grin broke over his face. "Over here, sir! See! These are the locked forms of the pages. They weren't harmed."

"Then get them boxed. You'll be leaving within an hour, Andy."

Tim O'Fallon did not respond to Parnell's excited reply, for a man, a cowboy named Noah who spent more time in the Mesita saloon than on his horse, was peering through one of the broken windows. The town builder motioned for him to come in. "Noah," he said hurriedly as the fellow approached, "go up to my house and ask Max Beasley to come down here on the double."

The other hesitated. "I don't think Beasley is in town."

"Yes, he is. He rode in late last night. Tell him I said *pronto*." He paused and then added, "And tell Margaret Hendricks I need her too."

As Noah turned and hurried up the street, O'Fallon removed his jacket and began righting overturned boxes. He judged that the damage had been done during the early morning hours, and that the perpetrators had gained access by using an iron bar to force the office lock. Replacement costs would run high, for both equipment and supplies would have to be shipped in from Denver or even more distant cities.

It was about fifteen minutes before Max Beasley came through the door. "Jesus." He shuddered. "Did the hordes of Genghis Khan overrun this place?"

"He isn't a suspect this time, Max. But there *is* someone I want to talk to right away. Not at my office, but right here. Max, look up Bob Delaney and ask him to come over here. Ride down to his sawmill if necessary. But make damn sure the man shows up.''

"I will see to it," Max Beasley answered quietly.

Max had no trouble locating Delaney; the lumberman was in his office in Mesita. Delaney was dour-faced and curt. "What can I do for you, Beasley?" he asked.

Max took an irritatingly long time before answering, causing Delaney to urge, "Well, speak up."

Slowly, mildly, Max said, "Tim O'Fallon wants to see you, Delaney."

"I'll be going by his office sometime this afternoon. Maybe I will have time to look in."

"That's not soon enough," Beasley replied. "Tim O'Fallon wants you at the *Messiah* office. Now."

Robert Delaney looked angry. "I said I would be out and around—later," he flared, then added, "Now Beasley, suppose you do your lackeying for old Time somewhere else. I'm busy."

Suddenly Max Beasley took on the aspect of a man who had killed and would not hesitate to kill again. "Delaney," he said in low and colorless tones, "get your fancy pants up from that chair. Tim O'Fallon wants you. He's the boss around here. And I would hate to have to bring you to him sprawled across the ass-end of my horse . . ."

"You bastard," Delaney growled. Nonetheless he pushed back his chair, grabbed his hat, and ambled to the door.

The Mesita plant was still in shambles by the time Delaney entered, followed closely by Max Beasley; the lumberman gave a startled glance around. His manner confirmed a suspicion already in O'Fallon's mind: Delaney had not personally taken part in the break-in; he was seeing the results for the first time. He appeared both furious and somewhat baffled as he barked, "Tim, how come you sent this . . . this gunslinger to force me down here? It's one hell of a way to treat a business associate and a friend. I resent it."

O'Fallon stared coldly at him and demanded, "Delaney, just how much do you know about this mess?"

Delaney banged a clenched fist on an empty wooden box. "O'Fallon, don't try to make me out to be the villian here. I hate this paper and the smartass you brought in to ramrod it, but last night I wasn't even in town. I have proof of that."

"Well, just be prepared to pay the bill I will be sending you—or withholding from your lumber account—to cover the complete cost of repairing this newspaper plant."

Delaney's face whitened with fury. "Tim, have you lost your mind? I said I didn't take part in this."

"Of course you weren't here, Delaney. Just as you weren't on the Plateau yesterday when your henchman Paul Gribble attacked and almost maimed Royce Milligan. You found out about that, though, didn't you? And about Lucy Lattamore learning of your duplicity. When Gribble decided on this break-in, you were aware of his plans, too, and yet you did nothing to stop him. Maybe you saw it as a way of getting even with Royce Milligan—by using Gribble."

"O'Fallon, I don't know what has gotten into you. After all, I have set prices much to your advantage. Perhaps I ought to—"

"Perhaps you'd best be looking for different customers," O'Fallon interrupted, "for a couple of reasons. Your method of logging may bring a couple of United States marshals onto the Uncompahgre Plateau to investigate. They'd shut your outfit down on the spot."

"Who's been feeding you all this bullshit about how I harvest lumber?" Delaney demanded.

"I've been getting reports—and not just from Royce Milligan either. I don't hold with cutting down trees on land that doesn't belong to you. And another thing, just last week I was offered prime spruce, pine, and fir for twenty percent less than you've been charging. As of right now, Delaney, I am giving notice—to be confirmed later today in writing—that I won't be buying any more lumber from you."

Delaney picked up a packing box and flung it to the floor. "Hell, my mill and I will survive without you," he boasted, but his face told a different and more somber story. He drew himself erect, cast an oblique stare toward Beasley, and strode from the building.

O'Fallon's gaze followed him through the open door and onto the sunlit street. Then he observed, "Max, you know what? There isn't much fun in stripping a man of his pride. You can clean him out of dollars or land or livestock, and he will get mad as hell. But humble him by striking down his pride and usually you've made a dangerous and mortal enemy."

"Delaney will survive," Beasley reasoned. "He's smart and knows how to influence people. Besides, Tim, he will soon figure out that logs from the Plateau will find a ready market in the Uncompahgre Valley; there is a lot of building going on there."

"He's a ruthless one," O'Fallon agreed thoughtfully. "With that phony deputy, Gribble, and that choice collection of no-account characters of his, Delaney is far from whipped. And he is going to strike back. At me. Perhaps at you, Max. And surer than hell at Royce Milligan."

Darkness was gathering when Royce and Lucy rode into Mesita. Their trip down from the Plateau had been a leisurely one, for each of them seemed intent on extending their hours together. They halted in surprise in front of the *Messiah* building upon noting that there were lamps still lit inside. They dismounted and tied up their horses, then Royce opened the door. Inside, they stood in mute astonishment. Much had been done during the day to clear away the mess left by the intruders, but it was still evident that the entire printing plant had been wrecked. Before either of them could speak, Margaret

Hendricks came over to them, her dress smudged and wrinkled.

"Margaret! What in the name of the Almighty has happened?" Royce managed to say.

"You were damned near wiped out, Royce. By somebody who doesn't seem to appreciate *The Mesita Messiah.*" She looked from one to the other of them in an appraising way. "But you two look great . . . discounting that messed-up face of yours, Royce."

"Where is Andy Parnell? Is he all right?" Royce inquired.

"Safe and sound. Right now he's down in Columbia having *The Messiah* printed from the locked-up type forms we salvaged. Tim O'Fallon sent him. There is going to be a newspaper this week despite a galavanting editor and a plant in shambles."

Lucy finally spoke, her eyes wide with apprehension. "Margaret, this is ghastly!"

"Isn't it?" she said dryly. "Now, suppose we head up to Tim's. He is expecting you, and I need to wash up and change." Margaret put out the lights and made for the doorway. When neither of them followed immediately, she turned back, and stood watching quietly as Royce held Lucy in his arms, wiped away a tear from her face and replaced it with a kiss.

"So this is what a trip into the woods did to the two of you."

"It is all right," Lucy responded, embarrassed, but smiling. Margaret, we love each other."

"And if I can convince this independent woman," Royce said, "we're going to be married." At that, Lucy's eyes widened and filled with fresh tears.

"I would recommend it," Margaret Hendricks replied. "And congratulations to both of you."

An hour later, when they were gathered in the dining room, Royce and Lucy took turns answering questions. Tim O'Fallon was anxious to know just what had happened to them up on the Plateau. He showed special interest in Paul Gribble's behavior, and shook his head in disgust when he neared Royce to inspect his cuts.

Then Lucy spoke up, telling of her decision to buy the forestland around the Three Rivulets park.

"That would be a wise move." O'Fallon nodded. Then he added thoughtfully, "But I would advise that you make the attempt to buy as quickly as you can. You see, Lucy, just this afternoon I severed relations with Bob Delaney."

All those listening registered surprise, causing him to explain. "You see, I've had firm offers of quality lumber at more reasonable prices than Delaney charges. But more important, I now believe—thanks to you, Royce—that the man's got no conscience. That's government land up there on the Uncompahgre, I know that now for a fact. I looked into it. And I don't want to see my town built out of stolen planks. Besides, what Delaney's men did to Royce and to the *Messiah* office . . . those are crimes, and I don't do business with a crook."

Royce looked at his employer affectionately. "Those are admirable words, Tim," he replied.

There was a short silence, and then Lucy said, "Margaret, we would like to study any maps you have of the Uncompahgre Plateau. We had no chance to set claim stakes, but we believe we can tie the legal description into Royce's mining claim. Do you suppose that would do?"

"I'm sure we can work something out, at least temporarily," the older woman said briskly. "How soon would you need this?"

Lucy's face shone with eagerness, though she hesitated before she spoke. "How soon would I like to offer to buy the forestlands? That would depend on you, sir," she said to Tim.

"On me?" O'Fallon gasped. "Why?"

"Because if you really want to put me under contract for a series of concerts, I can use your first payment to buy some timberlands. And with the contract to sing, maybe a bank—say in Denver—will loan me more."

The bluntness of her reply, and the intensity with which she now awaited O'Fallon's response, caused both Royce and Margaret to sit in stunned and expectant silence.

O'Fallon said nothing for a time, but rose and opened a window to let the cool late-evening breeze in. When he returned to his seat, he was grinning, but was still businesslike as he said, "Lucy, the plans are just about completed for our Mesita opera house; I believe you'll like what our architect has come up with. And maybe now is just the time for us to strike a deal. How much per concert will you charge . . . say for a series of six?"

Lucy gulped. This was the first time she had been asked to set a price for singing. She wondered if fifty dollars a night would be too much. Then she recalled that three hundred people had gathered to hear her at Columbia. She steeled herself and asked, "If I continue to draw good crowds, Mr. O'Fallon, don't you think I should be worth one hundred dollars per concert?"

"That would be six hundred dollars all told. That seems fair, Lucy, provided—"

"Provided what?" she breathed.

"Provided we go partners on this deal of buying forestland on the Plateau. I will match you dollar for dollar and we will seek joint ownership."

Lucy glanced at Royce, and then nodded eager acceptance. "Can we close the deal and then handle the purchase from here?"

"We might, but I wouldn't advise it. Lucy, I will advance you your fee so you can leave for Denver tomorrow. Ike Fenlon will be coming through with his stage just before noon. Go to the regional public-lands office; then insist on seeing the highest possible government official to handle your deal—if they *will* deal. I'll give you a letter that will let you draw on my Denver bank for my part of the payment, and for your trip expenses."

On sudden impulse Lucy rose, leaned across the table, and laid a kiss of delight and gratitude on Tim O'Fallon's brow. The hard-headed, ambitious builder of Mesita beamed.

They talked on, but after a time Margaret said, "We are all tired. I think we should go to bed." Then, as they put out the lamps and climbed the stairs, she whispered mischievously to Royce, "To our separate beds, that is."

In playful protest he replied, "I'm banished to my lonely room, with the company of only a mysterious young lady watching from a daguerreotype?"

Royce was utterly unprepared for her reaction to his light-hearted words. Her smile dissolved, and she became both grave and quiet.

"Have . . . have I said something wrong?" Royce asked in a bewildered way.

"Not knowingly. Not that you were aware of," she answered quietly as they came to a stop outside his door. By now, the others had disappeared into their rooms. At last Margaret spoke. "There is something I think you should know about Max and Tim and all of us here." She grabbed Royce's hand. "May we enter, Royce?" she asked, nodding toward his door.

"Of course." He motioned her inside. The room was in deep shadow; Royce touched a match to the circular wick of a lamp. When its glow sifted across the room, Margaret Hendricks moved to stand before the framed daguerreotype that had so often aroused Royce's curiosity. Her fingers lifted to touch the silver frame in a gesture of love, then gracefully, she took a seat in a chair beneath it. "Perhaps I should have told you sooner. You must have wondered about my presence here, and about Max Beasley—he is my nephew. Did you know that?"

Royce shook his head, amazed. "I have wondered about him, of course . . ."

"This," Margaret said, gesturing toward the photo, "is my younger sister, Julia, taken on her twenty-first birthday—Max's mother. She died a horrible and sense-less death at the hands of Quantrell's guerrillas."

Margaret turned almost blindly from the daguerreotype;

Royce reached to take her hands, helping her to regain control. After a few moments she went on. "We were living on a farm close to Lawrence, Kansas, at the time; Father had bought it and given it to Julia when she married Paul Beasley. Max was born a year later. It was just after sunset on August 21, 1863, that Quantrell's raiders hit our area. Most of them centered in on the town of Lawrence, but others scoured the surrounding farms in an orgy of plunder, rape, and murder." Margaret Hendricks closed her eyes and her voice dropped to a whisper, as waves of resurgent memories washed over her.

"We had a little forewarning, for a neighbor rode by on a sweaty horse and told us of the hell that had broken loose. Minutes later, three of the sons of bitches rode into our yard."

"None of your menfolk were around?" Royce asked.

"Julia's husband was with an infantry unit in Tennessee. I was not married."

"And then?" Royce gently urged her on.

"We had a ten-acre field of corn. It was thick and high, and we managed to flee into it before the plunderers arrived, but they saw us run to take refuge. We had nothing but the clothes on our backs and our father's old, long-barreled rifle and three spare bullets I dropped into an apron pocket." She clenched and unclenched her hands, and continued. "Oh, they hunted us down. First they found Julia. I heard her scream. Again and again. Then that awful silence. Somehow, Max, who was beside me, put on years in those terrible moments." Margaret Hendricks paused for breath and fortitude. "They came toward us, and I clutched Max's shoulder. He was less than seven years old, but I know he sensed that his mother was dead. Right then he grabbed the old rifle from me. I had loaded it. He stood white-faced and rooted as the animal who killed his mother appeared. Royce . . . that boy, Max, my nephew, shot and killed his mother's murderer. Somehow that stirred me to action, for with that old rifle we rid Kansas of three beasts unfit to live.''

"My God, what an ordeal,'' Royce gasped. "Didn't Quantrell's other desperadoes try to take revenge?''

"Of course they did . . . but not until dawn. Max and I dug a makeshift grave for Julia in the cornfield. Clawed it out with a bit of board and our bare hands. Then we took advantage of the night and put a few bits of this and that in packs on our two farm-horses. We rode all through the night, avoiding the town of Lawrence and heading for Topeka. We managed to get there at mid-morning.'' Now, with the story of her night of horror at an end, Margaret smiled tiredly.

"And you finally made it to Colorado?'' Royce marveled.

"By the care of God and with the help of Tim O'Fallon.'' She nodded. "We sold our horses to raise money for a few necessities. Some freighters were taking canned goods and whiskey through to Denver. By offering to do the cooking, I was able to arrange passage to Denver with them. Even before we reached Denver, though, I noticed the strangeness about Max. He had always been a fun-loving boy, but then he started to spend hours practicing with any weapon he could get hold of. He would back down from no one. A grimness came upon the boy. He would play childhood games, but if events took a menacing turn, he wouldn't hesitate to use force.'' There was a glimmer of tears in her eyes. "But he's like a son to me—and to Tim.''

"How did the two of you end up here in Mesita?'' Despite Margaret's sorrow, she seemed to want to talk, so Royce encouraged her.

"To make a long story short, I met Tim in Denver. I was cooking for a little place there and I guess he spotted me as perfect housekeeper material. I've been with him ever since.''

"I've wondered, Margaret, why—'' Royce paused and looked down at the floor.

"Why we didn't get married? Is that it, Royce?" She chuckled softly and shook her head. "I admit I had designs on him for a while. What sensible woman wouldn't? But Tim just isn't the marrying kind. He's a free spirit. Maybe that's why he came out west in the first place. You know, I think I could have gotten him to the altar, but I always knew I'd be manipulating him somehow. So I just let well enough alone . . ."

Royce could see the wistfulness in her eyes, and it moved him—this patient, talented woman had waited so long. "Maybe there's time for that yet. I mean if a cranky old bachelor like me can be making marriage plans . . ."

Composure and something of her usual good humor returned to Margaret Hendricks then. "When are you two plateau-riders planning to be married?" she asked.

"Soon . . . very soon," Royce said firmly. "But I suppose Lucy should get this land-buying trip to Denver out of the way first. Then I suppose I'll pin her down on the time and the place."

"Wouldn't it also be fitting for you to be married here? Tim could give Lucy away." Her eyes danced. "And Lucy and I could arrange it together. A beautiful wedding. But I warn you, I always cry at weddings."

Royce laughed. "I'll bet you do, Margaret. And that's a wonderful idea. I'll tell Lucy about it first thing tomorrow."

Chapter 12

Six days later, at mid-afternoon, Lucy arrived in Denver. Most of the trip, via Blue Mesa and then over lofty Cochetopa Pass, was again made on the swaying stagecoach of Ike Fenlon. From Pueblo north to Denver she traveled by railroad day-coach. As always, the sight of the Front Range Mountains stirred her. The San Juans were rugged and snow-crested, but not so massive as this north-south wall of peaks fronting onto the plains.

As the miles clicked off beneath the coach wheels, Lucy sat alone, pondering. On the way from Mesita, Fenlon had arranged for her to visit briefly with Phillip at the Military Cantonment. They sought out the quiet of Phillip's quarters, and he listened as she told of Royce, and their plans to marry.

He had been cautious at first over the news about Royce, saying he was happy for her, but he wished he knew the prospective bridegroom a little better.

She'd laughed at that. "Phillip Lattamore, you know better than to try to father me!"

"You're right about that, Sis," he'd replied, grinning ruefully. "And I can see you're in love. In my book, that's the most important thing. Congratulations, Lucy." He'd wrapped her in a bear hug. When they parted, he went on. "In a way, I'm relieved, Lucy. You see, I have a bit of news of my own."

"What is it, Phil?" Lucy exclaimed.

"Orders came through two days ago. As of June first, I'm being officially transferred to Fort Riley, Kansas. Probably for two years, until my time for promotion comes around."

"Oh, Phillip," she cried, grasping his hand, "I hate to see you go!"

"I know, Lucy. But I have my orders . . . Anyway, I guess with me going to Kansas and you marrying Royce Milligan, the orchard plans will have to go by the wayside—"

"No," Lucy interrupted adamantly. "Royce and I have talked about that. We're going to get the orchard started together somehow. Royce has made a claim on a beautiful plot of land adjoining my site." Then she'd told Phillip all about the incomparable beauty of Three Rivulets Glade and its strategic importance to the orchard lands below. He'd been amazed by her plan to buy land on the plateau, but was nonetheless approving.

Now, as the train ground steadily toward Denver, Lucy smiled to herself. So much had happened since her arrival—meeting Royce, her concerts, her plans, and this expedition to Denver. Out west she felt positively excited by the dawning of each new day.

She was so deep in thought that when the conductor announced that they were arriving in Denver, it startled her. With her two pieces of luggage in hand, she inquired of the Denver ticket-agent as to where clean and safe lodgings might be secured.

"Up Seventeenth Street to the Addison Hotel, ma'am. It's small but entirely respectable. Lately they have opened a dining room." He ran appraising eyes over her, nodded approval of her appearance, and added, "If you want I can have a boy help you to the cabbie waiting for passengers outside."

"I would appreciate that," she answered and then listened as he barked, "Joe, help this lady to a cab . . . get a move on!"

Her room at the Addison proved to be large, high-ceilinged, and comfortable. There was a spacious bathroom just two doors down the hall, with spotless fixtures and clean linens. Lucy bathed, changed into a street-dress of green linen and then found out from a helpful gentleman at the front desk that the Federal Land Bureau office was located in the Post Office building.

Lucy knew the location of the Denver Post Office, but decided to wait until morning to visit the Bureau of Public Lands, as it was getting close to the end of the day. She spent an hour shopping on Sixteenth Street and then returned, bundle-laden, to the Addison. Later she ate alone in the hotel dining room.

When she returned to her room, darkness had fallen. She felt too restless to read the romantic novel she had bought. She soon tossed it aside, for the author, in order to be discreet, had shown neither personal experience nor imagination in her handling of the relationship between men and women. Lucy prepared for bed, still thinking of the novel. *It is a far cry from that night of mine and of Royce's in the tent. That was real. Memorable.* Slowly, drowsiness overtook her, but only after her thoughts had dwelt longingly on the way Royce had set her aflame.

When the morning sun awoke her, she dressed carefully and brushed out the coppery tumbled mass of her hair. Then, just a few minutes after finishing a light breakfast, she walked to the Post Office.

When she arrived at the third-floor Land Bureau office, she found the inevitable counter dividing the office area from the reception room, but here there was no forbidding grillwork. She approached the counter and caught the attention of a gray-haired man whose face seemed florid from the restrictive tightness of a high, starched collar.

"Sir, I wish to speak to someone in charge of land sales."

He eyed her in a surprised way. "Sales, did you say? Madam, you can homestead up to three hundred and twenty acres, you know."

"Perhaps you don't understand," Lucy began patiently. "I want to buy timberland, perhaps a thousand acres or more."

He gulped in evident astonishment, then hastened to say, "This is quite extraordinary. Perhaps I should have you talk to our bureau manager, Mr. Pumphrey." He waved her toward a chair. "Have a seat, please, Miss . . . Miss—"

"Lattamore . . . Lucy Lattamore." Then as an afterthought she added, "You might tell Mr. Pumphrey that I represent Mr. Tim O'Fallon of Mesita."

Within five minutes she was ushered behind the counter, down a hall, and into an impressively furnished office. A short, heavyset man was watering some geraniums on the windowsill, but turned as the receptionist said, "Mr. Pumphrey, this is Miss Lucy Lattamore." He drew up a leather chair, placing it near a wide and orderly desk, and indicated that Lucy should be seated.

"Miss Lattamore." He smiled. "Am I to understand that you are here on a timberland-buying mission . . . all the way from the wonder-town of Mesita?"

"That is correct, sir. Tim O'Fallon and I are prepared to purchase up to a thousand acres of standing timber on the Uncompahgre Plateau."

He rose, selected a map from a rack, and spread it before her. "This is a map of the quadrants that include the Plateau. I'm afraid it won't be of much help, though, because most of that high country has never been adequately surveyed."

"But I know it, or at least part of it, quite well, Mr. Pumphrey." She drew from her handbag the map she had prepared with Margaret Hendricks' help. "There is a mining claim here," she pointed out. "It is owned by a Royce Milligan." Lucy laid her sketched map before him and continued. "We have tied all of our boundaries into the southeast corner of Mr. Milligan's claim. If Mr. O'Fallon and I obtain the land, we will immediately have it surveyed and provide you with section, township, and range references. Until then, a few blaze-marks and piles of rock will have to suffice.''

Pumphrey leaned back in his chair and studied her face. ''Miss Lattamore, I can understand Tim O'Fallon's wanting a source of logs. But you? What is your interest? I hope you don't mind me asking—''

Lucy gazed at him in a open and thoughtful way. ''Not at all, Mr. Pumphrey. As you know, there are valuable stands of pine, fir, and spruce within the land I have mapped. But my reason for being here isn't based on desire to exploit these resources. Rather, I want to save this area from impending disaster—that of being ruthlessly logged.''

He leaned forward. ''Is there such danger?''

''Indeed there is,'' she said forcefully. ''Already hundreds of acres have been cut over, devastated, and rendered worse than useless by a logging crew.''

''But no one has title or logging rights to a single acre on that area of the Uncompahgre Plateau.''

''I'm afraid the United States government has been blind in this regard,'' Lucy responded.

''That may be, Miss Lattamore. But this office has millions of acres of government land to administer. It extends over a dozen states; some of it hasn't even been explored. And to patrol it I have just twelve deputies.'' Pumphrey tapped his pencil reflectively on the desk. At length he said, a bit cautiously, ''Things will change, though. Already there is agitation for a national system of public forests such as have proven so productive in Germany. Suppose, Miss'' he went on cautiously, ''that we were to agree on a price and sell you the Plateau timberland. Would you agree to someday sell it back, at a reasonable price, to become part of a national forest?''

''Gladly.'' She nodded.

''It will cost you one dollar and twenty-five cents per acre.''

''Sold,'' she shouted.

He grinned at her alacrity, then said briskly, "Mind you, Miss Lattamore, before we can provide a deed or merchantable title, we must receive your legally referenced survey. I can give you a receipt and a memorandum of purchase. Now—how many acres?"

Lucy borrowed his pencil and made some quick calculations, then said, "Nine hundred and sixty. Half in my name and half in Tim O'Fallon's."

Pumphrey raised his eyebrows, made a notation, and replied, "Consider it done, then. And in the meantime, I'll dispatch a marshal to nose around the Plateau."

Lucy caught an evening train to Pueblo, knowing that Ike Fenlon must leave before noon the following day on his run back to Montrose, Columbia, Mesita, and other points westward. The train had scarcely cleared the Denver yards when a stooped man came down the aisle from the gent's room. Her eyes widened, for it was Pappy Loutsenhizer.

"Mr. Loutsenhizer! How nice to see you," she exclaimed.

He peered at her and his melancholy face lightened with a smile. "Why, it's Lucy Lattamore—"

"Please sit down with me," Lucy invited.

He complied happily. Once he was settled into the aisle seat she asked, "How are fruit prospects at your orchards?"

"The apple crop will be heavy, but the peach yield just tolerable. Our grape harvest was excellent."

Then, impulsively, she told him, "I have just bought some timberland on the Uncompahgre Plateau; that is why I was in Denver."

He studied her in a penetrating way. "Miss Lucy, you are very ambitious. Timberlands up there may prove a fine investment."

They talked of many things, for there seemed to be a strong bond between this copper-haired, vivacious girl and the aging pioneer whose eyes had scanned the west when it was still a pristine wilderness. She told him of Three Rivulets Glade, and how water would be brought from it to assure irrigation of orchards on Cedar's Edge Mesa. The possibility of using a flume proved of special interest to Loutsenhizer. "That will prevent much waste of water through evaporation and seepage." He nodded. "The entire Uncompahgre Valley must practice economy with water, until—"

"Until what?" she encouraged.

"Someday, Miss Lucy, a way will be found to bring water from the vast depth of the Gunnison River Canyon to the fertile miles of Uncompahgre Valley flat country."

Their train was nearing Pueblo when he prepared to return to his own seat. Lucy said, "I'm going on through to the Cantonment on Ike Fenlon's stage tomorrow. Are you?" But before he could answer, she spoke again. "Just in case you don't, I have a secret." She clung to his thin hand. "I am going to be married soon to Royce Milligan; you will get an invitation to the wedding. I want so much for you to be there."

He leaned close, and whispered, "Great happiness to you and your young man, my dear. I will come."

Surprisingly, Loutsenhizer and Lucy were the only passengers on Ike Fenlon's westward stage-run the following day. The road over Cochetopa Pass and on to Barnum Station was dry enough to be somewhat dusty. There was brilliant sunshine, but a coolness born of the high elevation.

As on her memorable first trip westward on this stage, driver Fenlon changed his tired team for fresh horses at Barnum. Their sandwiches seemed just as tasteless and the coffee as strong. With the added sack of mail, and half a dozen parcels, they began the climb onto Blue Mesa. This time, there was no indication of foul weather and they rolled swiftly ahead. Both she and Pappy Loutsenhizer nodded drowsily and then fell asleep to the jolting of the vehicle.

Two hours later the coach slowed, and after drawing to

a bit of a clearing, stopped, leaving the road clear. Lucy and Loutsenhizer had awakened when Ike Fenlon climbed down and opened the coach door. "I don't suppose you remember this spot, ma'am," he said, grinning, and then pointed with his whip.

"Of course I remember, Ike," she exclaimed excitedly. "Right there is where we built the lean-to that first night, huddled under a buffalo robe, and nearly froze in snow and wind."

"It weren't no picnic," Fenlon agreed.

Fenlon stretched his legs and tended to the horses. Lucy glanced up the slope, started to walk up it, and then seemed to hesitate. Half a minute later she called out, "Mr. Loutsenhizer, come up here, please—and you too, Ike."

Within minutes the three of them climbed the ridge, and at its crest came to the old rock cairn.

Lucy stopped behind the structure and laid her hands on the flat, thick capstone. "See, Mr. Loutsenhizer. This is the marker and the sighting device I described to you." She stooped and let her right eye search the V notch and roam along the mountain slope where just weeks ago, a mine portal had caught her attention. But now there was no such black rectangle. She squinted again and again, but there was only the gulch and a mass of talus rock and twisted, felled timber.

"But I don't understand," Lucy muttered. "It was so plain . . . that framed tunnel into the mountain . . . just before we took refuge in it."

Loutsenhizer crouched beside her and said quietly, "Suppose I take a look." For a time he scanned the gulch area, then he rose and smiled. "It is easy to figure out what has happened, Miss Lucy. There has been another slide; an avalanche has buried your mine opening."

"But how deep?" she asked.

"That is hard to say. Perhaps only a few feet. Perhaps fifty or more feet."

"Why would anyone have put a mine portal in such a dangerous and difficult location?" she queried.

"Probably because that was where the seam of gold or silver ore surfaced. Besides, mountains change; there may not have been avalanche danger when the Spaniards were working the mine many years ago."

Ike Fenlon had listened in silence, but now he asked, "Mind if I take a squint?" He studied the vista and then said excitedly, "Do you suppose that was one of those fabulous mines like the Spaniards stole from the Aztecs and them other tribes?"

"Perhaps. The conquistadores could take only very rich ores all the way back to Spain."

Fenlon was quiet, his expression was puzzled. "I should have paid attention and looked around that night we holed up from the storm. I wonder if anyone owns these diggings now. Seems I read a newspaper article about some old Spanish mine. I think there was map, too . . ."

The three then returned to the stagecoach and continued over Blue Mesa toward the Cantonment.

Despite her eagerness to return to Mesita and to Royce, Lucy also wanted to spend a few days with her brother before his impending transfer to Fort Riley. She mentioned this decision to remain with Phillip to Ike Fenlon just before he maneuvered his coach to a halt at the Cantonment guard station. She did wish for both Royce and Tim O'Fallon to learn immediately of her successful meeting with Mr. Pumphrey in Denver.

"Ike, could you possibly hold off an hour before leaving for Columbia and Mesita? It would give me time to write a couple of letters you can take. They are to Royce and—" She fell silent under his knowing grin and his nod.

"Royce will be disappointed not to see you, Miss Lucy."

She told him of Phillip's transfer and of her upcoming marriage.

Fenlon absorbed the news, and replied, "Changes. Always changes. I'm sure happy for you, but what about your plans for a big orchard?"

Lucy gazed at him fondly, then declared, "Oh, I'll have my orchard, all right, Ike. Just you watch."

Ike Fenlon scanned the horizon. "Take your time writing them letters, Miss Lucy. Being as I have no through passengers, I'm going into Pomona and put up for the night." He did not add that a mighty thirst was upon him, one that only the tent saloon of Pomona could satisfy.

Within that same hour, a horseback rider approached the settlement of Pomona from the opposite direction. It was Robert Delaney, tired and frustrated. He had ridden down the previous day from the Uncompahgre Plateau, intending to visit the towns along the Uncompahgre and Gunnison rivers and seek out markets for his lumber.

Delaney had spent the better part of the day in the settlement of Delta, twenty miles down the Uncompahgre Valley. He had made a deal there, but it seemed insignificant compared to the quantities of lumber Tim O'Fallon used to buy from him. It might be five to ten years before the Uncompahgre Valley towns would provide a market as lucrative as Tim's had been.

Still another problem was rankling Delaney as he rode into Pomona, stabled his horse, and entered the rough quarters of a makeshift hotel. Lately he had been having trouble with Paul Gribble. Just yesterday, in fact, he had listened while Gribble berated a lumberjack for stopping too often for water while at work. Under seemingly endless goading and curses from Gribble, the man had finally flung his axe in Gribble's direction, told the fat man to shove the job, and started to stalk away. "Get the hell back to work," Gribble had demanded. Then, when the retreating man paid no heed, Gribble raised his rifle and fired. The lead slug plowed through the timber-cutter's heel; it would be many days before the man would again fell a single tree.

Lying on his bunk in Pomona, Delaney tossed restlessly. He recalled the heated way he had torn into Gribble for such senseless wounding of a good work-hand. The fat man had turned insolent, demanding, ''I suppose you could have handled him better. Coddled the bastard.''

''Probably I could have. Your trouble, Gribble, is that you're too dammed fast with your rifle. Your knife. Your damned saddle quirt.''

''You'd pay hell running this operation without me,'' Gribble half-shouted.

''Let's find out,'' Delaney had answered. ''Right now I'm sending you away from this plateau to cool off. Don't show up here again for a week.''

''Shit! Maybe I'll never come back.''

''In that case,'' Delaney responded, ''you had better leave your badge with me,'' and he had reached out to unfasten the token of authority from Gribble's shirt. Then in a friendlier tone he added, ''Paul, you've got to get hold of yourself. Go up to Columbia. Get liquored up. Get laid. Get rid of what's eating you.''

Now, still unable to sleep, Robert Delaney rose from the lumpy, wrinkled bed. At another slab-sided building nearby he had seen a sign offering baths with clean water and towels. He dug into his pack for fresh clothing and a bar of soap. With any luck there would be water hot enough for a comfortable shave. After that he'd have supper, followed by a couple of whiskeys.

Almost two hours later Delaney entered the unpretentious saloon. Before claiming one of the few tables that were set close to the crowded bar, he looked about. At first he didn't see a single familiar face; but presently, through the tobacco smoke and the din of raucous voices, his attention centered on one patron—the mustached stage-driver, Ike Fenlon. Under ordinary circumstances, Robert Delaney would not have selected Fenlon as a drinking companion, but tonight he was interested in whatever news of the territory Fenlon had to tell. So he ordered two glasses of whiskey; with them in hand, he approached Ike Fenlon who stood at the crowded bar. "Hello, Ike," he said in a friendly manner. "Good to see you. Why not come on over to my table and take a load off your feet?"

Fenlon stared at him. "Mr. Delaney! Ain't you quite a way off your beat? You need a lift back to the San Miguel River country? I'll be rolling that way come morning." As he spoke, Fenlon drained a beer glass and got to his feet a bit unsteadily. Delaney helped him to thread a way through the crowd to the table, and set a whiskey glass before him. He smiled as Ike mumbled, "Thankee, sir."

Then the subtle probing began. "Ike, I hear there has been another issue of the newspaper at Mesita. Have you seen it?"

Ike nodded, then said, "I took a few and handed them out all the way to Pueblo."

"Oh? Did Milligan ask you to do that?"

"No, but it was a good idea, wasn't it, Mr. Delaney?"

The question drew no answer. "I hear that the singer—what's her name, Lucy Lattamore?—is going to give concerts for Tim O'Fallon." Delaney had ordered another round of drinks, but kept them just beyond Fenlon's reach. He was not yet ready for the stage driver to sink into a senseless stupor.

"Haven't you heard? Miss Lucy signed a contract. A big one, for six concerts." Fenlon lifted his head in a gesture of approval, then added, "She told me about it, when I took her to Pueblo on this last trip."

"To Pueblo? I suppose she went on a shopping spree."

"Nope. She was headed to Denver. But she got back to Pueblo and came on home with me. She and Pappy Loutsenhizer."

"You mean she is here in Pomona?" Delaney said.

"Hell no, Delaney. Why would she come here when she has a brother who is an officer at the Cantonment?"

Delaney was striving to put the pieces together, and asked, "Don't you usually head for Dallas, up by the divide, instead of taking your rest here?" He eyed Ike, noting his condition, then asked, "What happened?"

"We was late getting here. Old Pappy had to stop to piss at nigh every turn of the road. Then we spent maybe half an hour at the rock monument, up by the old mine."

"So you killed time at a rock pile and a worthless mine?" Delaney pried.

At that, the half-drunk driver bridled. "Worthless, hell. Not if what I read in that Pueblo paper means anything."

For the next ten minutes, Delaney managed to get all the information he needed from Ike, pouring nearly half a bottle of whiskey down him in the process. He was able to get a description and approximate location of the old Spanish mine on Blue Mesa, together with Fenlon's recollections of the cairn and its chiseled sighting groove. Further probing enabled Delaney to learn the contents of a certain article which, indeed, had appeared in the Pueblo paper, telling of skeletons, with the rusted trappings of the conquistadores found near an old Spanish grant in the San Luis Valley, of a map leading to a mine. Clearly Ike thought there was a connection between this and the mine on Blue Mesa. Delaney thought so, too.

When he was satisfied that no further information could be dragged from Ike Fenlon, Delaney made an excuse and left the saloon. Soon thereafter, Ike's head fell onto the table and he slept.

Delaney returned to his rented sleeping quarters, pulled off his clothes, and sought the scant comfort of the bed. For a long time he remained awake, sifting through every detail of what Ike Fenlon had revealed. There had been no hint of what sort of business had taken Lucy to Denver, but instinctively he reasoned that it had to do with her—and Royce Milligan—prowling around on the Uncompahgre Plateau.

Abruptly a possibility entered his mind, causing him to sit upright and swing his feet to the floor. Why not look into this business of an old mine, starting by hastening to the San Luis Valley to learn more of the unearthed skeletons? Such a mine would at present belong to no one, unless Lucy Lattamore's hasty trip to Denver had been to file claim to it. Even so, with fast work he could be in and out of the workings in a hurry, bringing forth any precious ore that might have been hidden in the depths. And with his lumbering business on the skids, he could use a little "buried treasure." The meddling of Lucy and the newspaperman he despised, Milligan, had brought about an end to his profitable arrangement for selling lumber to O'Fallon at Mesita. So maybe he should do some meddling on his own. . . . He had already reduced his crew on the Uncompahgre Plateau to a mere skeleton group, and replaced Paul Gribble with a more reasonable man. He should be able to leave for the San Luis Valley within the week.

Chapter 13

In Mesita, a quiet and lonesome Royce Milligan had kept himself busy repairing his printing plant, and putting out another issue of his *Mesita Messiah*. There were encouraging visits from a number of potential subscribers and advertisers. Several of them spoke favorably of his forceful pleas for conservation of the natural resources of the area surrounded by the San Juan Mountains.

On the day Royce thought Lucy might return, he ate an early breakfast and, accompanied by Margaret, who'd been writing articles for every issue, went to the newspaper office.

Scarcely an hour had passed when there was the clatter of horses' hooves in the street. Royce shot a glance out the window, and exclaimed, "What the hell?" Outside, Ike Fenlon was clambering down from one of his stage-horses that he'd unharnessed and ridden bareback. Without waiting to tie the sweating horse to a post, Fenlon burst through the door. Royce was aware of two things: the long coach-whip still dangling from Ike's hand, and the mixed fury and agony twisting his face.

Fenlon came to a halt only a couple of feet from where Royce and Margaret stood together in bewilderment. "Milligan," he panted, "he's coming here any minute. Drunk. Crazy. Saying he will kill you."

"Who, Ike? Who?"

That big fat son of a bitch, Gribble." Even as he

158

spoke, Ike Fenlon was peering out of the window. "He left Columbia before a posse got organized to nab and hang him."

"Posse? Hang him?" For what?" Royce asked.

"Later, Royce . . . later. See that rig headed here like a bat out of hell? It's him—Gribble."

"We'll settle it outside," Royce said in a hasty, but calm way. He motioned Margaret toward the safety of an inner room, but she would not budge.

When the light rig, driven by the fat ex-lawman, halted before the newspaper shop, Royce was standing on the sidewalk. Gribble started to raise a short-barreled rifle from the seat beside him, but Royce's voice sounded clearly through the morning quiet. "Point that at me, Gribble, and I'll shoot to kill."

Gribble seemed to hesitate, but not because of Royce Milligan's words. Instead, he was staring at Ike Fenlon. The whip-bearing stage driver had sprung from the office door, shouting, "Leave the bastard to me, Royce." And to Gribble he said, "Get the hell down from that buggy."

With unbelievable speed Paul Gribble jumped from the vehicle; at the same time his hand sought out the ugly black revolver at his belt. Margaret Hendricks, now standing in the *Messiah*'s doorway, screamed, then a single shot rang out.

Gribble's revolver broke from his grasp and clattered to the road; then the fat man fell to his knees and slowly collapsed into the dust.

Ike Fenlon looked up, confused. Royce Milligan was gently putting his smoking derringer back in its resting place beneath his belt. At his side now, Margaret said quietly, "He had it coming to him, Royce."

"You're damn right," Fenlon agreed. "The posse's gonna thank you for this."

"So there's really a posse coming after him?" Royce's voice was oddly toneless.

"There sure is," Ike replied. "Back in Columbia, Gribble raped a girl—a child, really—and then beat her to

death. Name of Felicidad, if I remember right . . . poor
kid never harmed anyone.''

The name clicked in Royce's brain . . . *Felicidad.* That
was the girl at Lucy's concert. He'd have to break the
news to her.

Royce looked back only once at Paul Gribble's body
before reentering the office. He wasn't happy to have been
the instrument of Gribble's death, but he was glad the
man was dead.

There was no stagecoach moving between Columbia,
Mesita, and the towns beyond the Dallas Divide for the
next four days, due to all the commotion. Royce Milligan
made a hasty trip on horseback to Columbia to learn the
details of Paul Gribble's rampage. Margaret Hendricks
accompanied him and they both attended the simple
funeral services for the Mexican girl, Felicidad, whose
death was still the talk of the town.

At Tim O'Fallon's insistence, a group of Mesita
residents was called together to determine what charges,
if any, should be brought against Royce. Such a hearing
was really just a formality. It took less than half an hour
for the citizens of Mesita to decide that Royce Milligan
had done the community a service by dispatching a rapist
and murderer, and, furthermore, that he'd acted in self-
defense.

That same afternoon, Royce was sitting at his desk
when Fenlon appeared at the office of *The Mesita
Messiah.*

''Isn't it about time to get the stagecoach rolling again,
Ike?'' Royce asked as his visitor pulled up a chair and
sat down.

''Yeah, but first I got to tell you what I came to say,
Royce. Likely you'll want to kick my ass all the way to
the Plateau and back.''

''What the devil are you talking about?'' Royce chided.

''Lemme catch my breath and I'll tell you. Royce, I

got drunk—and blabbed like an idiot. About you. About Miss Lucy.''

Royce looked up sharply. "I don't understand."

"It was after my last stage-run to Pueblo. On the way back I had a scad of mail and boxes, but just two passengers. Miss Lucy . . . and that old codger, Pappy Loutsenhizer, from Pomona. We stopped up there on Blue Mesa, right where we spent that freezin' night under a buffalo robe and snow piled up on us." Fenlon looked up in an ashamed way, then went on reluctantly. "Anyhow, Miss Lucy showed me and Loutsenhizer a pile of rock she called a cairn. On its top rock was a notch she sighted through. She said that was how she caught sight of the old mine where we spent the night."

"Did she let you sight through it this time?"

"Yeah, but I couldn't see any mine portal. Just a gulch full of slide rock and twisted timbers."

"Well, Ike, why are you worrying about that?"

"It ain't what I did or didn't see, Royce. It's what I said to Mr. Delaney—Robert Delaney, the lumberman."

"Delaney!" Royce echoed, startled. He had not seen Delaney for several days, or even given the timber baron much thought. "Where . . . and when did you talk to Delaney?"

"It was the night I laid over in Pomona, after Lucy and Pappy and me came down off Blue Mesa. I thought I'd have me just one drink. A nightcap. Delaney was in Pomona and came into the saloon. Royce, he was friendly and kept seeing I had plenty to drink—and he kept asking questions. It is kind of hazy as I think of it now, but I recall telling Delaney of the cairn and the mine, and of our stopping there. Maybe I even gave him directions."

"Well, likely no great damage can come of that," Royce said.

"But that ain't all, Royce. I even told Delaney about a piece in the Pueblo paper I saw. About the old skeletons they found down by that Spanish grant in the San Luis Valley."

Bewilderment touched Royce Milligan's face. "What are you trying to tell me, Ike? What skeletons? And how would that have anything to do with the mine where we stayed?"

Ike stared at the perplexed editor. "Royce, didn't I ever mention that newspaper piece to you?"

"Not a word, Ike. Suppose you start at the beginning and explain all this."

"It was in the Pueblo paper about six weeks ago. Told of a couple of old skeletons being found close to the base of the Sangre de Cristo Mountains, and maybe twenty miles from the big Spanish land-grant down there. They was Spaniards, with all the trappings of them old conquistadores. Right next to them they found a rusted iron box, holding a map and some small bars of silver and gold."

"Who got hold of all that?" Royce asked curiously.

"Damned if I know. Probably whoever found the remains. But Royce, listen to this: That map showed some of the country on Blue Mesa, west of where Barnum is nowadays. The article said so. The newspaper reporter fellow in Pueblo somehow got hold of the map. He had a man who can read Spanish study it. And get this, Royce—the reporter was told the map gave location of some sort of sighting device."

"You mean Lucy's cairn . . ." Royce half-whispered. Then he rose and stared at Fenlon. "And you told all of this to Robert Delaney?"

"Most of it, anyway," Fenlon admitted.

"I can't believe this, Ike. If only you'd told Lucy . . . or me about the article sooner."

"I know, but I forgot." Fenlon was silent for half a minute, then brightened. "There's one thing I didn't tell old Delaney, though, Royce."

"What?" Royce's single word implied there could have been little left untold.

"I didn't tell him that you can't see the mine anymore. Not even by squinting through that chiseled notch on the

top rock. Royce, I think there has been another rock-slide
. . . an avalanche . . . down that ravine where the portal
was. Now all a person can see is piled rock and a stack
of broken and uprooted trees.''

But the mine is still there, within the mountain, Royce
thought. *And what if the precious metals found in the old
iron box came from there?* Royce knew immediately what
he had to do; he must himself journey eastward to the
San Luis Valley, and to the place where skeletons had
come to light. But caution kept him from mentioning this
to Fenlon. Just now the man was contrite and remorseful.
But liquored-up, he'd been loose-lipped before. Common
sense warned that it might happen again. Ike must not
know of his plans—but somehow Lucy must be quickly
informed that the cairn and the mine were suddenly
extremely important, to them, and most likely to a certain
ruined lumber baron from Mesita.

"Ike, try to keep what we have been talking about a
secret. And something else. I'm going to the Cantonment
with you tomorrow morning."

Chapter 14

Lucy saw Phillip off for his new assignment on the morning of May 30. Two other Cantonment officers were also being transferred out. They and their baggage would be given an escort to the nearest railroad, at Gunnison. She held Phillip tight, then watched his conveyance disappear beyond the Cantonment gate. At that moment it seemed that her only link with family and childhood had vanished. Immediately, though, something else crowded upon her—the need to be with Royce, to have his arms about her again.

She returned to Phillip's quarters, where she planned to remain until the following day. For an hour she did final housecleaning and packed her belongings, but the loneliness about the Cantonment seemed unendurable. *Why not catch a ride into Pomona, find out when Ike Fenlon's stage would pass this way again heading for Mesita, and possibly look up Pappy Loutsenhizer,* she thought.

When she stepped outside, she found that the sky had clouded over and a strong, chilly wind had sprung up. She glanced up the valley toward the San Juan peaks. They seemed stern and remote to her.

There was no Cantonment vehicle headed into Pomona, but an officer-friend of Phillip's arranged for her to use a well-broken sorrel horse. On the ride toward town, she was glad for having brought a heavy coat. The wind was tearing leaves from trees and bushes and driving them in

164

bunches across the road. Watching them, Lucy thought gloomily how much needed to be done on Cedar's Edge Mesa.

It was nearly noon when she rode into Pomona. There was a corral at which she could unsaddle and feed her horse. She gazed about at the drabness of the settlement, noting its striking contrast to the beauty of the mountain-guarded valley. Smoke was swirling from the stovepipe of the half-tent, half-shack that served as an eating place. She walked toward it, suddenly feeling ravenously hungry.

She was near the cookshack door when a man fell into stride beside her. She glanced up, saw an unshaven face and gasped. She was staring at Robert Delaney. "What are you doing here?" she asked.

His face was bleak and inscrutable. "I might ask you the same thing, Miss Lattamore."

"I have been at the Cantonment; my brother, an officer there, was transferred out to an army post in Kansas this morning."

"How sad," Delaney responded. She couldn't tell from his tone whether the words were said sarcastically or sincerely. Presently he shrugged. "My reason for being here? I'm trying to find new markets for lumber, visiting every town and ranch this side of the Plateau." He paused and his voice hardened. "But right now I've just come from a meeting with the U.S. marshal you managed to send snooping into my affairs."

"Mr. Delaney, that is a lie. I never spoke to or even saw any such official."

"Oh, you didn't?" His response clearly indicated disbelief, and he continued, "I don't suppose you were in Denver either, or bought almost a thousand acres of timber on the edge of my cutting area. I suppose that was all just a load of lies the marshal fed me . . ."

Lucy's anger was mounting. They had reached the cookshack, but stood facing each other just outside the door. "Not that it is any of your business, Mr. Delaney, but I *was* in Denver. And the marshal was right, I bought that land as a buffer between your destructive, wasteful, and unlawful timber-slaughter—and the source of water for orchard lands I own. I said *bought*. Something you never thought of. Oh no! Mr. Delaney never buys what he can steal."

She fully expected that he would slap her.

But just then, two strangers suddenly burst through the cookshack door and Lucy heard the first one say to the other, "Do you know anything more of that woman being murdered up at Columbia—or of that newspaper fellow, Milligan, shooting Paul Gribble?"

An unbelieving gasp broke from Lucy Lattamore, and Delaney froze in his tracks. Then he turned to the two newcomers, his face white and tense. "Excuse me, gents. Did I hear you right? Did you say that Paul Gribble is dead?"

"I don't know much about it," one of the men said. "A fellow rode through our cattle-graze this morning, carrying mail himself from Mesita, because the stage hasn't run for a couple of days. Seems that this Gribble raped and murdered a Mexican gal up at Columbia. Then he headed for Mesita; he was crazy-like and threatening to shoot the newspaper man there."

A low cry escaped from Lucy's throat.

"Seems Milligan got to Gribble first. Shot him through the heart. Town council ruled it self-defense. Anyway, Gribble is deader than hell."

Robert Delaney's eyes had a hard gleam in them as he heard the news. Lucy glanced at him, knowing that Gribble's death would give him another score to settle with Royce. She shivered, then asked, "Did they say the name of the woman Gribble killed . . . the Mexican girl?" But Lucy didn't really need to ask. She had a feeling in the pit of her stomach.

"Not that I recall." The older man shook his head.

"Girl's name was Felicity or something," the other one offered.

The words confirmed what Lucy had already sensed. *Oh, God in heaven. Felicidad! A child within a woman's body . . . a loving, bewildered child.*

"You knew her?" the cowpoke asked.

"I met her only once . . . when I gave the concert at Columbia," she said sorrowfully. Then she looked up at the jagged San Juan mountains on the horizon, tears stinging her eyes. She blinked them back and swung around toward Robert Delaney. "This is what comes of your devilish work. You hire an animal like Paul Gribble and this is what you get," she spat out. "Well, I'll tell you something. I'm glad Royce Milligan killed him. Paul Gribble got what he deserved!"

The two cowpokes looked on in amazement, and Lucy was just about to walk away, but Delaney grabbed her tightly by the wrist.

His voice was a harsh, low whisper. "And you and Royce Milligan are going to get just what you deserve, too. I'll see to it!"

Before she could reply, he strode rapidly away.

Still shaken, Lucy retrieved her horse and started back to the Cantonment. Her thoughts were jumbled. What had driven Royce to shoot Paul Gribble? Was it really self-defense? Would the stage be running again soon? Right now she wanted more than anything to be in Mesita. And what about Robert Delaney? When and where would he take his revenge?

She rode slowly, through the windy, overcast afternoon. Rain was beginning to fall as she reached the Cantonment gate and guard station. An enlisted man with corporal's stripes accompanied her to what had been Phillip's quarters, offered to take care of her horse, and saw her safely to the door. She entered, touched a match to the wick of a lamp, and looked about. No fire had been lighted and the room's chilliness and silence seemed to make her lonelier than ever. Soon she sought the warmth of her blanketed bed. This would probably be her final night at the military post, and her thoughts turned to the eager happiness with which Phillip had welcomed her only a month previous. So much had happened since, and her life had been changed in so many ways. She wondered where, on this rain-swept night, the others might be: the Reverend Goodfroe, a Martin Goetz, Ike Fenlon . . . and Royce.

Lucy awoke to see rain still pelting against her window, and in the distance she heard thunder. Worried lines formed on her forehead. This was the day she had planned to travel to Mesita. It was a certainty, though, that no vehicles would cross Dallas Divide until the storm passed.

She donned some warm clothing and then started a fire in the kitchen. Practically all the food items had been packed, but she managed to heat coffee and stir up some oatmeal. So silent were the quarters, that she jumped in a startled way when a knock sounded on the door. It was the post commander; she held the door open as he dashed inside.

"Good morning, Miss Lucy," he greeted her. "We became a bit concerned about you . . . here all alone."

"And due to vacate these premises today, sir." She took his raingear and then motioned for him to sit down. "I would offer you some breakfast, but likely you would not be eager for coffee and oatmeal with canned milk."

"We suspected your shortage of victuals." He was placing an envelope in her hand. "Take this; it will permit you to take meals at the officers' mess until you leave the Cantonment. Also, feel free to stay in these quarters until you can arrange for transportation."

She grasped his hand. "Thank you . . . and your command. If only I could somehow repay you."

"But you can," he said without hesitation. "Would you consider singing tonight for a bunch of lonely military men again?"

"I would love to sing again, Major. When you have

made arrangements, just let me know the hour and place."

He got up to leave, but abruptly turned. "By the way, Miss, the storm brought in some others seeking shelter. Two of them claim to know you."

"Know me? Who are they, Major?"

"The Reverend Lucian Goodfroe and a prospector who signed our register as Martin Goetz."

"How their paths and mine seem to keep crossing," Lucy marveled. "Major Watson, I would love to see both of them."

"I'll have them meet you in the public lounge down at headquarters."

"I will be there shortly after one o'clock," she answered, and then showed the Major out.

It was still pouring when Lucy made her way to the building housing the officers' dining room. She ate a hearty lunch and then went to the headquarters building where Reverend Goodfroe and Martin Goetz were already awaiting her. Lucy was not surprised to see the Parson Goodfroe, for she had become accustomed to his erratic comings and goings as he attended to the spiritual needs of his flock. The last time she had seen Goetz, he was preparing to begin assessment on Royce Milligan's so-called coal shaft at Three Rivulets Glade atop the Plateau. Both men greeted her warmly, but Goodfroe seemed to her unusually quiet. Eventually she was moved to ask, "What is bothering you, Reverend Goodfroe? You seem so melancholy."

"The thought of my last service . . . the funeral rites for a young lady up at Columbia."

Lucy's throat grew tight and her voice uncertain. "Was it that of Felicidad, the young Mexican girl murdered by Paul Gribble?"

"Then you already know," he answered, and clasped her hand. In a consoling way, he added, "It was a quiet, lovely service."

Still shaken, Lucy turned to Goetz, who, as usual, was

clad in the rough and serviceable garb of a miner. "Mr. Goetz, I suppose you are still busy sinking a shaft for Royce Milligan."

He shook his head. "That is over until next spring, but there is plenty of footage to report as assessment work."

"Then you are working elsewhere?"

Goetz shook his head, and said, grinning, "Right now I'm heading down the valley. My two sons have jobs as black-powder men, blasting a road of sorts into the town of Delta. I aim to visit them."

"We met last evening, coming over Dallas Divide," the parson explained. The rain was terrible, so we hurried here for shelter."

"And what brings a pretty young lady like you here?" Goetz inquired.

"To spend a few days with my brother, who was an officer here."

"Was?" Goetz asked.

"He was transferred out, to Kansas, just yesterday."

"Then you will be leaving also?" Goodfroe questioned.

"When the stage is running again to Mesita, and after I give a concert tonight for the men here."

The face of each man took on eagerness, and Goetz asked, "If the reverend and I can arrange to stay—?" He paused, doubt overtaking him. "No . . . there wouldn't be a place for us. Men out of uniform, refugees from the storm."

"I am sure it could be arranged," she reassured them. Then she added, "What on earth are we doing . . . still standing here, when there are chairs and even a table?"

They made themselves comfortable, as Reverend Goodfroe remarked, "Even one chair or table would have been a sort of treasure that night in the old Spanish mine up on Blue Mesa."

His comment caused Lucy to glance about and make sure there were no strangers within hearing range, and then she said anxiously, "You know, sometimes that night and that old mine seem but a fantasy to me. Was it really there?"

"Our nearness to freezing was plenty real," Goodfroe said firmly. "You somehow led us to that portal in the nick of time."

"Yes, but it is no longer there; at least, it can't be *seen*," she mused. "Only a few days ago there was no sign of such a portal, or even an ore waste-dump."

Goetz had remained quiet, but now he spoke thoughtfully. "That may indicate a change in the terrain of the mountainside, Miss Lucy. As I recall, the portal was in a sort of gulch or ravine. Also, it had all the appearances of having been in an avalanche path."

Fascinated, Lucy asked, "You mean there may have been another avalanche . . . since we were there?"

"It is possible. If so, the rock, the broken timber, and other debris may have piled up and hidden the portal—or even swept the old entry timbers away."

Lucy studied Goetz's face, then began to speak again. "If the way into the tunnel is blocked by rock and earth and timber, what are our chances of blasting through? Of reopening the portal and gaining entry to the tunnel?"

Goetz toyed with a battered hat lying on his lap. It was a full minute before he answered. "There is always danger of setting off another slide by blasting. We have no idea of the depth of the jammed-up debris, or the exact location of the portal beneath it. Perhaps a new portal would be needed." He paused, and added, "It would be a challenge!"

"And a gamble," Lucy conceded. "I can pay our costs—and give each of you written agreement to percentages of whatever we uncover."

"How would I, a man of the cloth, be of value to you?" Goodfroe inquired.

Lucy's reply was light-hearted. "Perhaps by giving us spiritual advice." Then, more seriously, she said, "We'll need a lookout man, to warn us of any intruders."

"When would you want to head for Blue Mesa?"
Goodfroe asked.

"Within the week, providing this storm lets up. Her
mind was also warning: *What will Royce say to such
fantastic chance-taking?* She breathed deeply and then
asked, "Now let's figure out what sorts of supplies we'll
need."

The meeting with Goodfroe and Goetz lasted for
slightly more than two hours. When Lucy left the
headquarters building she was surprised to find that the
rain had petered off, replaced by sunshine, together with
a warm chinook wind; there were still large puddles of
water and an amazing amount of mud. She plodded
through it and returned to the quarters that she had shared
with Phillip. Inside, the devastating sense of loneliness
she had experienced during the hours just after his departure had fled, for today she had things to look forward
to—the concert scheduled for this evening, her own trip
to Mesita, and the effort to reenter the old Spanish mine.

For the concert she chose a well-tailored, blue skirt and
blouse, and ironed out a few wrinkles. She would also
keep handy a colorful shawl, as the building chosen and
prepared for her hour or more of singing would likely be
chilly.

Her remaining bits of packing proved negligible, for
she had already filled and secured all but one piece of
luggage. *Surely by tomorrow,* she thought, *there will be
some means of travel over Dallas Divide to the San
Miguel River Valley and to Mesita.*

The shadows of sunset, moving through a westward
window and up a wall, warned Lucy that only two hours
remained in which she might prepare for the concert. She
already had determined the songs she would sing tonight,
but nonetheless, she ran through them one more time.

That accomplished, she prepared for her bath. There
was hot water in the cast-iron reservoir of the kitchen
cookstove. She dipped it into a washtub, tempering it with
cold water. Then after making certain that the window

shades were drawn, she disrobed and stepped into the tub. She lowered herself down and then with a bar of soap lathered herself until her skin glowed.

Just then, there was an insistent knocking at the front door. "Oh, hell!" she muttered. "Anytime but now . . ." Again the door was hammered upon, this time more loudly. Aggravated, she stood up, foamy and dripping suds onto the kitchen floor. Another round of fist-beats on the door caused her to shout out, "All right . . . all right . . . I hear you. Just a minute."

She looked around for something to cover her nakedness. There were only the wrinkled and soiled garments she had cast aside, and the gown she would don for her concert. She grabbed a towel and flung it about her, but its scantiness made her abandon it. In desperation she glanced about. On the kitchen cabinet was a bedsheet which she had meant to wash out and hang to dry. She tossed the towel aside, wrapped the sheet about her, and made wet tracks toward the front door. Her sudsy condition caused the sheet to dampen and cling to her body in a revealing way.

She reached the door and fumbled with the lock as she called out, "Who is it?"

Lucy recognized the answering voice as that of the young corporal from headquarters. "It's me, Corporal Wolfe. There is a gentleman here to see you. Says his name is Milligan . . . Royce Milligan. Do you want—?"

The corporal's question broke abruptly off, for Lucy had squealed, "Oh . . . Royce . . . at last!" and pulled open the door.

"Do you know him?" Corporal Wolfe began, and then added, dazedly, "You must know him . . . that's for damn sure." He was staring at a half-soaked, sheeted woman; who was suddenly in her visitor's arms, on bare tiptoes to claim a prolonged kiss.

"God, wait'll I tell them down at headquarters!"

Royce pulled himself away from Lucy momentarily, and whispered something to the corporal about being Miss

Lattamore's fiancé. The soldier's face turned pink with embarrassment; he moved to leave. but not before taking a final look at the trim curve of Lucy's thigh.

Once inside and by themselves, Royce lifted her into his arms, heedless of her dampness. As her arms tightened about his neck, his hand caught at the sheet and cast it to the floor. He studied the perfection of her exposed body, and murmured. "Lucy . . . Lucy . . ."

"Royce," she whispered, coming to him. "If only we could make love. Here. Now. But it must be later. Right now I must dress for a concert I'm giving within the hour." She looked at him with love and longing, and let her hand caress his chest and face.

Later, when Royce Milligan had reluctantly left, and Lucy was putting final touches to her attire for the concert, a singular thought entered her mind. *He is here . . . my Royce. And I didn't ask him a solitary one of all the questions I have in mind. About Ike Fenlon's whereabouts . . . Gribble's death . . . the paper . . .*

The questions were still buzzing about her head when a military guard of honor appeared at her door to escort her to the concert stage.

With the knowledge of her lover's nearness, and the help of a young enlisted man's expertise at the piano, Lucy captivated her audience. As always, these soldiers applauded most vigorously for the heart-touching songs of the Civil War and the melodies of Stephen Foster. She varied the program with songs of Spanish and Italian origin. Later she urged every man present to join her in several hymns, and she closed with a moving rendition of Schubert's "*Ave Maria*".

Her singing was followed by a reception with the largest selection of food and drinks she had ever laid eyes on. The officers crowded about to congratulate her, but later she suggested that the enlisted men be permitted in so she could greet each one of them too. She broke into a gale of laughter when at the end of the line, three civilians appeared—the Reverend Goodfroe, Martin Goetz, and finally Royce Milligan, who leaned forward and whispered, "Miss Lattamore, I do believe there are still some soapsuds behind your left ear."

"You hush up," she murmured, and then spoke in an even lower tone. "There is a sort of guest lounge at headquarters. I can be there in about forty-five minutes. I've a million questions to ask."

"And perhaps I can evade every single one," he teased.

He was already waiting, sprawling in a comfortable cowhide chair, when she came into the lounge. Royce jumped to his feet, offering her the seat. Then suddenly he said, "Lord-a-mighty . . . you're more beautiful than ever."

She sat down, tired but exhilarated by the evening's activities, and gathered his hands into hers. "Royce, I am not—and was not—destined to be beautiful; but I love to hear you claim I am. Pull up another chair so we can talk." When he was seated close by, she drew a deep breath, and asked, "Tell me, dear, about Paul Gribble."

Royce became quiet and subdued. At last he said, "Gribble went berserk. If I hadn't killed him, someone else would have."

She shuddered and her face whitened. "And Felicidad—"

He lifted a restraining hand, and said, "Don't, Lucy. Don't torture yourself. She is beyond pain now."

"Somehow I hold Robert Delaney responsible for all this." She paused. "You know, I saw him in Pomona."

Royce shot a startled glance toward her. "You saw Delaney?"

"I ran into him at the cookshack there earlier this week. When he heard about Gribble he was furious. Needless to say, we didn't part friends."

The muscles in Royce Milligan's face tensed. "Lucy, did Delaney try to pry any information from you about the cairn and mine on Blue Mesa?"

Lucy looked thoughtful. "I don't know. I didn't give him much chance. Why do you ask?"

"Because I think I have a hunch the bastard is up to something, that he's out to get to the mine before we do." Royce said heatedly. He noted her utter bewilderment and explained, "Lucy, he got Ike Fenlon drunk and talking about the cairn and the old Spanish mine; Ike also told Delaney something strange that may reveal much more about the mine and its origin."

"Like what?" she breathed in amazement.

He told her then about the article that had appeared in a Pueblo newspaper; how Ike Fenlon had forgotten all about it until he visited the mine again; how it told of the skeletons of conquistadores found at the base of the Sangre de Cristo mountains, of the map that seemed to indicate the location of a rock marker atop Blue Mesa.

"How strange," Lucy commented as he finished. "Royce, is it possible that it contained directions to the cairn and the old mine where we waited out the storm?"

"That's what I hope to find out by going to the Sangre de Cristos. I am quite certain that Delaney is already en route there himself."

"That could be," she admitted. "He is pretty desperate about money matters." She studied Royce, and added, "And he threatened to get even with us somehow."

"This all may prove a wild goose chase," Royce said. Then he added, "On the other hand, Lord knows what may come of it. Lucy, you were the one who found the cairn and showed us the way to the mine. I think that you should file claim to it right away."

"I fully intend to. In fact, I have already asked Parson Goodfroe and Martin Goetz to join me in further exploration—if we can locate the portal beneath rock and other debris that a snow-slide has brought into the gulch."

"You should get mining claims filed first."

"But I can't without legal descriptions or boundary lines. If only I knew someone who could—"

Royce did not answer at once, for now an enlisted man

was standing ready to blow out the lamps and close the area for the night. Royce helped Lucy to her feet and they moved outside of the building. Then he said, "You have just the perfect fellow to do some surveying up there on Blue Mesa, Lucy."

She stared at him in the light of a waning moon and myriad stars. "Who? Don't tell me that you yourself—"

"No, Lucy, I'll be headed eastward to the Sangre de Cristos. But don't fret. Just send the Parson Goodfroe to mark off the lines for your claim. Then Margaret Hendricks can work out the details of filing."

"But Goodfroe is a preacher, not a surveyor."

"Granted. But who in hell would suspect that a man in minister's garb, prowling about, Bible in hand, is marking boundaries for a mining claim?"

Before Lucy could answer, two men clad in dark uniforms appeared out of the darkness. The taller of them spoke. "Miss Lattamore, if you are ready now to return to your quarters, we would be honored to escort you; your brother, Phillip, was a good friend of ours."

Momentarily Royce studied the two. With them, there would be no bargaining for time alone with this woman whose voice had entranced the Cantonment. He'd have to sleep in the quarters provided for transient guests.

Lucy seemed to fathom his thoughts. "Good night, Royce." Then her voice became a whisper as she drew him close, and added, "May fantasies see you through the night."

Chapter 15

Royce Milligan arrived in the railroad town of Salida, Colorado, three days later. Accompanying him was Max Beasley. When Tim O'Fallon heard that Royce was venturing to the San Luis Valley to learn more of the mysterious Spanish skeletons, he was adamant that Beasley go along.

They had boarded the Denver & Rio Grande train at Gunnison, hoping to save many hours of time and avert trail weariness. Later, if need be, they could buy horses in a village or at some remote San Luis Valley ranch.

Royce's knowledge of the San Luis Valley was limited to a few rather nebulous facts: It was a high, mountain-ringed expanse, with the Sangre de Cristo Mountains forming an eastern barrier, and the San Juan Ranges bordering it to the west; it reached a hundred miles from Poncha Pass to the New Mexico border.

Max Beasley was able to furnish some helpful information. "Royce, there is a town at the northwest end of the valley called Saguache, and there's a toll-road over Poncha Pass. If there is a stage route over there, why don't we make that our first stop?"

"I don't have a better idea," Royce agreed.

Inquiry at the railroad's baggage counter assured them that a daily stage ran to Saguache, and would leave in about two hours.

They arrived near noon the following day. The long

climb up Poncha Pass had proved interesting but slow; they'd spent the night at a shelter station at the crest of the pass, where the air was thin and the aspen green and graceful.

Their stage-driver was a morose and silent man who gave short and unwilling answers to their questions, but a whiskey salesman aboard was friendly and willing to supply information. From him, they learned about a mining town called Crestone on the east side of the valley. "It straddles Crestone Creek and is being built on a juniper-wooded slope right where the creek breaks out of the mountains. It's not far from the Ortega grant." The salesman went on, "One of those old Spanish land-grants, you know."

"I've heard of them," Royce answered. "Enormous blocks of land deeded by the ruler of Spain to a nobleman, because of service rendered to the crown."

The salesman was warming to his subject. "This Ortega grant, twenty thousand acres in one block, is a rancher's dream. It starts at the top of the Sangre de Cristos, drops along half a dozen big creeks and heavy forest, and down onto the meadowlands that extend out into the valley. It reaches practically to the Great Sand Dunes to the south."

Careful not to show undue interest, Royce fell silent. However, the liquor-drummer continued enthusiastically. "There's some boggy marshes, and even quicksand, surrounding the dunes, especially on the east. That's where they uncovered those old skeletons a while back."

"Old skeletons," Royce repeated, acting uninterested. "Likely that created excitement."

"For a time. Then it died down."

On the final few miles of the bumpy stagecoach ride into Saguache, Royce Milligan did some calculating. The skeletons had come to light near marshes abutting the Great Sand Dunes. This merely confirmed what Ike Fenlon had read in a Pueblo paper. There had been no mention of the Ortega land-grant, but it made sense to

Royce that the skeletons had been found so near the immense old Spanish ranch. It also made sense for them to head over there.

Their first stop in the town of Saguache was at a café where an attractive Mexican girl, clad in a flaming-red dress and ruffled white blouse, pointed them to a table and brought pottery cups of steaming coffee. When she approached to take their order, she worded her inquiry in softly musical Spanish. Royce looked up chagrined, and then listened in wonder as a short torrent of Spanish came out of Beasley. Presently he smiled at Royce. "The lady suggests that we have either a broiled steak or a mixed dinner of tacos, enchiladas, and tostadas. And a glass of tequila, of course."

Royce's eyes roamed the cool, shadowed depths of the café. "Please tell her that the mixed plate suits me, except—"

"Except what, Royce?"

"Tell her to leave out that bit of hellfire known as a chili pepper. You know, like those red ones hanging on the gatepost just outside."

When they finally left the café, Royce squinted at the sun and said, "Max, what say we look around for horses? Then first thing tomorrow morning we can head over toward the Sangre de Cristo Mountains and that settlement called Crestone."

It was when they went in search of horses that Royce first found confirmation of what he already suspected—that Robert Delaney was already in the San Luis Valley. Max and he were directed to extensive corrals on the irrigated meadows bordering the south edge of town. A bent old man with gnarled hands led them to a pen containing sturdy mares and geldings. By paying a reasonable deposit, they were able to rent the horses; saddles, blankets, and bridles were also available. They would pick up the horses and gear early the following morning.

They were preparing to return to their quarters in town

when the stableman asked, "What part of the valley do you gents hail from?"

Royce saw no reason to be evasive. "We're from a bit further off, a town called Mesita, over on the San Miguel River."

"I've heard of it." The man nodded, and then added, "In fact, a fellow was in here two days ago wanting a fast horse. He was from Mesita. Maybe you fellers know him."

"What was his name?" Royce asked quickly.

"I'm not sure. He bought the horse and asked that I make out a blank bill of sale. I told him that was against the law, so he said make the paper out to Ed Walton. I had an idea he was making up the name."

Beasley had listened with quiet interest, and now he asked, "He didn't happen to mention the name Delaney? Robert Delaney?"

"Nope. Just Ed Walton."

Beasley persisted, giving a detailed description of Delaney.

"That's him, all right. Big fellow. Sort of good-looking. Fancy breeches and jacket."

"Did he happen to say where he was headed?"

"I don't think . . . Wait!" The horse-tender scratched his head as though trying to recall something. "I think he said something about Crestone. . . ."

It wasn't until Royce and Beasley were out of the old man's hearing that they evaluated what he had told them. Max Beasley was the first to speak. "Royce, it's a sure thing that Delaney is over here, and that he has just one goal in mind . . . to somehow get hold of that map, and see if it's of the mine on Blue Mesa. He won't waste time."

"That's for sure," Royce agreed.

The following morning they had no trouble finding the trail across the valley to Crestone; as they rode eastward, the road left the meadowlands about Saguache and entered a vast expanse of sagebrush.

They rode for almost twenty miles across the sage-strewn levelness of the mountain-ringed valley, then passed a crossroads and began an upward climb. The Sangre de Cristo range was a mighty barrier before them; they seemed to be heading directly for the thin, needle-like summit of Crestone Peak. In the harsh light of midday, they now could see lines of trees marking the creeks by which water came from the wilderness to the gentle slopes at lower elevation. All around them, the sagebrush gave way to juniper, pine, and cedar trees. The height of this twisted timber increased as they climbed. What struck Royce was the awesome sweep of the valley as he turned to look backwards. *An inland, mountain-locked empire,* he thought. *No wonder the canny old Spanish dons were eager for land grants here. They realized they would become virtual rulers over vast domains.*

They were riding through meadows now, where water lay in cloud-reflecting patches, and cattle with wide-spread horns grazed in grass that often reached up to their bellies. They judged themselves to be within three miles of the village of Crestone.

Royce and Beasley rode slowly, excited by the views on every side. Presently a break in the bordering juniper revealed a well-laid-out road diverging to the south. There was also a gateway built of logs. Two of these acted as sturdy upright posts, and a trimmed log, more than a foot in diameter, had been raised some twenty feet to link the gateposts. They noted a hand-carved plank at the center of the gateway. It read: THE ORTEGA LAND GRANT, with the name repeated in Spanish beneath.

"Well! Imagine this." Royce spoke as if in disbelief. "No searching. No hassle. No having to sneak in." He reined his horse toward the gate, and asked, "Shall we, Max?"

"It could be dangerous, our riding in there and not really knowing what our reception might be." Beasley gazed toward the distant buildings of Crestone, and added, "Why don't we find some lodgings, look the town over, and then decide about barging into the Ortega spread?"

"You are probably right," Royce agreed. "Besides, we may be on a useless search. Perhaps all of the papers and gear found with those skeletons have been taken to one of the settlements south toward Santa Fe. Or perhaps to Pueblo or Denver."

"You sound about ready to give up already," Max said anxiously.

"No, we're going to see this thing through."

Thick timber surrounded them as they made their way through a sprinkling of tents, cabins, and shacks leading to Crestone's one business street. Royce and Beasley found lodgings above a dry-goods store. Entry to their quarters was by way of an outside stairway that clung to the building's side. Inside their high-ceilinged room were two double beds of burnished brass, neatly made up with heavy woolen blankets and pillowcases still carrying the printed design of flour sacks. The place was clean, and on the floor was a huge braided circular rag rug. For all this, they paid three dollars per night.

They found a restaurant where the odor of cabbage, onions, and roasting pork hung heavily in the air. They ate the tasteless food, and then strode out into afternoon sunlight.

They had moved only a dozen steps along the board sidewalk, when the door of a saloon opened and a man came toward them. Abruptly both he and Royce Milligan stopped and stared in mutual recognition. It was Robert Delaney, clad in dusty boots and a sweaty but well-cut woolen shirt. He seemed taken aback by their presence, but presently he spoke.

"So Tim O'Fallon's lackeys are branching out. What brings you to Crestone, Milligan?" As he spoke, Delaney's eyes were sweeping over Max Beasley, probing for any weapon the gunslinger might be carrying.

Royce studied the lumberman, knowing he had to be

handled with care. Only desperation could have caused him to take time away from his faltering logging camp and mill to chase the rainbow of a tenuous tale of dead men and their gold. Finally, he answered Delaney. "Suppose you and I lay our cards on the table. You rushed over here because of what Ike Fenlon told you of a newspaper story. You're hoping to uncover clues about a mine on Blue Mesa. I am after the same information, to feature as a lead story for *The Mesita Messiah*." Royce's expression gave no indication of his deliberate falsehood.

"And maybe to help Lucy Lattamore take a fortune out of the workings," Delaney answered.

"She seems to be pretty adept at taking care of her own business," Royce said. "Look, Delaney," he went on, "why don't you just call it quits? You aren't likely to gain one damned thing by coming here."

Delaney looked at him coldly. "The hell I won't. I've already met the man who holds the ace in this game . . . the gent with papers that are proof of title to that abandoned workings on Blue Mesa."

Royce's eyes widened in surprise. Then Robert Delaney, turned, laughed triumphantly, and strode toward his horse tied nearby. He mounted and rode up the busy street without looking back.

Royce and Max walked back to their boardinghouse, climbed the stairs, and spent half an hour trying to fathom Delaney's claim that someone else was now involved in the struggle for the old Spanish mine.

"Seems to me, Max, that maybe Delaney was bluffing. But we have to take that chance, and get whatever information we can. As quick as we can."

"I have an idea where to start, Royce."

"Out with it, then."

"We know pretty well about Crestone, and we've located the Ortega grant. But how about the Great Sand Dunes? That's where the skeletons were found."

"So you want to ride down that way?" Royce inquired.

"Not today. Likely it's too far. But let's climb a couple of miles onto the mountains and take a real look over the valley. I've an idea we can spot the dunes and calculate their distance. Then tomorrow we can head out early in the morning."

Royce grinned ruefully. "Why is it, Max, that when we travel you're the one who usually ends up leading the way?"

An hour later the two explorers stood atop a huge rock at the crest of a foothill lying immediately to the back of Crestone. Before them, the vast San Luis Valley seemed to stretch away to infinity.

The Great Sand Dunes were now clearly visible, a rippling mass of brightness surrounded by lowlands. Toward the eastern edge of the sands, a tree-bordered creek broke free of the mountains through a canyon with steep, forbidding walls. Beasley estimated that the dunes were in the neighborhood of seventeen miles south of Crestone.

After studying the vast piles of sand for several minutes, they discussed the route by which they'd approach the dunes on the morrow.

Before turning back toward Crestone, they noted another canyon and creek dropping swiftly into the valley. Its sheen was reflected as bright and shining silver in the light of late afternoon. Along it, there were a few buildings from which a wagon road winded toward Crestone. From somewhere in the canyon, a vast black pipe led down to hillocks at the valley's edge, and ended where there were raw, naked piles of rock and puddles of water.

Royce studied the heavy equipment. "Another placer-mining setup," he commented.

A quietness was upon them as they rode slowly back to Crestone. They came into the mining town just as the sun was edging close to other mountains far westward. They would have gone directly to their lodging, but instead they sat in silent wonder as they lifted their faces toward the high Sangre de Cristo Mountains. There was a mellow reddish glow on the high peaks, the strange and mystic light that had led the Spaniards to name these mountains Sangre de Cristo—*The Blood of Christ.*

Royce Milligan spent two hours restlessly tossing about before getting to sleep. He pondered Robert Delaney's enigmatic words: *"Already I've met the man who holds the ace in this game."* And he thought of Lucy. Was she awaiting news from him before starting her efforts to relocate and explore the mine on Blue Mesa? Had she been able to file for title to it and the ground about the cairn? Surely a gold or silver workings that had been deserted for a couple of hundred years would now be considered in the public domain and open to a new claim.

A mood of apprehension hung about Royce when shortly after sunrise he and Beasley rose, ate an indifferently prepared breakfast, and then claimed their horses at a small livery stable. Both men had brought pistols and a rifle; now they made sure the weapons were loaded and close at hand.

They left Crestone and skirted the foothills of the Sangre de Cristo Mountains, riding southward. They surmised they had soon crossed onto the landholdings of the Ortega grant, but along here there was an open and well-traveled wagon road leading to various mining claims.

An hour's riding brought them to the canyon and the stream where they had sighted the iron pipeline and the sluicing operations. This early, operations had not yet begun for the day. Royce was astonished by the size of the pipe and of the nozzle devices to which it brought a six-inch stream of water. "Max, that rigging could wash down a whole damn mountain," he said with awe.

"Or tear the head off anyone standing in its path." Beasley nodded.

They had halted their horses, and now a tall man in a slouch hat and faded leather jacket approached. "Can I help you fellows?" he asked.

"We're just riding through to the sand dunes," Beasley assured him.

"Are you gents part of that outfit that set up camp down at the dunes a couple of days ago?"

"We never heard of them," Royce said. And then he asked in what he hoped seemed an only mildly interested way, "You mean there are some prospectors down by the dunes?"

The tall stranger spat disgustedly into the dust. "Hell! Ever since them skeletons were found just east of the dunes, it seems there's been a stream of folks showing up here. Newspaper people. Gents from a museum over in Denver. And now this Spaniard—looks like some old don or nobleman, he does—comes and set up camp with a dozen or more Mexicans. They got rifles, so we've all been staying away."

"Maybe," Royce began cautiously, "you have seen a fellow who is an acquaintance of ours. We are hoping to catch up with him." He went on, describing Delaney.

After a little while the stranger nodded. "That one . . . sure I've seen him. Fact is, he rode through toward the dunes just about dark last night. Seemed to know just where he was headed."

Presently they were directed to a spot where dirt and rock had been piled to form a grade-crossing over the mammoth pipe. Warily, Royce recognized a grim possibility: If this means of crossing the pipe were either blocked or destroyed, there would be no ready means of crossing.

They were grimly watchful as they rode further toward the dunes. Their road was now but a tracery of wagon and hoof prints that moved in and out of the sage and piñon pines. The morning grew hot, and there were clouds of black gnats constantly swirling about their heads and turning their necks raw with stings.

Max Beasley had said little since their crossing of the placer-mining pipeline. Now, as they came to a clearing and paused atop a knoll, both men stared ahead. Perhaps five miles distant stood the white and shining Great Sand Dunes of the San Luis Valley.

Beasley pointed toward the green flatness at the dunes' base. "Take a look, Royce . . . just between the slough and the first mountain slope. Likely that is where we'll find Delaney, and perhaps the Spaniard. See? There are tents and a couple of wagons. Royce," Max went on urgently, "from now on we're in enemy territory . . ." He waited a bit and then asked, "Do we risk taking on maybe a dozen gunslinging Mexicans? Just to see what they're prodding for on the dune?"

"I think we already know. They want some absolute proof of the cairn and the mine and how to reach them, because they must not have the map. But who are they and where did they come from? Even more important, Max, has Delaney joined up with them?"

"Delaney knows the mine's on Blue Mesa," Max commented grimly.

There was a tense quiet, and then Royce spoke again. "I have an idea that within a day or so the whole outfit . . . men, guns, and loaded wagons . . . is going to make a trek toward Blue Mesa. We've got to either head them off or beat them there to the cairn and the old mine. But it would make matters simpler if we knew how many men they've got down there."

"All right, Royce. We ought to be able to size up the camp if we get say a mile or so closer. Then let's get the hell out of here."

They turned to backtrack a bit before moving further down the slope, but where the trail wound around a dense stand of piñon pine, four armed riders sat on impatient horses and watched as Royce and Beasley reined quickly to a halt. The men of the party showed no surprise, and Royce surmised that he and Max had been watched for some time.

There was no possibility of using their own weapons. Each of the four intruders had a rifle poised for instant use, as well as pistols and a bandolier of cartridges at his belt. Their garb and dark, unfriendly faces told Royce plainly that he and Beasley were now in the hands of Mexican *banditos*.

After running appraising eyes over their two captives, one rider, astride a clean-lined black gelding, motioned for Royce and Max to come closer. They did so with extreme care, for even the smallest incident might bring a hail of gunfire. The man was obviously leader of the brigands; at a distance of about eight yards, he motioned for them to stop.

Suddenly sharp and demanding Spanish words broke from him. When Royce remained quiet, the leader's rifle pointed in unerring aim at his chest. And then Max Beasley spoke up, his Spanish urgent and pleading.

The leader tossed his head in impatience, then lifting his weapon slightly he seemed to dismiss Royce and turned his attention to Beasley addressing him in rapid Spanish. After a few seconds, Max nodded and spoke cautiously. "Royce, he says for us to hand over our guns; then they'll tie our hands behind our back. And Royce, we'd better damn well do as he says."

It was thus that they were brought into the encampment on the edge of the sand dunes an hour later. When they arrived, their horses were taken from them and both Royce and Beasley were shoved inside a small, bare tent, with guards posted to prevent any escape attempts. The light was subdued and the air heavy with the scent of saddle gear and unwashed bodies.

After what seemed like hours, two men entered with hands on revolvers at their sides. Royce gave only momentary heed to the first intruder; he was the leader of the band who had brought them to this dismal place. But the second man was Robert Delaney. Now he asked, "Milligan, are you ready to answer some questions?"

When Royce remained silent, he and Max Beasley were pushed toward two armed guards waiting outside the door. "Take them to the tent of Don Felipe Jaramillo," Delaney commanded.

It was but a short walk to the large and handsome tent of Don Felipe Jaramillo. It was partially screened by a dense growth of piñon pine. Twice Royce brushed against branches heavily laden with piñon nuts, causing a handful to shower to the ground. It seemed an inconsequential thing, but it stayed in his mind.

Inside his tent, the Spanish leader was seated at a small table, scanning pages of handwritten script. Only Robert Delaney, Beasley, and Royce were admitted, but guards stood silent and alert at the tent's opening. For some time, Don Felipe Jaramillo seemed to ignore Delaney and the two prisoners. Finally he folded the written pages and laid them aside. He rose and looked searchingly at his two captives. Royce noted the man's trim and well-muscled physique and his air of proud reserve, an air like that of the famous Spanish conquerers: Cortés, Pizarro, and a legion of others.

Presently the Spaniard spoke, his tone that of a man used to obedience; his words were in English. "I need information which I am told one of you can supply." His gaze swept Royce Milligan, and he continued. "I am told that you, Señor Milligan, spent time in a mine belonging to the Spanish crown. That you know its location on a distant mesa. Also that you have knowledge of a stone marker, a monument some distance from the mine's portal. Is this true?"

Royce stood silent for a few seconds. Nothing could be achieved by denying facts already known. Too, lying to this man would be dangerous. So he said, "With several others, I took refuge from a blizzard in the mine. For only one night. I have never myself seen the stone marker of which you speak."

"But you could lead me . . . and my expedition . . . to the mine?"

"Hell's fire, Milligan," Delaney interrupted, "why not tell him the whole truth? About the sighting device and how Lucy Lattamore is planning to take a crew and explore those old workings."

Royce eyed him with contempt. "I imagine you have already given him that information, along with a line of pure bullshit." He turned back to the Spaniard. "If I answer questions, I will speak only the truth as I know it. Some questions I will not answer."

"We have means of forcing you to speak," Don Jaramillo reminded him in a causual manner.

A bold recklessness marked Royce's next words. "Then, Señor Jaramillo, I suggest you verify any facts given you by this man, Delaney. He is a crooked, two-faced bastard."

A short laugh broke from the Spaniard. "You are a spirited one. You will remain my prisoner, to be treated exactly as your conduct deserves. Later today we will leave here and proceed toward Blue Mesa—with you as our guide. If inquiry is made, we are but an elk-hunting party." Jaramillo paused, and studied Beasley, who had not yet spoken. "I understand that you are a superior rifleman. It is a pity we cannot make use of your expertise in securing wild game, but prisoners are denied firearms." He motioned to the guards still at the tent's opening. "Take these two back to their quarters."

The day dragged on, hour by hour. At midday a guard brought them tin plates of beans and bread. There had been sounds of considerable activity outside, but now they slackened. There would be a meal for the Mexicans and then a siesta. Presently Beasley spoke in a whisper. "Listen, Royce. I've an idea. If we can get outside, maybe tell them we've got to relieve ourselves, I think maybe we can bust out of here." Max explained his plan to Royce, then both men rose and moved to the door. In urgent Spanish, Max convinced the one guard on duty to let them visit a nearby piñon grove.

Minutes later when he and Royce had finished, Max studied the guard standing with rifle ready a few steps away. Causually he moved toward a heavily-boughed piñon tree, quietly indicating that Royce should follow. The guard stepped closer. Max appraised the gunman's stance. Then he reached out and picked a handful of ripe piñon nuts. Royce did likewise. They bit into the nuts and spit out the hulls in obvious enjoyment. Quickly Max picked another handful, then, moving cautiously toward the guard, he offered the man the tasty morsels. They were greedily accepted. In low-toned Spanish Beasley spoke, pointing at the guard's serape, "Your serape. If you'll spread it out, we can shake the tree for more nuts." He moved back and lifted a hand to a well-laden branch. And with caution overcome by appetite, the Mexican handed him the woolen blanket. Both Max and Royce worked together in placing the serape at a strategic angle. Then they shook the branches to bring down a cascade of ripe nuts.

Eagerly the guard knelt to gather the nuts up in his serape. Beasley and Royce edged into position behind him. Then, together, they seized the corners of the serape and jerked it to cover the stooped guard. Instantly Royce's hand shot out to cover the struggling man's mouth. Already Max had wrenched the rifle away; now he brought its heavy butt down upon the guard's skull; he slumped, limp and unconscious.

Max then rolled the guard from the serape, crammed his straw sombrero on his own head and threw the serape over his shoulder. "Quick," he whispered. "Help me lug him into the brush. Then I'm gonna get our horses out of that corral. Keep me in sight—and yourself out of sight. Take this rifle. Shoot if you have to." With that Beasley was already walking cautiously toward the corral, and Royce, left alone, breathed apprehensively. The words of Don Felipe Jaramillo were ringing through his mind. *"You will be treated exactly as your conduct deserves."* "Oh, Jesus," Royce murmured, "give us horses of speed."

The heat and silence of siesta-time continued. He saw Beasley single out their own horses and throw saddles on them. Moments later Max was approaching him, clutching the bridle reins of their two mounts. A sigh of relief escaped Royce as he swung onto his horse. Then abruptly he had to stifle a laugh. Max had left every corral gate open, and the entire remuda of Don Felipe Jaramillo was escaping into the forest of piñon.

They edged toward the place where trees would conceal their escape. Presently they touched spurs to their horses and moved swiftly up the trail toward the placer pipe, the safety of Crestone, and far beyond, the mine at Blue Mesa.

Chapter 16

Within two hours after Royce Milligan had departed on his journey to the San Luis Valley, Lucy Lattamore searched out Parson Goodfroe. Her plan of action had been formulated in the quiet hours of the night. Today she would leave the Cantonment, probably never again to see these quarters she had shared with Phillip.

Goodfroe met her in the officers' mess hall and they sat down to a late breakfast. "Your concert is the talk of the Cantonment, Lucy. And deservedly so." The tall, black-clad parson nodded proudly.

"You *do* have a way of cheering me up," she acknowledged. Then she asked, "Reverend, how soon do you suppose you could get up onto Blue Mesa and back here to Pomona?"

He studied her face, and asked, "You mean to where we were marooned?"

"Yes, and here is what I need . . ." Her voice lowered and she told him she wanted him to do some line-of-sight surveys. "There is a pile of rocks, a monument of sorts, just up the slope from where we slept that first night. Use it for a reference point."

"You intend to file some sort of land claims?"

"Yes, mining claims to be exact. But I need the surveying done in a hurry."

He pulled out a silver-cased watch and studied it. "Ike Fenlon is due at the Cantonment right about now; he's headed east. I'll ride along with him, and if the weather holds good we should be up there about this time tomorrow morning.'' He started to rise, then paused to ask, ''But Miss Lucy, I'm no surveyor. Why in all that's eternal are you sending me?''

She leaned forward to place her arm about his neck. ''Why, Reverend? Because no preacher is apt to be sized up as a prospector or land agent.'' She placed some folded U.S. currency in his hand. ''For expenses, Reverend,'' she whispered.

Later she walked with Goodfroe to where Ike Fenlon's stage was being loaded for its eastward climb. She had not seen Fenlon since her concert in Columbia. ''God, Miss Lucy,'' he exclaimed, ''I wish you was riding along today.''

''If only I could, Ike. Take good care of the parson; he's on a bit of business for me. And I tell you what, Ike. Get him back here as soon as you can, and I'll be packed and ready at Pomona to let you take me and my belongings to Mesita.''

When the stage had faded into the distance, she arranged transportation for herself and her baggage to Pomona. Surely she could find safe and suitable quarters in which to rest until the return of the gambling preacher and a stagecoach driver beloved by Columbia's ''ladies of quality.''

It was only two and a half days until an elated Parson Goodfroe returned from Blue Mesa. Lucy was sitting in a rickety armchair just outside a small but secure one-room shack that Pappy Loutsenhizer had helped her to locate. She had devoted most of her daylight hours to planning how to put together a crew to explore the old Spanish mine. Too, she had attempted to prepare a written estimate of the lumber she would need for a flume capable of bringing water to the orchard lands of Cedar's Edge Mesa.

And now Parson Goodfroe held out a small, grimy handful of papers toward her.

Lucy studied the handwritten notes eagerly. "Reverend Goodfroe! This is exactly what I need—even your small drawing estimating the distances to the cairn. Did you run into any difficulty?"

"Well . . . a little," he conceded. "There was this fellow with a rifle, who claimed he was hunting elk. He got right miffed at me. Asked me what in hell I was doing."

"What did you tell him?"

"I opened my Bible and read a bit from the thirteenth chapter of Leviticus, about people with the plague of leprosy being brought to Aaron, the priest. Then I looked him in the eye and told him I was Aaron, and that I would be glad to remove the curse from him. Miss Lucy, he took off running."

"Oh, my goodness," Lucy gasped, then exploded into laughter.

"You'd best be packing your gear if you're going to Mesita with Fenlon and me. We'll be heading up toward Dallas Divide in about half an hour."

Lucy stared at him in a speculative way. "Reverend, I don't suppose I can persuade you to stay here, and not to go on to Mesita."

"But why, Miss Lucy?"

"Because I can't stay here myself, and I desperately need to get a message to Martin Goetz. Just now he is staying down at a settlement called Delta; his two sons are working there."

Goodfroe placed a hand on her shoulder. "Don't fret, Miss Lucy. Write your message to Goetz and give it to me. Then you climb on Ike Fenlon's coach."

"Aren't you even going to ask what the rush message is about?" Lucy said with evident relief. When Goodfroe shook his head, she explained. "I want Martin Goetz and his two sons and you—and a couple of other men, if Goetz thinks we will need them—to meet me here in just three days. Parson Goodfroe, we are going to Blue Mesa. With men and tools and a lot of black powder. We're going to cut or tunnel or blast our way into that old mine and explore every possible inch. And God help us to be quick, for Robert Delaney is probably planning right now to play hell with our plans.''

The day was warm and clear as Ike Fenlon's stagecoach left Pomona and began the trip up the Uncompahgre Valley. Lucy chose to ride up-top with the driver, and her first words as they departed from Pomona came as an anxious question. ''Ike, have you seen . . . or heard anything of . . . Royce Milligan?''

''No. Nothing at all, Miss Lucy. That assistant of his over at Mesita, Andy Parnell, and Margaret Hendricks put out *The Messiah* last week.''

Apprehension touched her face. ''Then I can only wait . . . and hope . . . and pray.''

There were moments of silence as Lucy pondered every facet of the bold venture she would soon undertake on Blue Mesa. Finally she said, ''Ike, I wish you were going to be free of this stagecoach for a while.''

Fenlon touched the rump of a horse with the tip of his long whip. ''What's on your mind, Miss Lucy?''

Suddenly she was telling him of her decision to blast into the old Spanish mine, and how Parson Goodfroe and Martin Goetz would take part in the undertaking. ''If only Royce Milligan and you could take part too, Ike, we would all be there—just as we were when that old tunnel sheltered us from the blizzard.''

There was excitement in Fenlon's reply. ''Whoa up, Miss Lucy. I can't answer for Mr. Milligan, but I'm not going to miss out being there to help you.''

''But your work, this stagecoach route—'' she began.

Before answering, Fenlon stared at the butt-end of his whip. ''Most of the excitement of stagecoaching is gone. I guess I been at it too long.''

''But what would you do after we finish my risky business up there at the mine?''

"Something I've been thinking about for a long time . . . going into business in Columbia, or Telluride as it's called now."

"A livery stable?" she ventured.

"Nope. An investment office."

Lucy gasped. "Investments? Are you serious?"

He grinned at her, displaying the tooth that had been a gift of the Columbia Quality. "It ain't all that new to me, Miss Lucy. The ladies up at Columbia have had me doing most of their buying and banking for nigh on five years. You'd be surprised how much money some of them have in the bank. Together, my ladies own a good slice of Telluride's real estate. I'll be working to protect their interests."

They came into Mesita early the following day. As the stage rattled past the *Messiah* building, Lucy resisted an urge to have Fenlon draw his rig to a stop and let her go inside. She knew she wouldn't find Royce there; he was what now seemed half a world away. "Ike," she asked, "can you take me on up the hill? Let me off at Tim O'Fallon's?"

"And your baggage, Miss Lucy?"

"Take it to that little hotel down the block from the site of the new opera house." She dug into her purse and handed him ten dollars. "Have them save a room for me and put my luggage in it. I'll register later."

Fenlon nodded and then looked doubtful. "What are Mr. O'Fallon and Margaret going to say to such an arrangement?"

"I'll have to bear whatever they say, Ike; I have taken advantage of their hospitality too much already." She hesitated, and then added, "If any word comes through about Royce, do let me know right away."

"Okay," he agreed, and presently swung the coach expertly into the driveway of the O'Fallon home.

Tim O'Fallon, clad in a tattered coat and heavy gloves, was nearby trimming a hedge. He looked up and waved to Fenlon, and then, seeing Lucy Lattamore step from the rig, he hastened to embrace her. "Howdy, stranger, and welcome. I've been busting to tell you my plans for the interior of the opera house." He looked about, noted that already Fenlon was heading his rig down the driveway, and then asked, "Say, my dear, where are your boxes and bags?"

"On their way to the hotel, Tim, where I will be staying for the night."

He laughed aloud. "You can be stubborn, Lucy. Just so you come here for meals."

"I will," she assured him. "But tell me, have you heard from Royce?"

"Not since he left for the San Luis Valley." He noticed the tension on her face and spoke in an effort to ease it. "Don't worry so. After all, he has only been gone a few days. Besides, he isn't alone."

She caught his meaning. "Max Beasley is with Royce?"

"I thought it best," he answered quietly. He discarded the heavy pruning gloves and walked with her to the front door. Just inside, he called out, "Margaret, look who just fell from the sky."

Margaret Hendricks appeared at the top of the stairs and peered toward them. "Lucy . . . Lucy . . . you gadabout, you come up here right away." As Lucy climbed the steps to meet this usually staid and calm woman, she noticed that Margaret Hendricks looked anxious and upset. Lucy's arms went around her in a comforting way, and they moved to the sunporch. Margaret Hendricks still clung to Lucy's hand as they sat down in a comfortable pair of wicker chairs. "Don't mind my sniffling, honey, but I'm worried about Max . . . and your Royce, too. There are vicious men who will try to wrest information about your Spanish mine from them, and Robert Delaney is probably among them."

"Margaret, Robert Delaney isn't the murdering kind."

"I'm not so sure, Lucy. Not so sure at all."

In an effort to divert Margaret's mind from such dire possibilities, Lucy asked, "While we are waiting for some word of Max and Royce, can you help me prepare and file mining claims to some areas on Blue Mesa? I've had it surveyed now."

Composure was returning to Margaret Hendricks' face. "We'll get busy on it right away." She paused and her voice became touched with irony. "And Lucy Lattamore, I hope we make much faster progress on this than we have on your wedding plans."

Lucy rose, moved to a window and surveyed the sun-drenched town. Then she walked back and sat down to face her companion. "Margaret, I have a feeling that before long, this business will be settled, that all of this terrible waiting and tension will be resolved one way or another."

"What will bring that about?"

"Tomorrow I will return to Pomona; men will be waiting for me there, men who will help me gain entry to the old Spanish mine and explore it thoroughly."

Margaret studied the stubborn expression on Lucy's face, and said, "You expect trouble up there on the Mesa?"

"We are preparing for it. For any eventuality."

"You just be careful, honey." Margaret rose, and there seemed renewed assurance about her. "Now! Let's get these mining claims in order and filed today."

Two days later a small caravan composed of two heavy wagons and half a dozen horseback riders labored onto Blue Mesa. Before leaving Pomona, Lucy had called all of those in the expedition about her. "I can't promise you much. Each of you must undertake this venture knowing we may come away empty-handed. Also, I have reason to believe other men will oppose us. Armed men. Dangerous men." She paused, and seeing no fear or reluctance on their faces, added, "If there is buried treasure within the mine, we will divide it . . . equally.

That is all I can offer, except maybe an adventure each of you will remember for the rest of your life.''

Now, as the expedition crawled tediously up the switchbacks, she scanned those upon whom the success or failure of the mine's reopening rested. Most crucial to the attempt would be the old miner Martin Goetz. Both of his sons had chosen to accompany their father. They took turns sitting on wagons loaded with gear that the elder Goetz had rounded up; every so often they climbed down to walk out and gaze across meadows and ranges of hills that surrounded them.

Lucy was riding a black mare that Ike Fenlon had delighted her by offering. ''The fellow who's taking over my route sold me the mare and this sorrel I'm riding.'' Before she could thank him, Fenlon went on. ''Miss Lucy, I don't have any idea how I'll fit into this gamble you're taking. But I'm with you. All the way.''

''My sentiments exactly.'' The words came from Reverend Lucian Goodfroe, who had tied his burro to the tailgate of a wagon and was now striding beside Lucy.

Ike Fenlon sized up the circuit-riding parson and then grinned broadly. ''Parson, aren't you forgetting that Armageddon . . . and the second coming . . . may hinder our treasure hunt?''

Goodfroe drew himself up and replied, ''Friend Fenlon, at least I am prepared for that fateful day of judgment. Are you?''

They fell silent then, and Lucy studied the sky and the distant rise of snowy peaks off southward.

Sundown, with its softer light, was touching the trees and brush when they came to the spot where the blizzard had stalled their trek from Pueblo and Barnum. Ike Fenlon recognized the spot first, and said, ''Right here is where we left the coach and hiked down to that patch of timber you spotted, Miss Lucy.''

She looked ahead. ''Why don't we set up camp, at least for tonight, in the same spot. There is kindling, grass for our horses, and likely a little stream close at hand. And, Ike . . . it is almost within a stone's throw of the cairn.''

Fenlon nodded, then rode forward to tell the wagon drivers of her decision. He studied the two men Goetz had enlisted for the adventure. Most of the way they had ridden well in front of the vehicles, but now their mounts were tethered behind. *Lucy is taking no chances,* Ike Fenlon thought. *Those two strangers and their rifles. And sidearms. They aren't looking for rabbits.*

When the wagons had been drawn into the grove of spruce and fir trees, Lucy hurried up the slope. Her breathing was rapid as she approached the cairn and stooped to again sight through the V notch. Off on the mountain slope, she could clearly see the gulch and the debris strewn by a thundering avalanche, but still no dark rectangle marking the entry to a mine that had proved both a shelter and an enigma. She plodded down the slope, a mood of somberness upon her. *So tomorrow morning we get to work,* she told herself. *It is there, the mine, but hidden by the rubble of a snow-slide. Everything depends on Goetz, and the strong-backed pick-and-shovel men—and perhaps a god-awful charge of black powder.*

With ample food and bedding, plus a tent for Lucy's privacy, they spent a not uncomfortable night. After breakfast the next day there was a short discussion of how best to proceed. Goetz had easily taken command, and now he said, "First I want to get over there and size up the gulch. We need to be close."

"We also need to know if anyone else is prowling about," said Goetz's oldest son.

Lucy felt the urge to go with them, to take part in these all-important determinations. She sensed, however, their desire to work alone. "I'll do some chores around camp," she said, and reluctantly watched them mount horses and ride toward the gulch. Because of the industrious efforts of Parson Goodfroe and Ike Fenlon, she found little to do but wait and hope. As she walked restlessly about the little camp, she noticed that one of the two armed men Goetz had hired had chosen to walk halfway up the ridge to attain a better view. *Everyone is taking this project seriously,* she thought. *And that is good.*

Later, she tried to distract herself by reading, choosing a George Eliot novel. Unable to concentrate, she set it aside and her thoughts turned to the question of Royce Milligan's whereabouts. *Is our life together destined to always be like this, each of us coming or going, with precious little time together?* She found herself yearning for his arms about her. Hastily, she rose and again looked searchingly across the haze of the mesa.

Goetz, accompanied by his sons, the two pick-and-shovel men, and the quietly watchful rifleman, returned near mid-afternoon. "We can move camp now, Miss Lucy," he reported. "Just below, and off to the left of the gulch, is a clearing. Not comfortable like this, but we can make do."

"We didn't trek up here searching for comfort," she answered wryly. "Were you able to size up the avalanche debris?"

"Somewhat. But Miss Lucy, it would help to know just what one sees through that sighting device you mentioned."

With a quiet motion she signaled him to follow her and trudged up the ridge. When they reached the cairn, she first sighted through the V groove, and then said, "Take a look."

Goetz studied the distant gulch for almost five minutes; he drew out a notepad and made notations which he studied. Then he muttered, "If only there was some marker close to where you saw the portal."

Lucy again leveled her gaze through the V, letting her mind search the distant vista and also what it had revealed on the day of the blizzard. Suddenly she stiffened. "Mr. Goetz . . . there *is* something. That black thrust of rock on the edge of the gulch . . . it was almost part of the dark shadow of the portal."

"Good . . . damned good!" he whispered in hoarse excitement. "Now I believe we can blast through."

"How, Mr. Goetz?"

He again studied his notepad. "By a series of well-measured blasts of powder. Shots that will cause the rock and timber to slide away from the portal."

She faced him with excited eyes. "Can it be done, without starting another avalanche?"

"I think so," he replied.

Before nightfall their new camp had been set up within two hundred yards of the debris-clogged gulch. Tired, but filled with excited anticipation of the next day's blasting, Lucy sought out her tent and bedroll early. There was a chill in the air, and her blankets proved warm and comforting.

Next day, the work of placing measured charges of explosives among the tangle of boulders and broken trees proved more time-consuming than Lucy had predicted. It wasn't until near sunset that Goetz and his sons climbed out of the gulch; already the laborers were busy removing tools and bags of unused powder. To each explosive charge, sufficient fuse had been attached to allow a safe retreat when the time of detonation was at hand.

Exhausted, Goetz sought out Lucy. "We will fire the charges in about ten minutes. The first two, set to break the key timbers and boulders of the jam, will be big ones. Earth-shakers. Then, a few seconds apart, there will be other blasts. They will be of different strengths, meant to keep the plugged debris sliding below where we believe the portal is located. Lucy, keep clear, and warn the others to do the same. Soon we will know. Very soon."

"Who will light the fuses?" she asked in an awed voice.

"My two boys. They have done fuse-lighting many times. Besides, they can run like scared rabbits." There was jest in his voice, but grave concern and tension on his face as well.

Minutes later it seemed to Lucy that the whole of Blue Mesa shook beneath her, followed by a crashing crescendo of noise. Another similar blast caused her to crouch and fling her hands over her ears. And now her view of the gulch was lost in an acrid-smelling cloud of dust. Six blasts followed, and after each came the reverberations of sliding rock. She was aware of Parson Goodfroe and Ike Fenlon standing close by, and of the work crew gathered in what seemed to be perilous nearness to the gulch. And now a breeze sweeping up the gulch began to dispel the cloud of dust.

It was Goetz's younger son, Luther, a lanky teenager, who let out the first triumphant howl and rushed up to Lucy, pointing excitedly. "Look, Miss Lattamore. Over there in the gulch. There are timbers framing an old opening. Your mine, your lost Spanish diggings."

She peered at the opened portal and the dark depths it seemed to guard, then her arm went about the boy in sheer relief and ecstasy. Now there would be no need of slow and dangerous tunneling to reach the mine. If only Royce were here to share her moment of triumph.

Later Martin Goetz came again to her side, much of the anxiety gone from his face. "We will wait until morning, Lucy, to go inside. We must allow time for the powder fumes and dust to subside. Always we must be on the lookout for bad air. Yes, and rotted timbers."

"And men who would not hesitate at murder," she murmured.

They wakened the next morning to breakfast quickly on cold sandwiches and lukewarm coffee, then approached the tunnel's portal. There was still a great many scattered rocks and other debris about. They picked a cautious way through and came presently to the old hand-hewn timbers forming the entryway. Intent upon every detail, Lucy gazed at their size and strength; the morning light allowed her to look but a few yards into the rectangular low-ceilinged tunnel, but she marveled that long ago, men with little more than hand-tools had sledged and shoveled their way through solid rock in order to reach whatever treasure might lie deep in the mountain.

Martin Goetz was the first to enter the tunnel, telling the others to wait until he could determine the condition of the air and the possibility of cave-ins. He was back in a few minutes. "Light your lanterns and follow me. Keep close together. Watch your footing. If the lights begin to flicker or go out, we must get the hell out of this hole."

Lucy noticed that their armed guards did not follow. One took up a position near the portal. Goetz had posted the other guard to keep watch over their camp and belongings. It seemed as if Goetz was almost expecting a surprise attack.

There were six who trod their way into the gloom of the tunnel, and something about the place caused them either to speak in low tones or remain silent. Goetz and his younger son led the way, stopping often to let the rays of their lantern illuminate the detail of the walls, the ceiling, and the uneven floor beneath them. Lucy followed, knowing that both Parson Goodfroe and Ike Fenlon were close beside her. The older Goetz boy walked a few steps behind them.

It seemed but a short time until they came to the spot where she, Royce, and the others from the stalled stage-coach had spent the night. As he had done on that well-remembered first night, Goetz now made a minute examination of the room where a draft of fresh air indicated the presence of an opening to some point on the mountain slope above. The light he now carried was adequate to affirm what he had suspected: in the upward-reaching shaft there still remained an iron ladder. Probably a trapped man could use the device to climb to safety.

Nearby they came upon a room that they had previously missed. It was larger, and in the center there was a sort of circular path worn down from constant usage. Goetz nodded in fascination. "See. An *arrista*. A Spanish ore-crushing device. The burros—or the slaves—drug a heavy stone about the circle to crush ore." The others studied the smooth floor, hoping to see the glint of gold or silver particles, but there seemed to be none. Had every speck of valuable minerals already been mined?

Next they stopped close to the branch tunnel that Goetz had not previously entered because of apparent caving of its roof. "This one we must forget," he warned. "It is likely dangerous—a death trap." He paused, then sighed. "And too bad, Miss Lucy; it was here I picked up the piece of amalgamate ore which I gave you that night." The thought of what might lie in the caving area was tantalizing; it was also futile. They sensed that an entire rebuilding of these old and crumbling areas would be necessary to reopen and work the mine.

It was less than a hundred feet to the place where Goetz had come upon the dark and dangerous vertical shaft. He now cautioned them to keep well away from its edge and the sagging framework of old timbers that probably had been used for hoisting ore-buckets, and men as well. Goetz again tossed a fragment of rock into it. Presently there was the sound of its striking bottom, a dull thud that echoed up the dark reaches. It was Ike Fenlon, slight of build, who said, "With a strong rope you could let me down to take a look-see."

Before anyone replied, Lucy glanced at Goetz's face, revealed in the pale lantern light. The suggestion had clearly horrified him. She placed a restraining hand on Fenlon's arm. "You'll do nothing of the kind; I didn't bring you here to be killed."

Within half an hour Lucy's decision had firmed even more. "We are going to give up this search, Mr. Goetz. If there is anything of value here, it must still be locked in the bowels of the earth. And those old conquistadores weren't fools. Likely when they abandoned this mine they took every last iota of precious minerals with them."

They moved reluctantly back toward the portal in disappointed silence. Lucy was walking beside Luther Goetz, the bitterness of failure written on her face. The light grew stronger, the portal only a few steps away. And then Lucy Lattamore recoiled in horror and an anguished cry broke from her. The body of the guard they had posted now lay limp and bleeding just within the mine opening. And just beyond were the set and ugly faces of men blocking the way. In the numbness of utter shock, she stared at the features of Robert Delaney, and at a tall stranger she would later learn was of Spanish lineage, Don Felipe Jaramillo. Behind them, half a dozen grim and swarthy-faced Mexican *bandaleros* with rifles trained upon the others who clustered around her.

At that same moment, with daybreak only two hours past, Royce Milligan urged his saddle horses onto the high reaches of Blue Mesa. Royce sensed the weariness of the mount he was astride. He also morosely recalled all that had happened since he and Max escaped from the camp of Don Felipe Jaramillo.

He and Beasley had made haste in a direct line to Saguache to return their rented mounts, but had been delayed waiting for a stagecoach over Poncha Pass to Salida. More delay frustrated them at Salida, when their westbound train to Gunnison was held up half a day for the tracks to be cleared of a mud-slide. Within half an hour of reaching Gunnison, they managed to buy two sturdy-looking horses. But night was falling as they rode the high and lonesome trail that would lead to Blue Mesa, so they had laid over another night.

Royce was dead-tired now, but running on adrenaline as they rode westward, then paused at the grove where Ike Fenlon's stage passengers had huddled beneath a frayed and smelly buffalo robe. The traces of a recent camp caused Royce's face to fall in disappointment and concern. Apprehensively he searched the sweep of mountain off southward, but from this grove the timber beyond the trail blocked his view of the ravine and the dark opening to which Lucy had led them. Beasley began gathering bits of wood for a warming fire. They secured their horses to a large sapling and moved about to lessen the numbness born of hours in the saddle.

Then Royce walked slowly up the ridge, turning a couple of times to scan the widening vista of the distant slope. He gave scant thought to the stone monument. Then abruptly it loomed before him, a pyramid of boulders almost shoulder-high. He again turned toward the mountain slope that lay southward. Now he could see the gulch, and he realized it was from right there that Lucy had spotted the portal. Quickly, he walked to the cairn and moved behind it. He stared at the slab of stone forming the caprock and at the V-notch that resembled a rifle's rear sight. Then he stooped and peered through. His throat tightened, as he saw a small camp, with two wagons, close to the gulch—but no sign of human beings.

A conviction came upon Royce Milligan, a feeling that some disaster had struck there. As he continued to search the distant slope for any clue, Royce ran his fingers agitatedly along the bottom of the capstone. His hand tightened in helpless frustration—and suddenly, pieces of the old cementing material holding the cairn together fell loosely into his hand. In that same moment he felt the heavy capstone give beneath the pressure of his grasp. It moved but an inch or less. He glanced downward. At one corner of the cairn, a dark spot told him that this structure was not of solid rock. Instead it was hollow.

With heightening curiosity, Royce again pushed on the capstone; this time he exerted more force, and the stone slid almost a third of the way across the base of cemented boulders. Again Royce peered downward, into a cavity where the light of morning made the interior visible. His eyes widened and his jaw slackened. Then he muttered. "Oh, my God!"

After a time Royce slid the capstone carefully back into place. Max Beasley was calling from below. With awed reluctance, Royce began to walk down the slope. He was halfway to Beasley and the horses when he realized that he was still clutching loose pieces of old and rotten bonding material. He gazed at them in disbelief and then hurled them into the grass. It was Max's sharp words that brought Royce back to the reality of the moment. "Did you get a look over toward the gulch?"

Royce nodded. "Yes, and let's ride like hell up that way—praying we're not too late."

The desperate tone of his voice caused Max Beasley to draw his rifle from its sheath and hold it in readiness as they touched spurs to their horses.

Chapter 17

In that moment when Lucy Lattamore stood startled beside Luther Goetz, and helpless within arm's length of Robert Delaney and a tall and cruel-faced Spaniard, she knew the bitterness of utter defeat. Her anger flared and centered upon Delaney. Her clenched fist flashed upward to strike his mouth with a hard blow. His head jerked backward and blood marked a lip, torn by a ring she had worn since her school days. She stood ready for his retaliation, but he merely stood there. His face was stony and inscrutable as he said, "Enough of that, you silly woman. We'll have time for play after you and this German take us to the hidden ore."

Don Felipe Jaramillo had watched in an amused way. Now he spoke. "Señorita, your reckless cowboys eluded us at the Great Sand Dunes. But as it turned out, we found our way here anyway, with the help of Robert Delaney. We were half a mile away yesterday when we saw evidence of blasting. Have you opened a way for us, my dear?"

Lucy said nothing, only helplessly complied as she and her crew were forced to return into the tunnel. Delaney demanded that Martin Goetz lead them to where the gold and silver was hidden. As they toured the mine and found nothing, the captors became increasingly enraged.

Half an hour later they came to the vertical shaft. Aware of its danger, Lucy moved cautiously. Twice

Jaramillo turned to her with silent impatience. She was within arm's-length of the weakened hoist structure when she took a wary step backward. With the single word, and a toss of his head, he grabbed her arm and thrust her forward. A scream escaped Lucy, for she was momentarily thrown off balance. It was the hand of Robert Delaney that snaked out to clutch her jacket and pull her back from the shaft's brink. "Damn it, watch out!" he shouted at Don Jaramillo.

Utter ruthlessness and rage tore at Jaramillo. Then a pistol was in his hand, spitting a leaden slug through Delaney's heart. He fell backward, dead when he dropped to the floor. In that moment Don Felipe Jaramillo spoke with cold contempt. "The fool had worn out his usefulness." The pistol was still in his hand, and in terror Lucy struggled to shove past the cluster of bandits and run down the dark tunnel. She stumbled into the barrel of a rifle. Her movement caused its bearer to lose balance and clutch at Jaramillo's leg. Jaramillo bent to rid himself of this clinging burden. It was a fatal mistake, for Parson Lucian Goodfroe, who had been watching, leaped forward. With the strength of anger and fear, he swung at the Spanish nobleman, who tottered for only a second at the shaft's lip, and then, with a scream, fell into the unknown depths below. The sound of his striking bottom was followed by utter silence.

Of the captors, only two badly-shaken and bewildered *banditos* now remained, the others having run away. It was Ike Fenlon and the older Goetz son who maneuvered cautiously behind the leaderless Mexicans, seizing their rifles and pulling knives from their waistbands.

Relief surged through everyone in Lucy's expedition. Lucy's gaze moved to the body of Robert Delaney. She was remembering his last act, an effort to protect her. It had been quick and instinctive, born of some inherent decency that transcended his greed and ruthlessness. She vowed to bring his body out.

After a time Martin Goetz said, "We are not free yet.

That Spaniard would not have followed us inside without leaving a heavy guard at the portal.''

"But we had a guard at the camp," Ike Fenlon reminded him.

"I know . . . and likely he was overpowered." His words gave way to silence, for he saw no need to arouse fear that something worse than capture had overtaken the other of their party.

Within fifteen minutes Goetz led them to the hewn-out room that was cooler because of the air draft. Their return to this place, nearer the portal, was slowed by the fact that they had been taking turns to carry Delaney's body.

After a short rest, Martin Goetz and his older son sought out the air shaft and the old but sturdy iron ladder. "We'll take a look around," Goetz told them. "Stay here, and don't risk approaching the portal; if we should not return, each of you can climb to safety. But best you should wait until night."

Goetz counted the steps of the ladder, and found that a climb of fifty feet was necessary to bring them to the opening some distance above the mine's portal. They had only one rifle, having left the second captured weapon with those in the room below. Now both the old German and his son crawled to a spot where they could scan the slopes below without revealing their own position. As they had suspected, there were four or five Mexican *banditos* standing guard over the mine's portal. Then their surveillance of them was abruptly halted. Close at hand there was a movement in the brush, and presently the crouched form of a man climbing the slope could be seen. Within moments Goetz recognized the approaching man as a member of his own party, the guard who had been told to safeguard the wagons and gear. He stood up and motioned the guard to join him. Then he pointed toward the portal. "Are there more of the bastards hidden about?"

"Just one other that I know of," the guard responded. "Two of them tried to rush me. I took care of one with this," he said, slapping the stock of his rifle. "The other took off for his friends over by the portal."

They discussed the wisdom of trying to lay siege to those at the mine's entrance. But the plan seemed hopeless; the three of them, with only two rifles among them, stood no chance against the well-armed Mexicans.

Minutes later, they noticed two men riding swiftly from the clustered timber alongside the roadway below them. The Mexicans had also taken heed of the onrushing pair of horsemen, and now the sound of rifle shots rang through the thin air. Goetz saw a bullet kick up dust as it hit fifty feet short of the rider leading the way. Abruptly this rider halted his horse, dropped to the grassed slope and returned fire. Then Goetz and his two companions saw one of the portal guards stagger backwards, drop his weapon, and fall limply to the ground.

The action brought a cry of surprise from the younger Goetz. "Godamighty, Pa. That fellow in the grass—it's Max Beasley."

Soon the three of them were running excitedly down the slope. Despite a smattering of rifle fire from the portal guards, they were able to maneuver down the ridge and join Beasley and Milligan. Martin Goetz was the first to speak. "We ought to be able to circle—"

"Quick, Martin. Where is Lucy? Is she safe?" Royce interrupted.

"Likely so. She and my other boy, and Ike Fenlon and the preacher are inside the mine."

"Then Delaney and a Spanish fellow didn't get her, didn't harm her?"

"They tried, all right."

"Then what?" Royce demanded.

"That Spaniard shot Delaney."

"Jesus! Then what?" Royce gasped.

"Royce, you ain't going to believe it. That parson fellow pushed the Spanish gent into that deep shaft. Put an end to him." Goetz clearly wanted to postpone the questioning, for now he said, "We can wipe out those Mexicans still on watch up there."

"No, I think there is a better way," said Max tensely. "I can speak their language. Just keep me well-covered with your rifles as I belly my way up this slope to where they can hear me." Without waiting for their consent, he wormed his way from them. There was strained silence as they waited. Presently they heard the sound of Max Beasley shouting. In answer there was a volley of shots, and then they heard Beasley's rifle reply. Royce, waiting anxiously, was certain that another of the Mexican guards had fallen. There was the sound of excited voices from the portal area, and cold and demanding replies from Beasley.

This continued for perhaps two minutes, although it seemed longer. Then Max's voice was calling to them. "Okay, fellows, come on up."

They strode up the hill, amazed. Max Beasley stood close to the Mexican guards, and their weapons, rifles, and knives lay at his feet.

"How in hell—?" Royce began.

"Simple, my friend. I convinced them their leader is dead and that I had many many gringo gunmen ready to mow them down."

"What do we do with them now?" Goetz asked.

"I'd say we keep their artillery, give each of them a few pesos, and point them toward Santa Fe and points south."

Minutes later, all of them except Beasley and their rifleman entered the now-unobstructed tunnel. When they reappeared, Lucy was leaning heavily on the arms of both Parson Goodfroe and Royce. There was anguish on her face, and fatigue. Once free of the mine, she said brokenly, "Failure . . . desolation . . . death . . . all brought about because of my headstrong craving for treasure. Treasure that was only an illusion . . . a mirage." She raised her hands to cover her face, and then spoke again. "Royce, now I understand the lingering

sorrow on Pappy Loutsenhizer's face; it's a remnant of
the ordeal of seeing men suffer and die.''

Royce was silent, knowing that her outpouring of
frustration and grief would pass. They had stopped on the
slope, and she had sought the comfort of his arms when
she added, ''Do you know what Pappy Loutsenhizer said,
the last time I saw him? We were talking of the wedding
plans. Then he took me outside his little house to a
garden patch. There he showed me three ditches in which
he had placed shoots and slips and roots of fruit trees:
peach, plum, apple, pear, grape, cherry, and others. Then
he said, 'They are yours, Miss Lucy. You and your
husband can plant them up on Cedar's Edge Mesa next
spring.' Then he smiled softly, Royce, and laid a tender
hand on some of the seedlings. 'They will grow,' he said.
'And by the time your first-born is ready to trot off to
school, these will have become beautiful fruit trees and
vines.' ''

Others of the group had moved some distance away,
respecting their need for privacy, to talk and to dream.

''It is over now, Lucy,'' he assured her. ''We can tell
the men to load your wagons and then put this place and
its problems behind us.'' There was a short silence as he
saw the first hint of peace upon her face. Then Royce said
in a mysterious way, ''But right now I want you to ride
down to the grove with me and climb up to the rock
monument, the cairn.''

''What good would come of that?'' she protested.

''Let's do it anyhow, Lucy.''

They retrieved the horses that he and Beasley had
ridden up the slope, and seeing that Goetz and all of the
others had begun preparations to break camp, they headed
hastily for the trail and the grove below. Max Beasley
watched them ride off, but saw no need to follow. He
sensed that his time of riding as Royce Milligan's rifleman
had ended.

Lucy and Royce strode up to the old rock monument

hand in hand. When they reached the old heap of stones, Royce stepped behind it, but kept one arm tightly about Lucy. And then he gave the capstone a single hard shove. It slid almost halfway across the bouldered base, revealing the inner hollowness into which Royce had gazed earlier that morning. "Look, my dear," he said, and pointed into the cavity.

At first she seemed to see nothing, then there was growing comprehension and amazement in her eyes. "Royce . . . those bars . . . are they—?"

"Indeed they are, Lucy. Here is the hiding place chosen for their gold and silver by the Spaniards who worked the mine so many years ago." He drew her to him and kissed her forehead. "And all of it belongs to you." When she seemed overwhelmed and confused, he added, "You first found this cairn. You now hold title to it."

Her gaze held to the bars within the sturdy rock enclosure. She did not know their value, but she guessed it must be enormous.

With a firm pull, Royce slid the capstone back into position. "When Goetz and the others bring the wagons, we will load this. Then we'll head for home."

She looked into his face with a bit of reluctance, as though dreading how Royce might react to what she must say. "When we left to come up here and search the mine, Royce, I told the men who took the chance with me that we would share and share alike. Now I must—"

"Of course it must be split up, honey. But I'm sure you'll find yourself with enough of these metal bars to buy a lot of orchard lands."

"And to do something else, Royce. To start a newspaper for you in Montrose . . . that's what they're beginning to call Pomona. With a paper there, I'll have you handy. Royce, I want to settle down with you. Raise a family. Quit all this running around." She was encircling his neck tightly with both arms, and her lips sought his, as she added, "Maybe I'm tired of being a maverick."

Royce looked into her lovely face and thought, *All I dreamed about that night, that first cold night when she led us to the mine, is here now—in my arms. But God forbid she should ever stop being a maverick. This future wife of mine was born to keep reaching for a star—that's why I love her so.*

FROM THE NATIONAL
BESTSELLING AUTHOR

All the passions, adventure and romance of 18th century England are woven into this bestselling trilogy that captured the hearts of over 4 million readers.

MOONSTRUCK MADNESS, Book One
75994-2/$3.95US/$4.95Can
CHANCE THE WINDS OF FORTUNE, Book Two
79756-9/$3.95US/$4.95Can
DARK BEFORE THE RISING SUN, Book Three
78848-4/$3.95US/$4.95Can

More spellbinding stories

WILD BELLS TO THE WILD SKY
87387-7/$3.95US/$5.50Can
DEVIL'S DESIRE   00295-7/$4.50US/$5.50Can
TEARS OF GOLD   41475-9/$3.95US

And her newest bestseller

WHEN THE SPLENDOR FALLS
89826-8/$3.95US/$4.95Can

A powerful novel of unquenchable passions, of two mighty families swept by the raging winds of war to a destiny where only love can triumph!